PRAISE FOR RAGNAR JÓNASSON

'I enjoyed Ragnar Jónasson's *Snowblind* – a modern Icelandic take on an Agatha Christie-style mystery, as twisty as any slalom…' Ian Rankin

'A classic crime story seen through a uniquely Icelandic lens … first rate and highly recommended' Lee Child

'Jónasson skillfully alternates points of view and shifts of time … The action builds to a shattering climax' *Publishers Weekly*

'A tense and convincing thriller; Jónasson is a welcome addition to the roster of Scandi authors…' Susan Moody

'…a chiller of a thriller … It's good enough to share shelf space with the works of Yrsa Sigurðardóttir and Arnaldur Indriðason, Iceland's crime novel royalty' *Washington Post*

'Required reading' *New York Post*

'Puts a lively, sophisticated spin on the Agatha Christie model, taking it down intriguing dark alleys' *Kirkus Reviews*

'Economical and evocative prose, as well as some masterful prestidigitation' *Guardian*

'The best sort of gloomy storytelling' *Chicago Tribune*

'Ragnar Jónasson writes with a chilling, poetic beauty – a must-read addition to the growing canon of Iceland Noir' Peter James

'British aficionados of Nordic Noir are familiar with two excellent Icelandic writers, Arnaldur Indriðason and Yrsa Sigurðardóttir. Here's a third: Ragnar Jónasson … the darkness and cold are palpable' *The Times*

'A truly chilling debut, perfect for fans of Karin Fossum and Henning Mankell' Eva Dolan

'A challenging investigation that uncovers local secrets … Scandi Noir meets old-fashioned murder mystery in an atmospheric whodunnit' *Daily Express*

'Seductive … an old-fashioned murder mystery with a strong central character and the fascinating background of a small Icelandic town cut off by snow. Ragnar does claustrophobia beautifully' Ann Cleeves

'His first novel to be translated into English has all the skillful plotting of an old-fashioned whodunnit although it feels bitingly contemporary in setting and tone' *Sunday Express*

'On the face of it, *Snowblind* is a gigantic locked-room mystery, an investigation into murder and other crimes within a closed society with a limited number of suspects … Jónasson plays fair with the reader – his clues are traditional and beautifully finessed – and he keeps you turning the pages. *Snowblind* is morally more equivocal than most traditional whodunnits, and it offers alluring glimpses of darker, and infinitely more threatening horizons' *Independent*

'Ragnar Jónasson's *Snowblind* is as dazzling a novel as its title implies and the wonderful Ari Thór is a welcome addition to the pantheon of Scandinavian detectives. I can't wait until the sequel!' William Ryan

'*Whiteout* is all kinds of brilliant. Great characters, a gripping plot and a hauntingly atmospheric location. Another book added to my all-time favourites list' Bibliophile Book Club

'An isolated community, subtle clueing, clever misdirection and more than a few surprises combine to give a modern-day golden-age whodunnit. Well Done! I look forward to the next in the series' Dr John Curran

'This is almost a classic Scandinavian Noir setup, but Ragnar Jónasson is full of surprises … I loved it' *Mystery Scene Magazine*

'...brings you the chill of a snowbound Icelandic fishing village cut off from the outside world, and the warmth of a really well-crafted and translated murder mystery' Michael Ridpath

'Jónasson has taken the locked-room mystery and transformed it into a dark tale of isolation and intrigue that will keep readers guessing until the final page' *Library Journal*

'Jónasson spins an involving tale of small-town police work that vividly captures the snowy setting that so affects the rookie cop. Iceland Noir at its moodiest' Booklist

'A fantastic golden-age mystery novel with hard-hitting themes and a flawless writing style which lulled me into a false sense of security...' Chillers, Thrillers and Killers

'Elegantly and cleverly paced, with a plot that grips and a totally unexpected ending, this is crime writing of the highest quality' Random Things Through My Letterbox

'Beautifully evocative of place and character, these books are a pure delight to read' Louise Wykes

'Brilliantly atmospheric and claustrophobic' Have Books Will Read

'Crime fiction at its most exciting and storytelling at its most authentic ... The Dark Iceland series is fast becoming a book shelf collection classic' The Word's Shortlist

'The complex characters and absorbing plot make *Snowblind* memorable. Its setting – Siglufjördur, a small fishing village isolated in the depths of an Icelandic winter – makes it unforgettable. Let's hope that more of this Icelandic author's work will be translated' Sandra Balzo

'In Ari Thór Arason, Nordic Noir has a new hero as compelling and interesting as the Northern Icelandic setting' Nick Quantrill

'Jonasson's writing style is very purposeful and totally unmatched by anyone else. Every single word has a meaning deeper than its literal definition, yet there is a simplicity and a quiet gentleness about it … absolutely perfect' Novel Gossip

'Tense, thrilling and at times quite dark, *Rupture* delivers a GARGANTUAN five-star read!' Ronnie Turner

'With the lightest of descriptive touches and a melancholy colour scheme, Ragnar Jónasson leaves us with some open questions about the nature of justice and the power of redemption' Crime Fiction Lover

'A chilling, thrilling slice of Icelandic Noir' Thomas Enger

'A stunning murder mystery set in the northernmost town in Iceland, written by one of the country's finest crime writers. Ragnar has Nordic Noir down pat – a remote small-town mystery that is sure to please crime fiction aficionados' Yrsa Sigurðardóttir

'*Snowblind* is a brilliantly crafted crime story that gradually unravels old secrets in a small Icelandic town … an excellent debut from a talented Icelandic author. I can't wait to read more' Sarah Ward

'Is King Arnaldur Indriðason looking to his laurels? There is a young pretender beavering away, his eye on the crown: Ragnar Jónasson…' Barry Forshaw

'Ragnar Jónasson has delivered an intelligent whodunnit that updates, stretches, and redefines the locked-room mystery format. The author's cool clean prose constructs atmospheric word pictures that recreate the harshness of an Icelandic winter in the reader's mind. Destined to be an instant classic' EuroDrama

'A beautifully written thriller, as tense as it is terrifying – Jónasson is a writer with a big future' Luca Veste

'It sometimes feels as if everyone in Iceland is writing crime novels but the first appearance of Ragnar Jónasson in English translation (itself a fluid adaptation by British mystery writer Quentin Bates) is cause for celebration' Maxim Jakubowski

'*Snowblind* has given rise to one of the biggest buzzes in the crime fiction world, and refreshingly usurps the cast iron grip of the present obsession with domestic noir … a complex and perplexing case, in a claustrophobic and chilling setting…' Raven Crime Reads

'The intricate plotting is reminiscent of the great Christie but the setting is much more modern and darker. There is an increasing tension and threat that mirrors the developing snow storm and creates a sense of isolation and confinement, ensuring that the story develops strongly once the characters and scene are laid out' Live Many Lives

'A brooding, atmospheric book; with the darkness and constant snow there is a claustrophobic feel to everything' Reading Writes & For Reading Addicts

'It is surely only a matter of time before *Snowblind* and the rest of Ragnar's Dark Iceland series go on to take the Nordic Noir genre by storm. The rest of the world has been patiently waiting for a new author to emerge from Iceland and join the ranks of Indriðason and Sigurðardóttir and it appears that he is now here' Grant Nicol

'Jónasson's prose throughout this entire novel is captivating, and frequently borders on the poetic, constructing something that is both beautiful and uncomfortable for the reader' MadHatter Reviews

'A subtle, quiet mystery set in the most exquisite landscape – a slow burner that will suck you in and not let you go' Reading Room with a View

# WHITEOUT

# Whiteout

RAGNAR JÓNASSON

translated by Quentin Bates

**ORENDA
BOOKS**

Orenda Books
16 Carson Road
West Dulwich
London SE21 8HU
*www.orendabooks.co.uk*

First published in Icelandic as *Andköf* in 2013
Exclusive hardback edition published by Orenda Books
in association with Goldsboro Books in 2017
B-format paperback edition published by Orenda Books in 2017

Reprinted 2020

Hardback ISBN: 978-1-910633-88-5
B-format ISBN 978-1-910633-89-2
eISBN 978-1-910633-90-8

Typeset in Garamond by MacGuru Ltd
Printed and bound by CPI Group (UK) Ltd, Croydon CRO 4YY

This book has been translated with financial support from

 ICELANDIC LITERATURE CENTER

For sales and distribution, please contact *info@orendabooks.co.uk*

For my brother, Tómas.

'Come into my flower garden, black night!
I'll not miss your dewfall, now that all my flowers are dead...'

from *Haust*, Jóhann Jónsson (1896–1932)

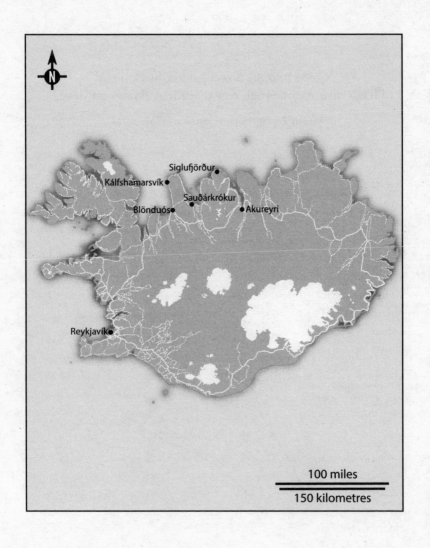

## Pronunciation guide

| | |
|---|---|
| Ari Thór | Ari Tho-wr |
| Arnór | Arn-oer |
| Ásta | Ow-sta |
| Blönduós | Bloen-du-ows |
| Hédinsfjördur | Hye-thins-fyoer-thur |
| Herjólfur Herjólfsson | Her-yol-fuur Her-yolf-son |
| Kálfshamarsvík | Cowls-Hamar-s-viek |
| Kristín | Christine |
| Óskar | Ow-skar |
| Reykjavík | Reyk-ya-viek |
| Siglufjördur | Siglue-fyoer-thur |
| Skagaströnd | Skaga-stroend |
| Thóra | Tho-ra |
| Tómas | Toe-mas |

Icelandic has a couple of letters that don't exist in other European languages and which are not always easy to replicate. The letter ð is generally replaced with a d in English, as in Gudmundur, Gudfinna, Hédinn and place names ending in -fjördur. In fact, its sound is closer to the hard *th* in English, as found in *th*us and ba*th*e.

Icelandic's letter þ reproduced as *th*, as in Ari *Th*ór, is equivalent to a soft *th* in English, as in *th*ing or *th*ump.

The letter *r* is generally rolled hard with the tongue against the roof of the mouth, and Icelandic words and are pronounced with the emphasis on the first syllable.

# PROLOGUE

The little girl stretched out her hands, and then everything happened so quickly that she had no chance to cry. Gravity took over and she simply fell.

The sea and the rocks were there right in front of her.

She was too young to recognise death as it approached.

The point, the beach, the lighthouse, the wonderland around her – all these had been her very own playground.

And then she hit the boulders below.

# PART ONE

# PRELUDE TO A DEATH

It was a sight Ásta Káradóttir would never forget, even though she had only been a child when she saw it – or maybe for that very reason.

She had been in her room in the attic when it happened. The door had been shut, as had the windows, and the air in the room was stale. She had been sitting on the old bed that would creak beneath her when she turned over in the night, staring out of the window. Maybe, or even probably, there were things that subsequently seeped into her recollection of that day, drawn from other childhood memories. But what she saw – the terrible event she witnessed – would never leave her.

She had never told a soul about it.

And now she had returned after a long exile.

It was December and the light snow – just a thin layer that covered everything – was a reminder that Christmas was almost here. There had been a drizzle of rain when she had driven up from the south, and the weather had been relatively warm. With the heater running to keep the windscreen clear, the car had become almost unbearably hot.

Ásta had found her way out of central Reykjavík without a hitch – driving up Ártúnsbrekka and leaving the city where life was like bad sex: better than nothing, but only just. Not that she was expecting to leave her life behind her completely. Her intention was to bid adieu to the monotonous reality – the dingy basement flat and the sixty-eight square metres of claustrophobia and darkness. Some-times, to alleviate the gloom, she would draw back the curtains, but that just meant that the passers-by on her busy street could peek in through the windows, spy on her comings and goings, and look down on her, as if she had given up on any claim to privacy by living in a basement and not drawing the curtains.

Then there were the guys she brought home sometimes at the weekend, when she was in the mood. Some of them wanted to keep the lights on and the curtains open – to make love in plain sight.

She was still young, only a few years past thirty, and while she was very aware she was not past the flush of youth, she was tired of the endless humdrum routine of temporary work and night shifts; fed up with scratching a living on benefits or minimum wage and living in a rented apartment in the centre of town.

To reach her destination, she had driven through the western part of Iceland and over the high mountain pass that led to the north, all the way up to the Skagi peninsula, to Kálfshamarsvík. She had never meant to come back, but here she was, carrying those old secrets with her. She had spent the day travelling, so when she arrived the bay was deep in evening darkness. She stood for a while and looked at the house. It was a fine building with two main floors, an attic and a basement. The architectural style probably pre-dated the house itself, even though it had been there for decades. It was painted a smart, clean white, with a dark-grey exposed foundation, and had curved balconies on the upper floor. Ásta and her sister had lived in the attic with their father and mother for a while. No expense had been spared when the house had been built.

There was a light on downstairs, where she recalled that the living room had been, and a lamp illuminated the front door. These two were the only lights, apart from the glow from the lighthouse on the point, of course. There was an undefinable grace to the interplay between light and shadow; the lights were unnaturally bright in the darkness. This was an area of great natural beauty and rich history, with remnants of disappeared houses hidden everywhere.

With no reason to hurry Ásta set off towards the house slowly, drinking in the fresh night air, and stopping occasionally to look at the sky and let the falling flakes of snow tickle her face.

She hesitated at the front door before knocking.

*Was this really a good idea?*

A sharp gust of wind sent a chill down her back, and she looked around quickly. The loud mutter of the wind had given her a sudden feeling of disquiet; it was as if someone was standing behind her.

Ásta looked around her, simply to convince herself that this wasn't the case.

The darkness greeted her. She was alone, the only footprints in the white snow were her own.

It was too late to turn back.

'He wouldn't have wanted you to stay here,' Thóra said, more to herself than to Ásta. This was the second, maybe the third time that she had said the same thing, in one form or another.

Thóra was well into her sixties but she hadn't changed much in the past twenty-five years. She had the same neutral expression, the same distant eyes and the same irritating, nagging voice.

Óskar, Thóra's elderly brother, sat at the piano at the far end of the living room and played the same quiet theme over and again. He had never been one for talking – was always quick to finish his coffee and make his way back to the piano.

Thóra seemed to be doing her best to make Ásta welcome. They had tried to reminisce about the old days, but the difference in their ages was too much for them to have many shared memories. The last time they had met, Ásta had been seven years old and Thóra around forty. What they did have in common, though, was that they both remembered Ásta's father, so naturally, part of the conversation was about him.

'He wouldn't have wanted it,' Thóra repeated.

Ásta nodded and smiled politely. 'It's not worth discussing,' she said finally. 'He's dead and Reynir offered me a place to stay.' She didn't mention that it wasn't Reynir who had broached the idea; rather that she had called him and asked if she could come for a few days.

'Well, that's the way it is,' Thóra replied.

Óskar continued to play the same theme, not badly, but competently enough, filling up the awkward gaps in the conversation.

'Does Reynir live here all year round?' Ásta asked, although she was sure of the answer. As the sole heir of a wealthy businessman, Reynir Ákason had been in the media spotlight for years. Ásta had read a few interviews with him in which he said that, when he was in Iceland, the only place he wanted to be was out in the countryside.

'More or less,' Thóra replied. 'That might change now that his old man is no longer with us. I expect you saw it in the papers a fortnight or so ago – that he passed away.' She dropped her voice in apparent respect for the deceased, but her tone sounded affected. 'Óskar and I were going to travel south for the funeral, but Reynir said there was no need for that. Reykjavík cathedral is such a small church anyway. And we didn't know him well – he wasn't here that much. As father and son they weren't much alike.' She paused before continuing. 'It must be a lot of work for Reynir taking over all that business, all those investments. I don't know how he manages it. But he's a smart one, that boy.'

*That boy*, Ásta thought. He couldn't have been much over twenty the last time they had met. Of course, back then he had been a grown man in the eyes of a girl of seven. Smart, yes, with an air of experience and ambition about him. He had been an enthusiastic yachtsman, clearly entranced by the sea, just as Ásta had.

'That boy,' she said aloud. 'How old is he now?'

'Getting on for fifty, I'd say. Not that he'd admit it.' Thóra tried to smile, but it was a half-hearted effort.

'He still lives in the basement?'

The offhand question swept like a cold blast of air through the room. Thóra stiffened and stayed silent for a long moment. Thankfully, as before, Óskar continued to play. Ásta glanced at him. Hunched over the piano keyboard, he had his back to them. Everything about his bearing was tired. He wore brown cord trousers and the same dark-blue rollneck sweater as he had worn in the old days; or maybe it was a close relative who'd worn those clothes.

'Óskar and I have moved in there,' Thóra said, her reply failing to sound as nonchalant as she clearly intended.

'You and Óskar?' Ásta asked. 'Surely it must be cramped for the two of you?'

'It's a change, but that's life. Reynir's going to live up here, and it's his house, of course.' She was quiet for a moment.

'We're just grateful to be able to stay,' Óskar broke in, surprisingly. 'We're fond of the point, in spite of everything.' He turned and stared hard at Ásta. His face was craggy, his hands bony. She saw immediately the sincerity in his face.

'I just assumed that you'd still have your space in the apartment up here, considering you brought me into the living room,' Ásta said awkwardly, even though their discomfort did give her some quiet amusement.

'No, no. We use the apartment up here when we eat together, all three of us, or when we have guests. The living room downstairs is darker than up here, not much good for entertaining,' Thóra smiled.

'I can imagine,' Ásta replied, speaking from her own experience of living in a dim basement flat.

'But I've done what I can to make it more comfortable,' Thóra said, almost by way of an apology.

Óskar had turned back to the piano and began playing the same tune as before.

Ásta looked around. The living room had hardly changed, although it certainly seemed smaller than before. As far as she could see, the same furniture was still where it always had been: the old Tudor-style sofa, the dark-brown wooden coffee table, the heavy bookshelves filled with Icelandic literature. The familiar smells played with her senses, creating an elusive aroma and feeling that were a part of the house. How remarkable it was that a smell could evoke long-forgotten memories. The handsome furnishings brought home to Ásta how bland, how depressing, her own apartment was with its cheap furniture – a ripped sofa, a table that she'd bought for almost nothing through an internet ad and the old kitchen chairs in a glaring yellow that had long gone out of fashion.

'You'll use your old room up in the attic, naturally,' Thóra said quietly.

'Really?' Ásta asked in surprise. She hadn't discussed the details of where she'd sleep when she had spoken to Reynir.

'Unless you'd prefer not to? We can put you up somewhere else.' Thóra looked nonplussed. 'Reynir thought that's where you'd want to be. We've stored stuff away up there these last few years, but we moved the boxes and things into the bedroom…' She looked down suddenly and hesitated. '…Into the bedroom that was your sister's.'

'It'll be fine,' Ásta said decisively. 'Don't worry about it.' It had not occurred to her that she would be able to stay, or would need to stay, in her old room. She would probably have preferred to be somewhere else, but she didn't want to ask; she needed to be strong.

'Don't take it the wrong way, my dear,' Thóra said with unaccustomed warmth. 'Although I said that your father wouldn't have wanted you to come back here, you're always welcome.'

*Generous of you, considering it's not your house*, Ásta wanted to say, but kept quiet. 'So what do you do here now?' she asked instead, and not particularly courteously.

'Much the same as ever … looking after the house. There isn't as much to be done as there used to be, and we're not as young as we were. Óskar's a sort of caretaker, like in the old days. Isn't that right, Óskar?'

He stood up from the piano and came over to them, supporting himself with a stick. 'I suppose so,' he mumbled.

'He can't do heavy work anymore, as you can see,' Thóra said with a glance at the stick. Óskar sat next to her but kept a distance. 'Broke his knee climbing those damned rocks.'

'It'll sort itself out sooner or later,' Óskar muttered.

Ásta's attention wandered from what Thóra was saying as she looked at the pair of them. The passing years had taken their toll, and the brother and sister seemed older and more worn than she had expected they would be. Like they'd just about had enough, she mused.

'And he looks after the lighthouse as much as his bad knee will let him. Took over from your father.'

Ásta was overwhelmed by a feeling of discomfort. It happened occasionally; she inhaled deeply, closing her eyes as a way of slowing her breathing.

'Are you tired, my dear?' Thóra asked.

Ásta was taken by surprise. 'No. Not at all.'

'Should I make something for you to eat? I cook for Reynir when he's here. Of course, he can look after himself, but I try and make an effort. It isn't as if he needs us any longer; he could throw us out to fend for ourselves if he felt like it.' She smiled. 'I'm not saying he would, just that he could…'

'Thanks,' Ásta said as she regained her composure. 'I had a sandwich on the way. That'll keep me going.'

Someone banged hard on the door and Ásta jumped. The elderly pair didn't seem surprised, though.

'I thought Reynir wasn't coming until tomorrow night?' Ásta asked.

'He doesn't make a habit of knocking,' Óskar mumbled.

'It must be Arnór, then,' Thóra said, getting to her feet.

Her brother sat immobile, staring into the distance and holding his knee, probably the damaged one, with a half apologetic look on his face. 'You remember Arnór?' he said in a low voice.

Ásta gave the old man a warm smile, thinking of him as old, even though he could hardly be seventy. He certainly looked older, without the lively spark in his eyes that had once been there.

She had always liked Óskar. He had been good to her, and on evenings when there had been fish for dinner, he'd made a point of bringing a glass of milk and some biscuits up to her room before bed. He knew that, despite the sea being so close by, or maybe because of it, little Ásta had never been able to stomach fish. She remembered the nausea she always suffered when there was fish on the table.

'Thank you,' she said to Óskar, having meant to say nothing more than a simple 'yes', and that of course she remembered Arnór.

'Thank you?' Óskar said, questioningly, still holding his knee and leaning towards her as if he had misheard and wanted to be sure not to let it happen again.

Ásta felt her face redden, something that rarely happened.

'I'm sorry. I was just thinking, you know, about the old days. You always used to bring me milk and biscuits … But, yes, I remember Arnór.'

Arnór lived on a farm nearby. He was Heidar's boy, although he must be no more a boy now than Reynir was, despite being ten years younger. She could see him in her mind's eye; a few years older than her, tall and chubby, he had been a shy and clumsy lad. The sisters had seen him around a lot, but he had never played with them. Maybe he thought it was silly to be playing with younger kids, especially girls; or maybe he was just shy.

She thought she saw a light in Óskar's eyes. He looked at her fondly and then dropped his gaze. 'So you remember, do you?' he said. Then added, 'It's good to see that you've turned out so well.'

She smiled out of pure courtesy. *Turned out so well?* she thought and felt she could hardly agree with the sentiment. It was clear that he had no notion of the monotonous existence waiting for her back in that miserable apartment in Reykjavík; the unrelenting struggle to break free of the humdrum and do something with herself. She felt so depressed some evenings, lying on the sofa and staring into the darkness beyond the window, watching people hurry along while life passed her by, that she desperately wanted to break out of her own apartment – smash the windows and crawl out, scratched and bloody from the broken glass. That would make her feel something; and that would have to be better than feeling nothing at all.

'He still lives in the same place?' She could hear the murmur of conversation from the hall: Thóra and her visitor talking.

'Oh, yes. He took over the farm after his father died a few years ago. Heidar was an old man by then, bless him. Arnór looks after Reynir's horses for him. And he helps us out a lot here, especially with the lighthouse. I'm supposed to be the lighthouse keeper, but you can see that I'm past climbing all those stairs. He's a good lad,' Óskar concluded, with emphasis.

She looked up as Thóra and Arnór came into the living room, and saw a young man, tall and slim, with the older woman. She almost didn't recognise him; it was only because she knew who he was that she could see the resemblance behind the bright smile. Otherwise, he had changed completely. He had become a handsome man – it was hard to see in him the clumsy boy she remembered.

'Ásta,' he declared confidently, as if he had seen her only the day before, out on the point, perhaps. Back then he was silent and hesitant, the sisters scampering around him as if their lives depended on it. Now he was self-assured. 'Good to see you,' he said.

As she stepped towards him, she put out a hand, intending that he should shake it. Instead she found herself being hugged affectionately. His embrace was so warm, she couldn't help responding, automatically drawing him closer. Then, realising what she was doing, she pulled away, uncertain.

She looked at him awkwardly and said, 'Good to see you too,' almost in a whisper, following it with a shy smile.

There was nothing awkward about Arnór, though. He stood stock still while she fidgeted and wondered where to look.

It occurred to her to say something about his father, to offer condolences, but she decided against it. She had no idea how long ago Heidar had passed away, or how, so she would have sounded insincere. Her own father had also died since the last time she had seen Arnór. Maybe those two deaths could cancel each other out? Neither she nor Arnór needed to mention them.

He glanced at Óskar. 'I brought the tools, so shall we have a quick look at that window in the lighthouse? We need to fix it soon.'

'It broke in the bad weather yesterday,' Óskar said to Ásta before turning to Arnór. 'Of course, not that I'll be a lot of help.'

'You'd better come anyway. I'll need you to show me what needs doing,' Arnór said, so politely that Ásta was almost convinced he was sincere, although she was sure he was just trying not to hurt Óskar's feelings.

The two men left Ásta and Thóra standing wordlessly in the living room.

'I think I'll go up to bed,' Ásta said finally, when the silence had become too awkward. She picked up her case.

'All right,' Thóra said. 'The stairs to the attic—'

Ásta interrupted her. 'I know the way,' she said in a heavy voice.

## III

She switched on the light and the weak bulb illuminated the narrow staircase, the walls grey and decorated with a tree-branch pattern. A closer look showed a few red berries on the green boughs. The carpet was worn and the wooden handrail was past its prime. From somewhere came a slight draught – enough to set her shivering again.

She knew that there were plenty of other unoccupied rooms in the house. She didn't have to agree to stay in her old attic room. But, in spite of everything, it had been her room, and she wasn't one to imagine that any lingering ghosts from her past were going to keep her awake. She was stronger than that. Once she was up in the attic, however, standing in front of the room's closed door, she wondered if she was doing the right thing. Was this a mistake? She had an uncomfortable feeling that it was all going to end badly. Wouldn't it be better to leave old stones unturned and go back home?

It wasn't too late. She could easily turn around, go downstairs and say goodbye to Thóra, telling her that something had come up in Reykjavík that meant she had to go. There would be no need to say anything to Óskar or Arnór.

She hesitated before opening the door and looked around. To the right were the doors to the main bedroom and the little bathroom. Behind Ásta was the corner that served as a kitchen and … she turned very slowly. The door to her sister's bedroom was shut. She wanted to look inside, just for a moment, but decided against it. Instead she opened the door to her old bedroom.

The attic room wasn't as large as it had been in her memory. There was nowhere she could stand upright anymore. The air was stuffy, with an almost mouldy scent to it, so she hurried to switch on the light and open the window.

That was better. The mutter of waves drifted in through the window, familiar and calming. She looked out and down at the edge of the cliff. Here, from this very window, she had seen something she shouldn't. Oddly, it didn't seem painful to recall it, even though the shock of it had been devastating.

There wasn't much to see in the evening gloom. The lighthouse on the point helped, though. Darkness never had the upper hand here, she thought, but then smiled grimly. In this house, and in this place, there was nothing but darkness.

The house seemed uncomfortably quiet. Thóra must have gone down to her rooms in the basement. Moving must have been difficult for her, but Ásta struggled to feel any sympathy for the old woman.

Her old bed was in the same place. Fortunately, even though it wasn't exactly big, it wasn't a child's bed. Still fully clothed, and leaving the light on, she lay down cautiously. The bed creaked loudly, as it always had. Ásta made herself more comfortable, the bed groaning beneath her.

Physically she was exhausted, but her mind was buzzing, and sleep was unlikely to come straightaway, so she got up again, remembering the steep spiral staircase that led from the little attic flat, if it could be called that, straight down to the back door and out into the open. Trying to throw off her fatigue, she went down the stairs. This had been a lot of steps for small feet all those years ago. But it was no distance at all now, and within a moment she was stepping out into the gently falling snow.

She took slow strides away from the house and out into the darkness, not because of the snow underfoot but due to the weight of so many memories. She inhaled and the cold air brought back even more, sudden and sharp now: those nights spent in the little attic room with the calls of the gulls and the rolling crash of waves preventing her from falling asleep. In fact, the sound of the sea was less a memory, more an all-encompassing presence that now rumbled in competition with the wind.

Once more she had the feeling that coming to this place was tempting fate. But making an effort to shake off her disquiet, she began to make her way to the lighthouse.

The path was difficult to make out in the darkness. Not that it mattered – Ásta could have found the way blindfold. And she wasn't afraid of the dark, never had been. Yet still she felt uneasy, as if the ghosts of the past were calling out to her, following her ... warning her. Soon the lighthouse began to emerge gradually from the gloom in front of her, on the high ground of the point. She had spent a lot of time around this tall building, sometimes basking in the sunshine under its southern face, more often in the cold shadow of the northern side.

She would have liked to walk right up to the lighthouse, but Óskar and Arnór were there, repairing the window and she had no desire to meet them. So instead she made her way towards the rocks to her left – a steep escarpment that weather, wind and sea had ravaged into jagged boulders over the centuries.

Before she knew it, she was at the cliff edge. She leaned forwards, holding her breath and gazing down as the wind buffeted her face and the snow stung her skin. Below was the unforgiving sea, illuminated by the lighthouse, and straightaway she felt the presence of death.

A strong gust all but pushed her off the edge of the cliff. She backed away, having no intention of ending her life here. All the same, she was not frightened; she enjoyed the feeling of blood pulsing through her veins. The thought of death had brought a sudden rush of energy.

The sea had always mesmerised her. Sometimes she had sat here on the clifftop and watched it, sometimes going down to the beach in the bay. When the waves were at their greatest and most fierce, there was no place she would rather be. White was the colour of an angry sea, and thus, little by little, in the small girl's eyes, white had become the colour of anger. Standing close to the waves in a violent storm, the salty sea would fill her being – she would become almost at one with the ocean. She remembered well now how she had watched spellbound as the gulls fought with the gusts of wind, trying with all their strength to stay in the air. Often she knew just how they felt.

Turning away at last, she started walking back to the house. As she went, she took a last glance at the lighthouse and saw Óskar and Arnór coming the same way. They saw her immediately and Arnór waved. She hesitated, waved back and then hurried onwards.

Back in her room, she drew the curtains, pulled on a sweater to drive out the chill and stretched out under the duvet. It was pitch dark now, but still she tossed and turned before finally managing to fall asleep.

She awoke suddenly, unsure how long she had slept, and had the feeling that she was struggling to breathe. She opened her eyes but the darkness overwhelmed her. She sat up with a jerk, breathing short, shallow breaths. It was far too hot, the air was heavy and stifling.

Pulling off the sweater and her shirt, she pushed the duvet off and sat there for a moment in her underwear, before reaching out to draw back the curtains and open the window. Cold air rushed in and the darkness was lifted as the lighthouse flooded the room with light.

She lay back on the bed, wondering for a moment whether to fetch her mobile phone from the pocket of her jeans to check the time. But time didn't matter, she decided. She closed her eyes, her breathing returning to normal once more, and settled into a new calmness. She wasn't used to sleeping with an open window these days – it just wasn't possible in her basement flat – but now the fresh air came like a saviour, and finally she fell asleep, the memories of the past leaving her in peace, allowing her to sleep soundly.

# IV

The next day passed uncomfortably slowly. Ásta slept in late and ate a midday meal with Thóra and Óskar in an almost overpowering silence. Reynir had still not arrived and Arnór had not made another appearance. After lunch she went for a short walk and then tried to rest in the attic, but with little success. There was too much on her mind.

At around six in the evening she went outside again, walking once more towards the lighthouse. Arriving in front of it, she tried to open the door, but it was locked – a change from the time when her father had been the lighthouse keeper. He had never locked the door; he simply trusted his daughters not to put themselves in any danger. So Ásta had been able to sneak inside occasionally, when she wanted to hide away or felt the need for solitude. It had been a refuge for a small girl. She had been careful never to fiddle with anything, normally just closing the door behind her and sitting on the steps to relax and think. She thought now that her father must have realised she did this, but he'd never said a word about it.

Ásta vaguely remembered him, at least once, and probably more often than that, taking her for a walk around the point and trying to tell her some of the history of the place. Back then she'd had little interest in what he told her, but now she somehow recalled it easily. She had always found the lighthouse to be a particularly beautiful building, though, its long black pillars contrasting strongly with the white walls. And its height could become overwhelming if you stood close to it. She took a few steps back, looking skywards and letting her eyes travel up the walls, allowing the feeling of being a tiny part of the wholeness of everything sink into her.

'It's locked,' she heard someone say behind her.

She jumped in surprise and spun around. She'd not heard anyone approach.

Arnór was coming towards her, wrapped up in a heavy down coat. He was bare-headed, even though there was no shelter here from the open sea, and his cheeks were red. He looked even more handsome than he had the evening before.

'Yes, I noticed,' she said sharply. 'Things have changed.'

'We're not all as casual as your father was,' he shot back.

'You remember him, then?' she asked, her tone a little more subdued.

'Of course. He was a wonderful man. Not the kind of person you forget in a hurry. It's a while since he died, isn't it?'

She looked on in surprise as Arnór took a seat on the little concrete platform that surrounded the lighthouse, choosing the view over the bay, rather than sitting next to the door and looking inland.

After a moment Ásta sat down next to him, taking care not to get too close.

'Yes and no,' she said. 'I wasn't twenty when he died, but you could say he left us long before.'

'He died far too early,' Arnór said thoughtfully.

'Yes.'

They were silent for a while.

'He was a real hard worker,' Arnór said at last. 'Right up until...' His voice faded away.

'Exactly.' Ásta nodded in agreement and looked around. Her father had been an outdoorsman through and through, and he'd loved the place at first ... but not afterwards, of course.

She spoke again. 'I used to...' she began, and was silent; she breathed in deeply, filling her lungs with cold air. 'I used to sneak...'

And that was all she could say before Arnór finished the sentence for her: '...sneak inside. Yes. I know. I used to watch you do it.'

She smiled.

'I used to find it a little strange,' Arnór continued, 'that a six- or

seven-year-old girl wanted to shut herself away in an old lighthouse.'
He paused. 'But, then again, you were always distant and mysterious.
You still are – even now, when I'm sitting right next to you.'

Ásta stood up, more abruptly than she intended to – she hadn't
meant to be rude. Arnór stayed where he was.

'Could you lend me a key to the lighthouse, please?' she asked,
smiling an apology for her brusqueness. 'Just for the weekend. It
would be interesting to take a look inside again.'

'Sure, no problem.' Arnór got to his feet, and stood in the lee of
the towering lighthouse. 'I don't have one with me, though, it's in
the car. I'll get it for you later.'

'Thanks.'

'Anyway, I came out here to fetch you,' he said.

'To fetch me?'

'Yes. Reynir has arrived. I've just been into the village with him, to
help him move a huge Christmas tree he bought on Skagaströnd. He
couldn't get it into that luxury SUV of his, so I had to take the truck.
There's no room in those fancy SUVs, and I don't think he wanted to
get his nice clean car all filthy by trying to get a Christmas tree inside.
Anyway, he wants to invite you for an early dinner. He's asked Thóra
to prepare something. There's some lovely smells coming out of the
kitchen, I can tell you.'

'Great. What are we waiting for?' Ásta replied with a smile.

The tree lay in the middle of the living-room floor, its branches
exuding a sharp scent.

Thóra greeted Ásta and Arnór, and then urged Arnór, who was
looking like he was about to leave, to stay and eat with them. 'There's
plenty of room,' she said, 'and far too much food.'

'Fair enough,' Arnór replied, clearly needing little encouragement,
and they all took their seats at the table, even though Reynir was
nowhere to be seen.

As Ásta sat down, someone placed their hands on her shoulders – lightly rather than firmly, but nevertheless she jumped in surprise and looked around quickly, getting half out of her seat.

Her first sight of Reynir after all these years was a bit of a shock. He clearly had a good press agent working for him, she thought. The pictures of the prominent figure of the business world that appeared in the papers suggested a younger, slimmer and better-groomed man than the one who now stood in front of her. His hair was tousled, shot with grey and starting to thin. And the shirt tucked into his tight jeans revealed a paunch that he might have been able to hide in a photograph, but was making no attempt to conceal now.

'Hello, Ásta,' he said warmly. 'It's good to see you again.' He took his hands from her shoulders and offered her one to shake – it seemed a more formal gesture than the circumstances required.

Nevertheless, she shook his hand, with its limp grip, and said, 'Thank you for letting me stay.' It was the only thing that entered her head to say. She had invited herself, so it wasn't as if she could thank him for any invitation.

'You're always welcome, my dear,' he replied. 'I hope you're comfortable? You're in your old room, I presume?'

'Yes, that's right,' she said. And then added, 'Lots of memories,' almost unconsciously giving weight to her words.

An awkward silence followed. Thóra broke it by announcing it was time to serve the first course: a rice pudding with a hint of cinnamon; Ásta hadn't tasted the dish in years.

'Just because it's Christmas,' Thóra said, as if reading her thoughts.

'Cold today,' Reynir said for no apparent reason once the pudding was served. 'There's no shelter anywhere out here.' He smiled at Ásta and then looked over at Óskar. 'Been in the water today, Óskar?'

Óskar glanced up from his plate as if surprised to be the centre of attention. He coughed and wiped a trace of rice pudding from his lower lip. 'No. No, I'm not doing any swimming at the moment,' he mumbled. 'Nothing to speak of, anyway.'

'"Nothing to speak of", what do you mean?' Reynir asked.

'I've hardly dipped a toe in the water recently,' Óskar answered.

'Not in the sea, surely?' Ásta said. But then, once again, it was as if old memories were struggling to the surface: hadn't the old man taken up some damned fool thing like swimming in the sea back in the old days? Yes, she vaguely remembered something like that, now. It had been a fairly uncommon thing for anyone to do at the time – immersing yourself in the bitterly cold Icelandic waters – but it had become much more popular these days. Some people thought it was healthy and refreshing, apparently, although Ásta couldn't for the life of her understand why. Swimming in the sea should be reserved for warmer climates.

'Yes, yes, in the sea,' Óskar mumbled. 'Always the sea.' After a pause, he spoke again: 'I have trouble swimming properly, though, now that my leg's as bad as it is. I'm giving it a chance to sort itself out before I go back in the water again.'

'So what brings you back here?' Arnór asked, his eyes on Ásta.

Her heart picked up a beat. She wasn't pleased about the question but had an answer ready; it was the same one she had given Reynir when she had contacted him. 'I'm working on a project.'

'A project?'

'Yes. I'm studying Icelandic at the university, and I'm writing a thesis about my father. I'm finding it hard to finish it, so I thought I'd come up north to do it properly.'

'It's Christmas break now, isn't it?' Arnór asked.

She hesitated. 'Well, yes. I don't need to hand it in until January. So I decided I'd kill two birds with one stone: finish my thesis and get out of the city for a while.'

Arnór gave her a broad smile, but there was something odd about his expression that made her uncomfortable.

'Well, then,' Reynir said and, turning to Thóra, added lightly: 'You're so good with words, Thóra, maybe you should have gone to university, like Ásta, here.'

Thóra started but said nothing in reply. An uncomfortable silence followed.

'That was the intention,' Thóra finally muttered.

'Really?' Reynir said.

'Thóra was taken ill before she could finish college,' Óskar said, clearly wading in to save his sister's dignity.

'It's a long time ago, now,' Thóra said sharply, and made as if to stand up.

Reynir leaned back in his chair, his hands folded over his belly. 'What bad luck. You would have done well at university. You could have come back here, bursting with knowledge, and taught us all something.'

'No,' Thóra said, quietly but firmly.

'How so?'

'Because I wouldn't have come back here.' Now she did stand up. 'I'll fetch the lamb,' she said, even though they had hardly finished the first course.

Ásta helped herself to more rice pudding. This was the kind of old-style home cooking she missed. She had no particular culinary skills of her own and nobody had ever taken the time to teach her them. And, anyway, who was there that could have done it? She had lost her parents too early. Maybe her aunt should have taught her, the person who had raised her from the age of seven? 'Raised her' was maybe not the right expression. Her aunt had simply provided her with a place to stay, taking her in out of duty alone – first as a temporary measure and then permanently. She had always been a cold and distant woman, and had certainly never taught Ásta anything, except, perhaps, to look out for herself. Ásta had moved out at the first opportunity.

She bore no grudge against her aunt, though, and still less against her parents. She didn't exactly miss them, either. She had no special feelings about them at all, in fact, and felt no bitterness that she had had so few opportunities in life.

But tonight she intended to take action. There was no point in waiting.

Thóra brought some red wine in with the lamb. She made a point of saying, almost as if she had been asked to do so, that it came from Reynir's personal cellar.

'It's a fine wine,' Reynir said. 'A good wine for a welcome guest.' He smiled at Ásta, but it looked insincere.

'What's it like, living in Reykjavík?' Arnór asked politely as Thóra filled Ásta's glass.

'It's not bad,' she replied, wondering whether she should have any wine at all.

'You don't miss the peace and quiet of the countryside?' Reynir added.

She smiled. This was a question she had no difficulty answering. 'No, not at all,' she said, and took her first sip of wine.

# V

Later that evening, an unexpected guest paid a visit to Ásta's attic room. After the initial surprise, she found the company welcome, as she would have struggled to get to sleep anyway; her mind had been racing all evening and her heart was still beating rapidly.

Ásta and her guest talked for a while in the narrow passage outside her bedroom, the soft smell of aftershave becoming gradually stronger as he inched closer to her. Then he kissed her – politely, almost coldly to begin with, and then with growing passion. A hand on the small of her back made its way downwards and drew her to him. She could feel her heart hammering and tried to think clearly through the alcohol-induced fog.

Was this a good idea? She hardly knew the man. But, she could not bring herself to pull away from him – not yet anyway. She felt at ease with him, this ghost from the distant past. And the pulse that vibrated through her was too hot, too strong. There was no hesitation as he unzipped her trousers and his fingers slid inside. Returning the favour, she unfastened his trouser buttons.

Their clothes were soon scattered on the floor, and he led her into the bedroom. It wasn't until they were standing naked by her old bed that she finally held him away.

'We can't do this here,' she whispered, kissing his earlobe tenderly. 'This old bed is falling apart. It makes a terrible noise.'

'OK, no problem,' he said. 'But we don't have to let that stop us.'

He pushed her up against the cold wall. She felt the sudden chill of it like a thousand needles pricking her defenceless body, but the discomfort passed quickly enough.

The pain simply reminded her that she was alive.

It was a fantastic feeling.

# PART TWO
# LIES

# I

'Good morning, my boy.' Tómas greeted Ari Thór in his familiar, warm, cheerful bass, as if he were picking up a conversation they had been having only an hour or two before.

It had, in fact, been some time since Ari Thór had heard from his old boss. A year and a half had passed since Tómas, then Siglufjördur's senior police officer, had sold up, resigned his post and moved south to Reykjavík to salvage the remnants of his marriage before it was too late. Fortunately, everything had worked out well: Tómas had been able to land a good job in the Serious Crimes Department of the city police force.

Having sorted his own life out, Tómas had then encouraged Ari Thór to apply for the inspector's position he had just vacated at the Siglufjördur station; he'd even recommended him highly to his superiors. However, grateful as he was to his former colleague, Ari Thór found the decision about whether or not he should put himself forward for the inspector post a difficult one. Should he take this opportunity and move back to Reykjavík himself, or should he gamble on a long-term career in Siglufjördur? Even after several years here, he hadn't learned to live comfortably in the shadow of the high mountains and in the endless, suffocating winter darkness. There was also the question of his girlfriend, Kristín, who had landed a good job at the hospital in Akureyri, which, since the opening of the new tunnel, was now an easy drive away. Eventually he decided he would apply for the job – or rather, Kristín and he took the decision between them. An inspector's job for someone so young was a significant step up the promotion ladder, even though

he wouldn't have a large team working under him – just two officers, at most.

Having made his application, Ari Thór had innocently believed
that he had an excellent chance of success, but things hadn't turned
out that way. One Herjólfur Herjólfsson had got the job. Herjólfur
had been with the Reykjavík force for many years, interrupted only
by a single leave of absence. Ari Thór had never asked him about this
gap in his record, and Herjólfur had never volunteered any explanation for it. Whatever the reason, his greater experience, longer service
and good connections down south had all probably combined to tip
the balance in his favour. Ari Thór had been deeply disappointed.
He'd even considered resigning, but Kristín had persuaded him to
stay on, gather more experience and not be tempted to drop a secure
job just as the force was going through a round of cuts.

Now, sitting at his desk in the Siglufjördur station, Ari Thór wondered why on earth Tómas was calling – two days before Christmas?

'Hello there,' he said to his former boss. 'Haven't heard from you
for a while.' He glanced over to Herjólfur, who hadn't even looked
up when the phone rang.

'Do you have a couple of spare minutes?' Tómas asked, his tone
turning serious. It sounded like he was in a car.

'Yes…' Ari Thór hesitated, and, deciding it might be better to continue the conversation outside, he stood up and pulled on his jacket.
It had snowed heavily over the past few days – a gentle, even snowfall
that had left Siglufjördur clothed in white. There was usually no
escaping the snow in wintertime in this, the northernmost town in
Iceland, which was so close to the Arctic Circle, the sun disappeared
behind the mountains in the depths of winter. Now, though, there
had been no raging blizzards and, the people of the town accepting
this inevitable part of winter with their usual stoicism, a calm had
descended on the town as Christmas approached.

In fact it was impossible to escape Christmas. Decorations hung
in all the windows, and strings of lights adorned the houses and trees,
and had even been stretched between the roofs and the lamp posts.

The usual magnificent tree stood in the centre of the Town Hall Square. The people of Siglufjördur were quietly getting ready for the holiday, which in Iceland was celebrated on Christmas Eve, with evening mass at the old church and then dinner and the unwrapping of presents, followed by what in Ari Thór's mind was one of the most important Christmas Eve traditions of all – the reading of a book well into the night.

Ari Thór stood on the snow-covered pavement and listened to what Tómas had to say as he took breaths of the fresh northerly air.

'I finally managed to get somewhere with your transfer application,' Tómas said.

At Tómas's instigation, shortly after Herjólfur's appointment Ari Thór had applied for a temporary transfer to Reykjavík, but without any real hope that a new role would be the magic bullet that would cure his disappointment. Still, he felt a surge of anticipation.

'I told you at the time that applying for the inspector's post wouldn't be much more than a formality ... So I still feel a little guilty you didn't get it...'

'That's rubbish,' Ari Thór said, with more determination than he had allowed himself when they had worked together. 'You're not responsible for my future.'

'All the same,' Tómas said and cleared his throat. 'We have some room to manoeuvre here.' He fell silent and Ari Thór could hear the hum of an engine.

He looked along the street to the snow-clad mountain slopes that gave the town a picture-postcard feel.

'There's been a sudden death not far from Skagaströnd, at Kálfshamarsvík. You know the place?'

Ari Thór thought for a moment. 'I can't say I do,' he said at last.

'Oh, well. That shouldn't matter too much. But keep that to yourself. I had to spice things up a little so I could pull you in on this with me: I told them that you knew the area.'

'Pull me in?' Ari Thór repeated in surprise, excited and nervous at the same time. 'When?' he asked at last.

'Now. Right away. I'm on my way north. Don't worry, I'll have a word with Herjólfur for you.'

'Now?' Ari Thór asked again. 'But it's almost Christmas,' he added without thinking.

'I know. This investigation could take a couple of days, so any Christmas celebrations are going to be on the modest side. That's just why it's been such a struggle to find someone for this job.'

'Why didn't the Akureyri force take it on?'

'There's some narcotics bust going on up there; I gather it's a big investigation so they don't have any spare manpower. There was the option of calling in an officer without a family who could come up north with me, but it's someone I don't get on all that well with. Then I mentioned you – a young officer with some solid experience behind him, a nose for sniffing out the truth and, what's more, is already in the north…'

'I'm not even in the same county as this … this—'

'Kálfshamarsvík,' Tómas said, finishing his sentence for him.

'Exactly.'

'It makes no difference,' Tómas said, and Ari Thór could imagine the amiable grin on his face. 'All the same, it worked out and you're coming with me.'

A series of thoughts flashed through Ari Thór's mind. One thing at a time, he told himself. One thing at a time.

'Who's the victim?'

'A young woman,' Tómas replied, his voice grave again.

'And what do you mean by a sudden death? An accident? Suicide?' But Ari Thór knew what the answer would be. Tómas's department would hardly be called in for either incident.

'It looked like suicide to start with, and that still hasn't been ruled out. She died on the twentieth, but it took the local police three days to call us in, as they assumed she simply took her own life,' Tómas answered heavily. 'But the post-mortem showed up marks on the body that raised a few questions…' He paused briefly, leaving the rest unsaid, before continuing, his tone unusually earnest. 'There's something sinister about all this, damned sinister.'

'Something sinister about the injuries?' Ari Thór asked, thinking Tómas was leaving too many things hanging in the air.

Tómas paused once more. 'That wasn't what I meant,' he said. 'It's more the circumstances, the back story. The terrible things that happened to the mother and her daughters.'

'Mother and her daughters?'

'Look, I'll tell you the whole story when we meet,' Tómas said with finality.

'OK, but I need to talk to Kristín first,' Ari Thór said, 'before I make any decision.'

Four years ago he had accepted the position with the Siglufjördur police without consulting Kristín. And everything had gone wrong after that – they'd even split up for a while. He was reluctant to make the same mistake twice. Now they were back together he had no intention of jeopardising the relationship. As often as she could, she stayed with him in the house in Siglufjördur and he stayed with her at her little flat in Akureyri whenever he had the chance. He didn't want to do anything to disrupt their life together.

'This isn't an opportunity you want to miss,' Tómas said.

'Any chance of running back to Siglufjördur for the evening on Christmas Eve?'

'Yes – depending on the weather and the conditions,' Tómas replied sternly. This was the senior man back in his former role. 'But I'm sure she'll manage just fine without you.'

'Yes, of course she can. But I'd prefer not to take the chance. After all the preparations, it will be a shame for Christmas to be ruined,' Ari Thór said. Then, aware of how little weight this excuse was likely to carry with Tómas, he decided to get straight to the point – to tell his old friend what was at the forefront of his mind. 'Then there's … Kristín … She's pregnant.'

'Pregnant?' Tómas was clearly taken by surprise. 'That's wonderful news. Congratulations.'

'Thanks,' Ari Thór murmured in reply.

'I had no idea,' Tómas said, and there was a hint of rebuke in his voice that Ari Thór hadn't passed on such momentous news.

'It's a long time since we've talked,' Ari Thór said, taking the unspoken hint. 'I kept meaning to call you, but you know how time runs away. Last time we spoke the pregnancy was still so early that we didn't want to tell anyone.'

'Don't worry about it. How far along is she?'

'Eight months,' Ari Thór replied with pride in his voice.

'Well, that's close enough! A little Siglufjördur lad arriving any minute,' Tómas said cheerfully.

Ari Thór decided against commenting on this last remark. He was, it was true, feeling more at home in Siglufjördur, enjoying its remoteness and stillness and the proximity of nature. He even liked engrossing himself in the small-town nature of the place. Yet there was still a restlessness inside him, even an occasional sense of despair.

'So, you'll understand why I don't really want to leave Kristín behind,' he said. And then he added, as an afterthought, 'Could I bring her with me?'

'Bring her with you?' Tómas asked, the question clearly taking him by surprise. He was silent for a moment. 'Sure. If you're certain she won't get bored there. We'll be staying in Blönduós. You two can have the big room. Can you get yourselves over there?' he asked. 'As soon as possible?'

As he put the phone down, Ari Thór knew that the hard part would be to convince Kristín that she would be spending the night, and maybe the whole of Christmas, in Blönduós.

They had been looking forward to their first Christmas together in their own home. The previous year, when they had just rekindled their relationship, Kristín had been on a shift at the hospital in Akureyri over Christmas so Ari Thór had volunteered for shifts at the same time, and there had been little in the way of any proper celebrations. This year they had been determined to make up for it. They had been out to the wooded region at the edge of town the previous weekend and chosen a tree. They had strolled through the woods, in no hurry to pick the best or the biggest tree, giving themselves time to take in the scent of pine around them, to enjoy being together, to make the most of this brief moment of daylight in the dead of winter; they'd even relished the chill that pinched their cheeks. Once the modest tree they had chosen had been cut down and the snow brushed off its branches, they went home discussing where the best place for it would be. On the way it occurred to Ari Thór that this was the first time he had bought his own Christmas tree; in fact it was the first time for years that he could look forward to a proper Christmas with a proper tree. His parents had always had a real tree for Christmas, never a plastic one, and always made sure it was the traditional type. They had bought the tree from a friendly seller who appeared year after year and made his pitch on the same spot. But then Ari Thór's parents had died, and he was left alone. He went to live with his paternal grandmother, until she died too. At her house a plastic tree was always good enough.

He hoped that Kristín would be understanding about this trip. Tómas was right – this was an opportunity not to be missed. However, Kristín's pregnancy meant that she was sometimes so emotionally and physically drained, no suggestion was likely to be well received.

As he mulled over how best to broach the subject to her, he was reminded of another effect the pregnancy was having on her. Clearly thinking about the new baby's heritage, she had become increasingly curious about his upbringing, and seemed particularly interested in his late father. She had recently asked how well he remembered him. Ari Thór would rather have avoided the subject, but humoured her by recalling a few memories. One that sprang to mind was of a visit to a playground when Ari Thór had been only four years old. It was only later he realised that at that time his father – and namesake – must have been twenty-eight years old, the same age Ari Thór was now. It was as if the passage of time were playing tricks on him – making him remember that specific and seemingly innocuous incident and treating it like some kind of milestone.

It was this same damned time that kept slipping past, however much he cursed and railed against it, making him wonder what he had achieved in those twenty-eight years. Would his father have been proud of him? And his mother? His father had been just thirty-seven when he died. Ari Thór didn't expect the same fate to befall him, but it was difficult not to let his thoughts wander in that direction. At the very age, Ari Thór was now, his father had fewer than ten years left to live.

Was he using his time as well as he could?

## II

Thóra smiled to herself. The dining table in the basement could hardly be cleaner, but she still polished it hard, as if it was very grubby. She had to keep herself busy, in spite of being so tired. It wasn't an option to sit idle, staring out of the window, thinking about the girl who had died.

In fact, it wasn't as if she could even stare out of the window – they didn't have much of a view now Reynir had made them move down into the basement.

They hadn't said a word in protest, though; they'd just let it happen.

Óskar always gave in. There wasn't an ounce of pluck in the man.

She would have complained herself, but her fondness for Reynir outweighed her inclination to resist him.

He must have understood how demeaning it was for them, though; how unfair it was to have them spend their declining years down in the basement after all those decades of service, even though she fully realised that this was Reynir's house, not theirs.

Pure coincidence had put them in the main apartment for all that time. The owners had occupied the upper floor, and she and Óskar had been on the lower one, the ground floor. To begin with they had lived in the attic, but they'd had to move out when Ásta's father, Kári, came to work there as the lighthouse keeper, bringing his wife, Sæunn, and their little girls with them. The only remaining space was in the main apartment itself, so she and Óskar had shared it with Reynir's father, while Reynir, who was a teenager at the time, had taken over the basement.

How quickly time passed. She was so tired these days, and this wretched illness didn't help. She tried to put it out of her mind, but it was difficult.

On top of all that, any Christmas spirit there had been in the house had now vanished. The house was usually so festive at this time of year; the old Christmas ornaments were brought down from the attic, old records of Christmas carols were played in the living room, lots of chocolates were enjoyed, and the smell of baking *laufabraud*, the traditional Icelandic flatbread, filled every room. And then, on Christmas Eve, the holiest of nights, quiet and beautiful, there was a delicious dinner followed by a few presents.

But this year everything would be different. The girl was dead and the police were on their way from Reykjavík 'to have a quiet word with them', as they put it.

She sat back on the sofa and tried to relax.

Everything in the basement was ready for Christmas. The plastic Christmas tree had been taken from its box, the old string of Christmas lights was in its place, as were her mother's tarnished baubles. Óskar had decorated the tree, as he always did, never departing from tradition. They held on tight to their old memories – the warmth of their childhood Christmases, when everything was just as it ought to be; back when she had high hopes for the future. That was before everything went so badly wrong.

Óskar had never been one to let life disappoint him, certainly not as far as she was aware. He was so easily satisfied and lacking in ambition. He was never angry; at least, he never showed it.

As siblings they were completely different. In fact, they were so dissimilar that it occasionally occurred to her that they might be half-siblings. There were two years separating them – Óskar was born during the war and she arrived shortly after it had ended.

Thóra had been told that their father, having worked for the US army during the war, had gone to America, leaving his wife and the two children behind him. Thóra had been just a year old, and her only memories of him were in photographs. Considering he had made himself scarce not long after her birth, could he have been Óskar's father but not hers? It was something the two of them had never discussed, although she was sure it must have occurred to Óskar too. He was such a trusting character, though, with a kind heart.

She had set her sights higher than his, and was duly punished for it. She had been a promising student, completing school with good grades in all her exams, and with well-wishers offering support so that she could go to college. But it was as if fate had decided that she could only go so far and no further. It had all turned out for the worse, and she had returned to Kálfshamarsvík and had been stuck there ever since.

That was the word: stuck. There was no other way to describe it. Life had conspired to place them there, out on the point at Kálfshamarsvík.

There had been a small village here in the early part of the twentieth century, but it had been abandoned around 1940. Ten years later a fine gentleman from Reykjavík had decided that this was the place to build a magnificent house. This was where she had lived, apart from one short break, for nearly sixty years. *Sixty years*.

Her mother had been taken on as the housekeeper not long after the house was built. She had lived sparingly on a meagre income all her life, supporting two children by herself, so when she died there was little left for Óskar and Thóra to inherit. By then they had both been in their twenties and had started working there themselves. Óskar had already been looking after the horses for Áki, Reynir's father. Áki had offered them both permanent positions and they had accepted, Óskar because he seemed to have no real interest in making his mark anywhere else, and Thóra because she had already tried to break free and failed. She was ashamed of herself and so decided to remain out of sight at the house.

Then – she wasn't sure how – it had become too late to leave. She had put down roots there, she supposed. She hadn't noticed it happening – it must have occurred gradually. She had become comfortable over the years, and it was a peaceful place, or it had been to begin with, at least.

The bad luck had moved in along with Kári and Sæunn. Hopefully Ásta's death would end it, closing the circle for good.

She smiled bitterly. She knew better than that. Lies don't go away and the sins of the past don't disappear that easily. The guilt was all around her.

Óskar had always been happier here than she had been, that was obvious. He loved the sea, the magnificent columns of rock – dangerous, but stunning to look at – and the lighthouse, of course. And while Thóra couldn't deny that there was something mesmerising about the twisted basalt formations, she wasn't given to an outdoor life. She would have preferred a life spent in the city, but early on she realised that would never happen.

Óskar's reaction to Ásta's death had been muted, not that he ever had much to say about anything. All the same, the two of them had been good friends at one time, despite the difference in their ages – she only a child and he around forty. Scurrilous whispers had put it about that his interest in the girl had been something … well … sinister. Thóra had told herself she didn't believe the rumours, but she couldn't be entirely sure she was right…

He had always been slightly odd. For instance, this winter he had developed the strange habit of locking himself in his room at the same time every working day. It was a combination of a bedroom and a study, and contained their television, radio, a modest library and the telephone. These days people wanted their televisions in the living room, but Thóra wouldn't have that. The living room was for receiving guests. That was the way it had been in the old days, and that was the way it would be as long as she had anything to say in the matter.

It was a mystery to Thóra just why Óskar had decided to shut himself away at the same time every day. The heavy door was a solid piece of work but she could still hear murmurs behind it, so he wasn't sitting there in silence. She was curious to know what he was doing, as well as apprehensive.

She didn't want to ask him about it. They each gave the other space, just like any old couple.

She had never had the opportunity to set up a home of her own. She knew that if her studies in Reykjavík had not ended so calamitously, she could have become a happy wife and mother. It was all down to one vile man. The bastard was long dead now, but she still kept the obituaries from the papers, keeping alive her virulent hatred for him.

Maybe she should have forgiven him after all this time – but that was such a difficult thing to do.

## III

'Being on duty at Christmas can happen to anyone, especially people in our lines of work,' Kristín said good-naturedly.

Her response was the opposite of what Ari Thór had expected. There were no recriminations and no disappointment, at least not on the surface. Maybe he didn't know Kristín as well as he imagined, in spite of everything. All the same, he had been careful to dress the plan up as a suggestion rather than a decision that had already been taken, and that may have made the difference.

'Of course, we can come home for a few hours on Christmas Eve,' Ari Thór said. The idea of going home was now synonymous in his mind with going to Siglufjördur, something he would never have been able to imagine before moving to the north. 'We can still have Christmas here.'

'We?' Kristín asked quizzically.

'You're coming with me, aren't you?'

'There's room for me there?' she asked. 'I was just going to take it easy by the tree with a box of chocolates and a book.'

'Tómas said it was fine for you to come as well and stay with us in Blönduós. Of course, you can't come with us to the place – the murder scene, I mean … if it is a murder,' he added, as he still knew so little about the case.

She seemed doubtful. 'Well, I suppose it's an option.'

'Tómas half promised that I could come home for Christmas Eve, but if anything were to come up, maybe it's best that we're together, even if we're just in some hotel. And … you know … as you're pregnant…'

'You're romance personified,' she smiled.

Ari Thór felt he could breathe more easily. She was taking it well.

'We need to go right away, though. Can you be ready in ten minutes?'

'Ten minutes? Are you out of your mind?'

⊕

'The roads might be bad, even if it's clear weather, so it might be best if I drive,' Ari Thór said, even though it was Kristín's car, anxious that she should not overtire herself in her condition.

'Don't be so old-fashioned,' she told him, but let him have his way on the condition that they stopped at the Co-op. 'I'm eating for two,' she reminded him.

Ari Thór drove unusually slowly along the Siglufjördur road, which was made treacherous by patches of ice; he was unwilling to take any risks with his pregnant girlfriend at his side. The snow on the mountain slopes glittered in the sunshine and, despite it being the purpose of their trip, the disturbing murder case was as far from Ari Thór's thoughts as it could be. They had bought a box of *laufabraud* in the Co-op and ate it on the way, accompanied by a cosy soundtrack of the Christmas greetings being read out on the radio. Every year, throughout the 23rd of December, the National Radio of Iceland broadcast nothing but Christmas greetings, sent in from people all over the country. Even in the age of social media, this tradition seemed to be stronger than ever. There was still something comforting and old-fashioned about these warm greetings.

The sun hung low in the sky, breaking occasionally through the clouds. The mountains were almost completely white, dotted at intervals by bright-red tractors, a few ewes and the odd house; even an old snow plough looked more decorative than useful in the perfect scene. The trip would take them from Siglufjördur, through the vast fjord of Skagafjördur, down to the town of Saudárkrókur, about an hour and a half from Siglufjördur, and then to Blönduós town, another forty-five minutes or so of driving.

An hour into the journey, Kristín interrupted one of the Christmas greetings. 'Can we stop in Saudárkrókur?'

'What for?'

'I'd like to meet an old man there, now we're up this way.'

'An old man?' Ari Thór asked in surprise.

'Yes ... I've been doing a little research into my family tree...'

Ari Thór sighed. Kristín's hobbies could sometimes be so strange. As her pregnancy advanced, she had been putting more and more effort into digging into the past. For as long as Ari Thór had known her, she had found it difficult to be idle, and right now she had far too much time on her hands. She had reduced her working hours and now only two sessions of pre-natal yoga each week had replaced her usual daily workouts.

'Is it just a quick stop?' he asked.

'No...' she said slowly. 'I'm going to need an hour. I want to find out about something that's in one of my great-grandfather's diaries. He lived not far from Blönduós.'

'We don't have time now, my love,' he said. But then, in an effort to show an interest added, 'You haven't mentioned a diary before.'

'My great-grandfather kept a diary,' she said, brightening. 'He wrote about the family, the weather, the farm and all the trouble they had to go through. Droughts and floods, snow and blizzards ... prices at the slaughterhouse, prices of imported goods...'

'Some things never change,' Ari Thór remarked.

'Listen,' Kristín said, reaching into the footwell for her bag and retrieving a battered book. She opened it to show Ari Thór the crabbed, faded handwriting before reading a section out loud.

*There has been terrible unrest abroad. It began in August, leaving trade in disarray, as ships dare not sail and prices have risen sharply. We have all been distressed by the sudden shortage of goods in every town. It has been wet since the tenth and has remained so for the rest*

*of the month. I was able to gather sixty horses but they were in poor*
*condition, and I can't collect more until the round-up. The haymak-*
*ing has been very poor and badly done and I was only able to bring*
*in the hay in the 24th week of the summer. Trade has been good,*
*though, as far as we are concerned, with meat fetching 27–28 aurar,*
*sheepskins 45 aurar and wool 80 aurar. Foreign goods have been costly*
*and there is little available thanks to the war. The harvest has been*
*poor, and hasn't happened in some countries again because of the war.*
*Farmers have slaughtered many of their animals due to the scarcity of*
*hay so there are fewer sheep. Times are hard for many. I slaughtered*
*90 sheep.'*

'"Unrest abroad". That's the First World War, right?' Ari Thór
asked.

'That's right,' she replied. 'And it seems to have been cold all the
time in Blönduós, just constant cold, storms, snowfalls, blizzards and
all sorts. Sometimes he mentions the sea ice in the bay – it seemed to
have made things difficult for people…'

'Did he write anything about Christmas?' Ari Thór asked. The
greetings being read out on the radio formed a background to their
conversation.

'Well … not really. He and his wife go to church, but not all
that often, and when it comes to Christmas all he mentions is the
weather. Everything revolves around the weather,' she said, looking
through the text. 'Christmas 1915: bare ground up until Christmas,
then sleet and ground frost, sheets of ice. And then there's the winter
of 1918…'

'The great frost winter?' Ari Thór said. 'Isn't that right?' The great
frost winter of 1918 was written about in all Icelandic history books.
The January that year had been the coldest of the century. The rest
of 1918 was notorious too, as later that year Iceland was gripped by
the Spanish flu, leaving hundreds of people dead.

Ari Thór glanced sideways out of the window. A few lonely horses
stood on the frost-bitten ground, reminding him of the print of a

painting by Jón Stefánsson that had hung on his grandmother's wall when he had lived with her after the deaths of his parents.

'That's right,' Kristín said and read again out loud.

*'On the thirteenth night began a blizzard from the north with frost, and there has been a temperature of 26 degrees below zero for many days. There had been two days of such frost over Christmas. This continued into the second month of winter and it even got as cold as 30 degrees below zero. The coldest temperature in the country was 38 degrees below, and all the ships in harbour were frozen fast and the bay of Húnaflói was filled with ice. This was the case to the north. One polar bear was seen near Skagaströnd and was shot and two whales were shot from the ice. With the coming of February it started milder, with thawing, but then there were blizzards, a weight of snow and a bitter cold. The outlook is poor and unrelentingly so.'*

'Well, this Kálfshamarsvík place is close to Skagaströnd, or so Tómas told me. There's a chance we might finally get to see a polar bear,' Ari Thór said.

'Then there's a mystery,' Kristín said, as if she had not heard him. 'The last entry in the diary is in 1918, when he says that, after a trip to Saudárkrókur, everything changed. I've done some research and found out that, while he was travelling, his wife was taken ill and she died. I know that his daughter always blamed him for that and never forgave him for being away. I want to know what took him to Saudárkrókur, so I've tracked down the old man I mentioned. Apparently he knows something about all this. I'm intrigued. It seems there's some secret hidden away under the surface. And anyway, everyone wants to know about their roots, don't they?'

'I suppose so,' Ari Thór replied. He had made efforts himself, not long after meeting Kristín, to find out why his own father had disappeared without trace when Ari Thór had been a child. He had solved that mystery, but a few things had come to light that should have been let lie.

'Maybe it's best not to know the truth,' he said without thinking.

# IV

Tómas was waiting for them when they reached Blönduós, sitting over a late lunch in a corner of the hotel's dining room – the only guest there – enjoying his soup. The restaurant was colourful, with dark wooden fittings around the bar and a parquet floor scattered with blue and wine-red rugs. An old-fashioned chandelier hung over a circular table. The smell of skate was overpowering. Ari Thór had tasted it a few times and, refusing to let the strong smell put him off, had actually quite liked it.

'We'll smell of skate for the rest of the day,' he said as he greeted Tómas.

'Welcome, my boy,' Tómas replied. 'They were holding a Christmas skate lunch here today.' It was an old Icelandic tradition to eat fermented skate the day before Christmas Eve, in spite of the strong smell that came with it.

'And you're sitting here with just bread, water and soup?' Ari Thór said with a grin.

'They were all out of skate. But this is no ordinary soup – it's proper Icelandic meat soup of the best kind, with excellent pieces of lamb. Come and sit down with me,' he said and then met Kristín's eyes. 'Hello, Kristín. Good to see you,' he said, failing to sound completely genuine. Tómas and Kristín hardly knew each other and on the few occasions they had met it seemed that they hadn't connected, as if they were not on the same wavelength.

'Hello, Tómas,' she replied, as she and Ari Thór took their seats.

'Soup?' Tómas waved to the waiter and ordered soup for two more, water and more bread. 'It's damned good,' he added and spooned a chunk of lamb from his bowl with obvious enjoyment. He looked to Ari Thór to have put on a few kilos.

'That's a handsome bump,' Tómas said, glancing at Kristín.

Ari Thór refrained from remarking that the same could be said of Tómas's paunch.

'Yes. Not long to go now,' she said.

'A boy or a girl?'

'We don't know,' Kristín said. 'I don't want to find out until it arrives.'

'Good for you,' Tómas agreed. 'That's the way we did it as well.'

'How's it going down south?' Ari Thór asked, before realising that his question could be interpreted as an impertinent enquiry into Tómas's personal life. 'The new job, I mean,' he hastily added.

'Pretty good,' Tómas said, after a moment's hesitation. 'Pretty good.'

'Detective Superintendent. That's not bad,' Ari Thór said.

'Well, yes. Maybe too good.'

'Why do you say that?' Ari Thór asked in surprise.

'Not everyone was delighted, if you see what I mean?'

'By your appointment?'

'I wasn't the only one who applied. And some of them had a lot more experience.'

'But hardly more *police* experience?' Ari Thór said.

'No, but that was taken into account. Ach, it's a mess…' Tómas sounded unusually downbeat. 'Two of the officers who applied are now working under me. So I feel that I have to prove myself every single day, as ridiculous as that may sound.'

'And this case? The fatality?' Ari Thór asked, suspecting that there could be more to this than Tómas had so far told him.

'The truth is, I could do with a good result, and preferably under my own steam,' Tómas said with an awkward smile.

'It didn't take you long to find your way around the office politics down south,' Ari Thór said with a grin. 'I can see now why you called me in rather than ask someone down there who was on leave … Am I right?'

Tómas left the question unanswered, so Ari Thór changed the subject rather than press the point. 'Do we have time for soup? Don't we have people waiting for us?'

'The poor woman is already dead,' Tómas said placidly, dipping bread into the little that was left of his soup. 'This case isn't going to run away from us. I'll go over the main points while you're eating.' He seemed to have no concerns about discussing the case with Kristín present. 'It's a strange one, that's for sure,' he added.

The waiter returned with a tray bearing two bowls of soup, glasses of water and a basket of bread. Once he had retreated to a reasonable distance, Tómas dropped his voice and continued.

'Her name was Ásta Káradóttir. Thirty-three years old. Orphaned.'

Ari Thór's heart jumped. Orphaned. Would he be described like that if he were found dead?

*The deceased has been identified as Ari Thór Arason. Twenty-eight years old. Orphaned.*

'By that I mean,' Tómas went on, 'she lost her parents early, her mother when she was five and her father before she turned twenty.'

It occurred to Ari Thór that this could be another reason why Tómas had wanted him as part of the investigation; Tómas imagined that he could in some way put himself in the victim's position. He quickly stifled these thoughts; he was allowing his imagination to run away with him.

'She lived in Reykjavík, a basement flat on Ránargata. The place has been searched and didn't turn up anything relevant.'

It took Ari Thór a moment to digest this information. 'Ránargata, you said?' he asked in a low voice, but with an unusually sharp edge to his words.

'That's right,' Tómas said, eyeing him. 'Anything significant about that?'

'Nothing,' Ari Thór replied, trying to hide his surprise and look as if nothing had perturbed him. 'Nothing at all.'

The truth was, there were two uncomfortable coincidences here: first, the victim had lost her parents at a young age; and second, she

lived in a basement apartment at the western end of Reykjavík. Ari
Thór had lived on Öldugata before moving to the north, a stone's
throw from Ránargata where the young woman had lived. Could
he have seen this Ásta out and about? Could he have seen her in the
street, or in the corner shop? It was a coincidence, he told himself,
and nothing more than that. All the same, the thought was disquiet-
ing, almost as if he had walked in her footsteps.

He wanted to know more about her, now, where she had come
from and why she had lost her life.

'No brothers or sisters?' Ari Thór asked, and flinched when Tómas
said that she had none. Once again Ásta's background seemed to
mirror his own.

'Not living, at any rate,' Tómas continued, to Ari Thór's relief,
even though the answer was a tragic one. 'She did have a sister…'

'…who died?' Ari Thór said, finishing his sentence for him.

'I'll fill you in on the details later. As I told you on the phone,
this is a pretty unpleasant affair, and this is what we are spending
Christmas on. What do you think of that?'

It was clear from the look on his face that he wasn't expecting an
answer and Ari Thór made no attempt to give him one.

'She was in a bad way financially, poor girl,' Tómas went on,
heavily. 'She rented her place in Reykjavík and she owed quite a bit
of back rent. Plus, she'd been out of work so she'd been doing relief
shifts at a supermarket at the beginning of the month.'

'So what was she doing up here in the north?'

'This is where she was brought up. She hadn't been back here for
a long time, though – around twenty-five years, or so I understand.
But it's hardly surprising…' He lapsed into silence again, finishing
his soup and draining the water from his glass before continuing.
'Her parents moved here in 1983, when she was four years old. The
reason she gave people for her recent visit was that she was studying
language and literature at university and came back to finish writing
a thesis about her father.'

'So she was a student?' Ari Thór asked.

'No,' Tómas replied arching his eyebrows. 'We've found out that she had her school certificate and that's all. She never went to college, let alone university. It was all a lie. So we have no idea why she came all this way, up to the north. Whatever her reason, it ended badly for her.'

'Financial problems, unemployed…' Kristín said. 'Has suicide been ruled out?'

'Ruled out?' There was a thoughtful look on Tómas's face. 'Not exactly. But we have to go into this with open minds.' He directed his words at Ari Thór.

'Of course,' he replied shortly.

'But I have to confess something,' Tómas added. 'I don't have a good feeling about this. I worry that I might end up regretting getting involved.'

'Isn't it exactly the kind of case a police officer should want to get his teeth into?' Kristín asked.

'Precisely,' Tómas replied with an uncomfortable smile. 'Right, let's get down to the details. She was found, or rather, her body was found, at the bottom of a steep cliff that runs between the point at Kálfshamarsvík and down to the bay. It's a very dangerous place if you're not careful. Maybe she tripped, or just went too close to the edge in the darkness, but that's pretty unlikely. She'd grown up there, so I'm sure she was fully aware of the dangers.' He furrowed his brow, a deadly serious expression on his face. 'She was staying in the only house out there on the point. The local police interviewed all the people who live there and also spoke to a young man who lives nearby. One of them found the body. They told the police it was a suicide, which does seem the most obvious explanation.'

'Who are these witnesses?'

'There's a brother and sister in their sixties who live permanently in the house, but it belongs to someone you'll have seen on the news: Reynir Ákason.'

'That's interesting,' Ari Thór said. 'He's rolling in money, isn't he?'

'So I understand. His father was a rich man, at least, so the boy must have inherited a decent amount. He took on the house and he spends a lot of time there.' Tómas paused before continuing. 'Now, here's the thing: we received the preliminary results of the post-mortem this morning. As I told you before, there are marks on the body that don't tie in with the suicide theory. There's bruising to the neck, as if someone grabbed her by the throat, although that wasn't the cause of death. What killed her were probably the head injuries. The current theory is that she received a fatal blow to the back of the head, and then the other injuries were a result of hitting the rocks and the cliff post-mortem. The pathologist didn't want to be pinned down on this so early, but it's enough for us to be suspicious.'

'I agree,' Ari Thór said.

'The forensic team is already at the cliff – two of them; they left Reykjavík before I did this morning. They'll be looking for anything that can tell us exactly where the murder took place – assuming it is a murder.' Tómas paused again and then spoke more slowly. 'There are a few more intriguing aspects to the case. She appears to have had sex shortly before her death.'

'Any idea who she was sleeping with?' Ari Thór asked.

'We still don't know. It'll take a while for the samples to be ana-lysed. There's nothing to indicate that there were any other visitors from elsewhere around, so we have to start from the assumption that it was either Reynir or the other guy, Arnór – the young man who lives nearby. He had a meal with them all the evening before her death.'

'Didn't you say there were a brother and sister living there?' Kristín asked.

'Well, yes. But I reckon the brother – Óskar – is an unlikely suspect,' Tómas replied. 'He's sixty-eight years old and walks with a stick. We're not ruling anything out, though.'

Kristín looked ready to add something, but stayed silent.

'Now I can see why you said it was an unusual case, or an unpleasant one, at least,' Ari Thór said. 'The poor woman must have experienced a dreadful death.'

'No, that's not what I was talking about,' Tómas said firmly, looking at Ari Thór. 'That wasn't what I meant at all.'

There was a dark, heavy silence, and Ari Thór began to feel a strong sense of disquiet. He could not explain exactly why, but he felt Tómas was about to tell them something terrible.

'Ásta had a sister, Tinna,' Tómas began, his eyes cast down. 'She died in 1986, which is—'

'Twenty-seven years ago,' Kristín said, without having to stop to think.

'Exactly. Twenty-seven years.'

'So she was a child when she died?' Ari Thór said, hesitantly.

'Yes, just five years old.'

'And how… How did she lose her life?' he asked, certain that he had no desire to hear the answer.

'She fell from the same cliff,' Tómas said. His voice was clipped, expressionless, as if he felt it tasteless to make such a tragic revelation overly dramatic. His words hung like ice in the air, striking and poignant.

'The same cliff?' Ari Thór repeated. 'Twenty-six years later, Ásta suffers the same fate as her sister. That's unbelievable. It's almost too far-fetched.'

'It makes you stop and think, though,' Tómas said.

'It's as if someone or something – fate maybe – had decided they would come to the same end.'

Tómas made no reply, clearly not inclined to interrupt his story.

'Two years before that the two sisters had lost their mother,' he continued. 'The family had not long arrived in Kálfshamarsvík back then.'

'Losing their mother – that's quite a burden for two little girls to carry,' Kristín observed.

'How did she die – their mother? Ari Thór asked, but as the words left his lips, the look on Tómas's face told him the answer. He shivered.

'She fell from the cliff as well,' said Tómas in a flat, quiet voice.

Ari Thór thought that he was prepared for the truth, but he wasn't. He stayed silent for a moment, gathering his emotions.

'All three of them … they all fell from the same cliff?' he finally muttered, shaken. 'All three?' he asked again, this time speaking to himself rather than to Tómas or Kristín.

'That's right. All over a twenty-eight-year period. I told you it was an unusual case.' Tómas smiled wearily and Ari Thór now saw why he had said this was a case that might have been better avoided – that he might regret getting involved.

'Where's the girls' father?' Kristín asked, breaking the silence.

'He's dead as well. He never got over Tinna's death and after a long stay in hospital – in a psychiatric ward, in fact – he died. He was still only a young man. As far as I can make out, he lost the will to live, little by little. He stayed on as the lighthouse keeper for a year after Tinna died, but he was never the same man. Before he gave up completely, he had sorted out a home down south in Reykjavík for the elder daughter, Ásta. She was only seven years old then. I can't help feeling that…' He sighed and started again. 'I can't get away from the suspicion that he wanted to protect her from something – or someone. Maybe they both took their own lives, his wife and his daughter. It may well be that he feared Ásta would go the same way.'

'So was this the first time she'd been to Kálfshamarsvík after moving away when she was seven?' Kristín asked.

'We think so. The first time she'd come back to where she had grown up, as far as I'm aware. Damn it – there's something very wrong about all this,' Tómas growled and suddenly slapped the table with his hand. 'How the hell are we supposed to find out what caused three women in the same family to throw themselves off the same cliff? And do we really want to know?'

'It's so disturbing,' Kristín said, and Ari Thór couldn't help thinking that he should not have involved his heavily pregnant girlfriend in such a dark affair. Normally, Kristín was tough, but recently even trivial things would badly upset her.

'Thrown themselves off, you just said,' Ari Thór said. 'But what if they were murdered – all three? Or simply fell?'

'That's precisely what we're here to find out,' Tómas said with a hint of self-importance.

'What about the other people you mentioned before – the ones who live there now?' Kristín broke in. 'Reynir Ákason, the brother and sister, and the younger man who lives nearby. Did any of them live there when Ásta's sister and mother died?'

Ari Thór glanced at Tómas, waiting for a reply. He could feel a spark of tension in the air. Tómas looked down and then up again.

'Yes. As far we know, all four of them,' he said, once again adopting his cold, calm voice.

## V

Ari Thór left Kristín outside the hotel in Blönduós with a stern warning to take it easy. But although he meant what he said, he knew there was little point saying it. Pregnant or not, Kristín had always been the type to do what she wanted.

She was a determined character, he accepted that, but soon they would have to make some decisions that would shape the next few years of their lives. Before she fell pregnant, she had talked about going abroad to specialise, but only half-heartedly. In fact, she did not seem entirely satisfied with a career in medicine, but she probably saw little sense in abandoning such a solid qualification and the long course of study she'd had to do to achieve it, just to turn to something else. And where did her interests really lie? He struggled to think. She had remarkably few pastimes, and when they had first met she had been so deep in her studies, there was little time for much else. Then, once she'd started work, she took all the long and most challenging shifts. He wasn't even sure she was that excited about becoming a mother. Perhaps he had pushed her too hard when they were discussing starting a family, and, not for the first time, he wondered if she was making his dreams come true rather than her own.

He and Tómas drove in silence, with Tómas, as always, behind the wheel. The road was good to begin with, and Ari Thór was wrapped up in his thoughts about Kristín. He was startled out of them when the car left the tarmac and they headed down a gravel country road. It reminded Ari Thór faintly of trips he'd taken long ago with his parents, back when there had been quaint, pot-holed gravel roads crisscrossing a lot of the country.

He switched on the radio to break the silence in the car. The Christmas greetings were still in full swing: 'We'd like to send friends and relatives, near and far, our wholehearted Christmas best wishes,' a smooth voice said.

*But why?* thought Ari Thór. He didn't see any point in sending any such greetings himself. He had few friends, and even his closest friendships had fizzled out after he moved north to Siglufjördur. He did have a few relatives, but he'd lost contact with them long ago, after his parents died. It had happened gradually, but it had happened all the same. His mother's sister had been in touch occasionally, inviting him round for a meal with her family, but he had never accepted the invitations and after a while they stopped coming.

'Can't we turn that off?' Tómas asked, his eyes glued to the road. The late-afternoon darkness was closing in, surrounding the car. The shortest day of the year was only just behind them.

The midwinter gloom had always felt like a burden to Ari Thór, bringing shadows into his thoughts, and this had become increasingly pronounced after his move north to Siglufjördur. He had hoped that the tranquillity and the brightness of the Christmas celebrations would lighten his mood.

'Well, well, so we have old Scrooge in the car with us,' Ari Thór said with a sly smile.

Tómas's request to turn off the Christmas greetings on the radio hadn't taken Ari Thór by surprise. He was too down-to-earth to let Christmas have much of an effect on him and had probably never even believed in Father Christmas.

'Do you want to take a look at the case files?' he asked, ignoring Ari Thór's comment. 'Use the time while you have it. The file's on the back seat. We have to talk to these people today and see what we can get out of them. There are only four of them, so we ought to be able to manage that, don't you think?'

'Definitely.'

Ari Thór reached behind him for the file, opened it and extracted the wad of documents. They had been put in plastic sleeves, but not in order, some sideways and others upside down. He flicked through the files. There were reports from the police officers who had been first on the scene. These pointed to suicide – or even simply a tragic accident – as the most likely reasons for the victim's death. There were also photographs of the area, and brief descriptions of four people; Arnór Heidarsson, Reynir Ákason, Thóra Óskarsdóttir and Óskar Óskarsson.

Ari Thór looked closely at two or three of the photographs of these people; they appeared to have been printed from the internet. Then he came to a picture that made him catch his breath.

It was a monochrome portrait of a young woman with dark hair that fell past her shoulders, sharp cheekbones and eyes that were half closed. She seemed to be looking straight at him, as if she were teasing him – a sexy, enticing look, but at the same time distant. There was something intriguing about the set of her lips – serious but with a smile behind them. He felt his heart suddenly beat faster.

The photograph was not as clear as it could have been, but it seemed to have a disturbingly strong effect on him.

'Who's this?' he asked Tómas, holding the photograph up, and dreading the answer.

Tómas glanced over. 'That's her, of course.'

There was an uncomfortable silence. Then Tómas said, his eyes on the road ahead: 'The woman who died. Ásta.'

Ari Thór quickly closed the folder. 'Of course. She was … beautiful.'

The distant glow of the lighthouse greeted them through the twilight as Tómas slowed down and turned off the road onto the track that led towards Kálfshamarsvík.

'I've only ever seen pictures of it before,' said Tómas, as they approached. 'It's magnificent in real life, isn't it?'

They drove along the track out to the point, where a thin covering of snow still lay on the road. It was beautiful winter weather; Ari Thór could practically see the chill that enveloped the place, almost feel it seeping into the car.

'Yes, it's quite a sight,' he said, gazing out over the bay, the calm sea and the point.

Tómas took the last turning. Here the track became increasingly rutted as they slowed along the final stretch leading to the house by the sea. It was as if they were coming not only to the end of the road, but to the end of the world.

'You could say that,' Tómas muttered, his eyes fixed on what passed for a road.

'Just two buildings, that's all there is out here.'

'There used to be more. I don't know the full story, but there was a village here at one time.'

'A village?' Ari Thór glanced at Tómas with widened eyes. 'Out here on the point? Where are all the houses, then?'

'They've pretty much all gone. There are supposed to be a few ruins. But, like I said, I haven't been here before.'

They came to the end of the track and he parked the car. There was one car there already; a smart, luxury 4×4 sitting next to the barbed wire that fenced off the point.

'Look, my boy,' Tómas said as they got out of the car, pointing to the bay. 'Column basalt. It's a fantastic sight. It looks almost magical, don't you think? As if the columns were made by trolls, playing around with nature.'

Ari Thór nodded but said nothing, huddling deeper into his jacket to shelter from the bitter cold.

A man was jogging towards them down the path from the house. Ari Thór hurried over to the gate to meet him, watching the man approach.

'Hello there,' the man puffed, and Ari Thór quickly realised that this was Reynir Ákason – his face familiar from his many appearances in the newspaper columns over the years, although now, in the flesh, he looked distinctly older.

'My name's Reynir,' he said, opening the gate and gesturing them inside as if the entire point was his personal property.

'It's a beautiful place you have here,' Ari Thór said, giving into temptation. 'The house and the lighthouse…'

Reynir gave a slightly forced laugh. 'It's just the house that's mine, but we have always been responsible for maintaining the lighthouse,' he said, the chill wind doing its best to sweep his words away. 'But there was a whole village here at one time,' he added as the silence between them became uncomfortable.

'So I hear,' Ari Thór replied.

Reynir led the way to the house and once they were inside, out of the biting cold, Ari Thór thought he could hear the familiar tinkling notes of a piano. Reynir beckoned them into a living room and, sure enough, an elderly man sat at a venerable black piano. He was no concert pianist, but still reasonably competent, Ari Thór thought. The living room was itself was respectable, but had something of an artificial feel to it. The furniture was far from new but had clearly not been cheap when it had been bought, and the overall effect made the room feel cold, with a heavy atmosphere and dim lights, as if the house was lacking any spirit of its own.

'Schubert,' Ari Thór said. His observation was meant for Tómas, but the effect was that the man stopped playing in the middle of a bar. *Ave*, but no *Maria*. He looked over at Ari Thór and nodded. It was a piece of music that Ari Thór knew well, one that his mother had often played on the violin at Christmas, being a member of the Iceland Symphony Orchestra.

'The old boy plays that tune again and again all through Advent,' Reynir said in a derisive tone.

Ari Thór guessed the 'old boy' had to be the sixty-eight-year-old Óskar. A woman of roughly the same age sat at the table – most likely the sister.

'Your colleagues are upstairs,' Reynir said to Tómas, and Ari Thór realised he must be referring to their forensic team.

'Thanks. What's up there, then?' Tómas asked.

'Ásta's room. That's where she lived in the old days, when she was a little girl,' Reynir replied, a certain self-conscious politeness entering his tone now.

Tómas nodded. The three of them – Tómas, Ari Thór and Reynir – stood in the middle of the room, in silence for a moment, while the elderly brother and sister sat stock still, as if awaiting a judgement.

'I'm sorry to have to disturb you so shortly before Christmas,' Tómas said at last, raising his voice and sounding formal. 'But I assume you understand how important it is that we get to the bottom of this as quickly as possible.'

'Didn't she just jump into the sea?' the woman asked, speaking slowly. 'This mother and her daughters, I've always felt they were cursed, in a way.'

'You're Thóra?' Tómas asked, examining her. 'Thóra Óskarsdóttir?'

'That's right.' There was an arrogant look on her face, as if she were determined not to let Tómas get the better of her.

'We have to use our time wisely,' Tómas went on. 'We'd like to get home before Christmas, and I'm sure you'd like to be rid of us before Christmas Eve. So we'll certainly be here well into the evening, and we need to interview you all,' he said. 'We need to speak to Arnór Heiðarsson, too. Is he around?'

'I expect he's at home. It's not far away,' Thóra said.

'We'll call on him this evening on the way back,' Tómas said with a glance at Ari Thór.

'You didn't answer Thóra's question just now,' Reynir said quietly. 'Are we to understand that this wasn't suicide?'

'We can't make any assumptions,' Tómas said, turning to face him, and clearly not prepared to give too much away. 'Could you give us some space to work – an office or another room that we can use?'

'Well, yes. You can use this living room, or you can use my office,' Reynir said. He pointed across the corridor. 'That's just over there.'

'Fine, we'll use that. And can we use your internet connection?'

'I'm sorry,' Reynir replied quickly, 'but I don't have a computer here.'

Ari Thór noticed that Óskar seemed about to say something but instead remained silent.

'We have a computer with us,' Ari Thór said. 'But it would be useful to have access to your wifi.'

'Oh, yes, of course,' Reynir said. 'I'll sort that out for you.'

'Perhaps you can sit down for a talk with us first,' Tómas said in a voice that made it plain this was more than a polite request. 'To begin with though, we need to see what our colleagues are doing. Could you show us the way upstairs?'

## VI

Tómas and Ari Thór clambered up the old spiral staircase into an attic, where they found a young woman from forensics, along with an older male colleague. She told them her name was Hanna. She seemed to be in charge, speaking for them both. She reminded Ari Thór of a well-known singer, whose name escaped him for the moment.

'That's where the deceased slept,' Hanna said, pointing to a small room that would have been suitable for a child but wasn't really big enough for an adult. A narrow bed that was probably the last place Ásta had slept occupied the space below the dormer window.

'We found traces of semen on the floor, not far from the wall,' Hanna said, getting straight the point. 'We'll test them, but it usually takes time to get a definite match.'

'That fits with what we know: she slept with someone shortly before her death,' Tómas said.

'We're collecting fingerprints from the room – as many as we can – and we've taken prints and DNA samples from everyone in the house.'

'And from the guy who lives nearby – Arnór?' Ari Thór asked.

'Yes. Mummi went over there to take his sample just now,' she said, with a nod to her colleague.

'Is there any indication that she might have been murdered up here?' Ari Thór asked.

'Not so far. There's no blood, and no sign of a struggle anywhere, but we'll keep searching. There's no sign of force being used on the spiral staircase, either.'

'Could you take a quick look at Reynir's office downstairs? We'll be using it until this evening and we need to be sure that we're not disturbing any evidence in there.'

'Mummi and I already went through the apartment downstairs before you got here. We weren't as thorough as we're being up here, but as far as I understand it, there's no reason to think that anything suspicious happened down there.'

Tómas nodded. 'And the basement?'

'That's next on our list.' She smiled, just like the singer, but Ari Thór still couldn't recall her name. He just remembered that he couldn't stand the woman's music.

It was clear that every effort had been made to furnish Reynir's office in a way that would give it some warmth, yet it remained an unfriendly room. It was also obvious no expense had been spared. The dark-brown wooden desk was an antique, and behind it was a plush leather office chair. On the wall behind the desk were shelves of carefully bound old books that looked like they had been passed down the generations. There were heavy curtains over the windows and in one corner were a leather sofa and a fashionable-looking glass coffee table.

Tómas took the big chair behind the desk. Ari Thór fetched two more chairs from the living room, sat on one of them himself and gestured to Reynir to take a seat.

'Thanks for letting us use your office,' Tómas said amiably. 'When did you move in here?'

'I've been coming up here now and then for as long as I remember, especially during the summer, but I've always lived in Reykjavík. I've spent more time here in the last few years, though. I'm more than half a country boy, I suppose…' Reynir said, trying to smile. 'My grandfather built the house in 1951. There had been a village here, as I said earlier, but by then everyone had moved away.'

'Why was that?' Ari Thór asked.

'You'd best ask old Óskar about all that; he knows the story better than anyone. I'm not much of a one for history.' He fell silent for a moment, squirming in his seat, seeming ill at ease. 'But I know another story from this area well enough. There's a farm just north of here that's famous for having been haunted. It's supposed to be one of the best-known examples of paranormal activity in recent years.'

'When did that first happen?' Ari Thór asked, certain that this was something he had never heard about.

'Nineteen sixty-four, the same year I was born. In March, in fact, the very same month. My parents were staying here with my grandfather at the time – they'd come up here to relax for a while. My mother hadn't expected me to arrive until early May, but I was born very prematurely at the end of March. Maybe all the talk of ghosts in the district set her off.' He smiled awkwardly. 'It made front-page news back then. Tables and chairs moving around of their own accord, again and again; crockery broken, a cupboard that toppled onto the floor, if the papers are anything to go by, anyway. I find that kind of thing fascinating. A bunch of newspaper reporters turned up to cover it.'

'It wasn't just an earthquake?' Ari Thór asked.

'No. A geologist was sent up here to investigate, but it was just individual items that had moved each time. So anything like that was ruled out. It even made international news: the *New York Times* ran a story about it.'

'Have you experienced anything of that nature here?' Ari Thór glanced at Tómas and saw from the expression on his face that there had been enough of this talk.

'Not exactly ... but the fate of the three women is extremely ... sinister,' he said, his tone serious.

'Are you single, Reynir?' Tómas asked.

'Yes. But I don't see how that's relevant,' he said sharply, the question clearly having taken him by surprise.

'What was your relationship with Ásta?'

'Relationship?' His voice rose in volume. 'There was no damned relationship. She asked if she could stay here, and I said yes. I could hardly refuse her. I hadn't seen her since she moved away from here about twenty-five years ago.'

'Did you sleep together?' Tómas asked, as if it were nothing out of the ordinary.

Ari Thór watched Reynir's reaction carefully; he seemed astounded at the suggestion. 'What? Of course not.'

'Is that such a far-fetched idea?'

'What makes you think I slept with her?' Reynir demanded, his anger rising.

'If you did, then it's as well to say so right away,' Tómas told him calmly. 'We'll find out soon enough.'

'I didn't sleep with her!' he said, his voice almost a shout. 'Was she murdered? Raped? You haven't told us anything.'

'What do you think?'

'I think she jumped off the damned cliff, just like her sister and her mother.'

'Tell us what happened when they died,' Tómas said, his voice relaxed. Ari Thór realised that he was taking care not to let Reynir become too agitated.

'Well...' Reynir coughed. 'To begin at the beginning. My family has been responsible for the lighthouse for years, but neither my grandfather nor my father did the lighthouse keeping themselves – they always had more than enough to do, both down south in Reykjavík and overseas. So, around thirty years ago they took Kári on as the lighthouse keeper, and he moved in here with his wife and Ásta and her sister. At the time we weren't aware that the main reason they moved here was that his wife had been suffering from depression and wanted a change of scenery. Kári only told us about it after her death.' Reynir leaned forwards before straightening his back again and crossing his ankles. 'She jumped off the cliff, just like Ásta.'

'Were you here when that happened?' Ari Thór asked in an offhand way, as if the question was unimportant.

Reynir looked at him suspiciously. 'I was, as it happens. I'd been staying up here with my grandfather after I had finished college and didn't go on to university until the following year. Sæunn, Kári's wife, died at the end of June. I remember there was a storm blowing that night. The cliffs are beyond the house, not far away. She jumped off in the middle of the night.'

'Were there any witnesses? Did anyone hear her?' Tómas asked.

'Not as far as I know. Thóra says she heard a cry, or so I remember her saying, but she said she didn't take any notice as it could just as easily have been the wind.'

'Who else was here back then?' Tómas asked, frowning in concentration.

'Thóra and Óskar, of course. They more or less grew up with my father and have always been part of the household. By then Thóra had taken over from her mother as the housekeeper – the old lady had died and it seemed the natural thing to take Thóra on in her place. She had been away to study down south, but something went wrong. She's as sharp as a knife, even though she comes across as quite hostile. I think maybe she's a little bitter at life in general.' He sighed. 'She has always been good to me though. My mother died quite young, so Thóra was a sort of surrogate mother when I was up here, even though she's not the warmest of people. Perhaps I was the son she never had.' Reynir paused for a moment before continuing. 'We've never done the usual kind of farming up here. My father was a great horseman. I inherited more horses than I could count, I can tell you. Óskar looked after them for a while, and now Arnór does it. So Óskar is just a sort of caretaker. I have to say, he's an odd character, solitary, quiet, doesn't say a lot, but he's a hard worker and as strong as an ox. I pay the two of them practically nothing for all their work, but they've lived here for free their whole lives. When I was younger, I lived in the basement and had that to myself. Kári and Sæunn lived in the attic with their daughters, Ásta and Tinna. That was the arrangement back then...'

'Was your father here when Sæunn died?'

'No, he wasn't.'

'And Arnór?'

'Yes, I think so. He lived with his parents on their farm close by, but he's always been like part of our household. He was just a boy when Sæunn died…' He thought for a moment. 'He must have been around eight years old I suppose.'

'And then Ásta's sister died, didn't she, about three years later?' Tómas asked, his voice low but firm.

'Yes … she died,' Reynir answered. 'That was a huge shock.'

'Do you remember it?' Ari Thór asked, although he could as easily have asked Reynir outright if he had been here too when it happened.

'Yes. That was in the summer as well, a beautiful summer's evening. The sisters were playing together after dinner. Ásta was a clever girl with a mind of her own, and her father trusted her to look after her sister. Of course he should have moved away after his wife died, but he was contracted to work here. I don't think he was from a well-off family and he probably had nowhere else to go, so I don't imagine that he wanted to risk being out of work with two small children to support. He had told the girls again and again not to play close to the cliffs. This time they were playing hide-and-seek. Ásta went inside while her sister hid.'

'How old was Tinna?' Ari Thór asked.

'About five, I think. There were around two years between them.'

'And she fell from the cliff as well?' said Ari Thór, although he knew the answer.

'That's it. There's something about the cliffs that called to them all,' Reynir said, making Ari Thór shiver. 'Ásta came into my place in the basement in tears, saying that they had been playing hide-and-seek, and she couldn't find her sister.'

'Nobody saw what happened?' Ari Thór asked, taking over the role of interrogator, as Tómas did not seem inclined to interrupt.

'No. There was nobody behind the house apart from Tinna. Well, Óskar was there, but he was taking a swim in the sea and didn't see anything. There's no view over the cliffs from the house except from

Ásta's attic window. I was down in the basement. Their father was somewhere outside, in front of the house, and he was sure that the two girls were playing at the back. He didn't see Ásta go in through the back door, where the spiral staircase is. Kári himself had been sunk in depression ever since his wife's death. He managed to keep going as the lighthouse keeper, but he was pretty much on autopilot. He didn't do much more than he had to. He had little time for his daughters, slept a lot, and just sat in front of the television night after night without seeming to see a thing. Then Tinna died too, and it seemed that it shook him up. It was as if he latched onto the thought that he had to save Ásta from the same fate. It was as if he thought that she … that she would go the same way.' Reynir hung his head, a gesture that Ari Thór felt was contrived. 'He finally managed to find a home for Ásta with his sister down south.'

Ari Thór felt a deep pang of sympathy for Ásta, not only for having suffered such a dismal end, but because of the series of tragedies that had made up her life – losing her whole family in such a short time. The thought occurred to him that he was also feeling a level of sympathy for himself.

'It seems to have been a bad decision for everyone concerned,' Reynir continued. 'Her aunt didn't seem to have much time for her…'

'How do you know?' Ari Thór broke in. 'Didn't you say just now that you hadn't seen Ásta for years?'

For a moment it seemed that Reynir was about to try and duck the question. 'We talked,' he replied at last. 'Before she died…'

'Privately?' Ari Thór asked.

'Yes. Just once,' Reynir said slowly and calmly.

'When was that?'

'After dinner. We all had a meal together here the second evening she was here. The evening before she died, I mean. The party broke up. But then she came downstairs a little later for something she had forgotten and we talked for a while. And, of course, I asked what had become of her over the years since she had left. She gave me a very short history, to the effect that her life hadn't been a bed of roses.'

'Was that late in the evening?' Ari Thór asked.

'Well…' Reynir replied thoughtfully. 'I don't remember what time it was. She went back upstairs to bed afterwards.'

Ari Thór caught Tómas's eye. According to the post-mortem results, Ásta had probably died late that night, although the pathologist had been reluctant to be precise about the time.

'She came here on the eighteenth of December,' Tómas said. 'You all had a meal together on the evening of the nineteenth and the following morning she was found dead. Right?'

'That's right.'

'And when did she contact you?'

'A few days before. She emailed me, or rather, she emailed my company and asked for the message to be forwarded to me. She simply asked to stay here for a few days, something to do with a thesis she was writing.'

'We need to see a copy of the email.'

'I'll sort that out for you,' Reynir said with decision.

'What's it like living here?' Ari Thór asked. He had both direct and indirect experience of how isolation could affect people.

'It's a beautiful place,' Reynir said. 'We get tourists coming here occasionally to take a look at the lighthouse and the basalt formations. There's hardly anywhere with finer column basalt than here.'

'Isn't it difficult to live here, though? Lonely?'

'No, not really. We're not that far from a village, Skagaströnd, and there are people living on the farms round about. It is isolated though, I suppose. There's no fire service out here, so if there was a fire, the place would burn to the ground before the fire brigade from Skagaströnd could get here.' He gave them a careless smile. 'And there's deep snow sometimes during the winter, but the sea is close by.'

'The call of the sea?' Tómas suggested.

'Yes…' Reynir seemed to be at a loss for a moment. 'It brings a certain freedom with it.'

## VII

While Tómas went to fetch Thóra Óskarsdóttir, Ari Thór opened the little office window. As the old lady sat down, a cold, fresh blast of sea air came into the room.

'We didn't talk a lot during those two days, before she lost her life, the poor girl.'

Thóra's manner was abrupt, as Reynir had described, but Ari Thór felt it was more a habit than that she was trying to send them any particular message.

Tómas leaned back in his chair, keeping his eyes on Thóra but not saying a word. It was Ari Thór's turn to lead again. It wasn't as if he had been plucked from Siglufjördur and summoned to this remote point to be simply an observer, he supposed.

'Had you been close in the past?' he asked.

'Close?' She shrugged. 'No, I can't say that we were. She was closer to Óskar, to tell the truth. He's always been good with children.'

Ari Thór was sure he could detect a moment's hesitation in these last few words.

'Weren't you surprised that she came back here, after all these years…?'

She shrugged again. 'I suppose so. She said she was writing some thesis, but I wasn't convinced. If I were her, I'd have stayed as far away from here as possible. It hasn't been a lucky place for her family,' she said with a sniff.

'Well, no. Clearly not,' Ari Thór said amiably. 'What explanation can you give us for this … ill fortune, if we can call it that?'

'I don't have any explanations,' she replied quickly. 'Maybe they all jumped off the cliff in a trance. What do I know? But I'm convinced that there's nothing … supernatural … going on here,' she said and then fell silent.

'What makes you so sure?' Ari Thór asked, more to keep the conversation going than because he wanted to hear ghost stories.

'I'm a down-to-earth person. I don't believe in all that stuff.'

'Reynir said there's a farm not far away that made news around the world years ago because it was haunted.'

'Did he, now?' she smiled. 'I'm surprised he said that. If there's anyone more sceptical than I am, then it's Reynir. There are no evil spirits at work here, just the usual human failings.'

'What do you mean?' Ari Thór held her gaze, but she let neither his intense stare nor his tone ruffle her composure. 'What do you think happened?' he pressed.

'I don't know anything about it. I wasn't the one who pushed her,' she said sharply. 'But I couldn't help wondering about it all when the little girl went over the cliff.' She crossed herself. 'May she rest in peace.'

Ari Thór waited patiently, knowing something more was coming.

'I think Ásta saw something,' Thóra said at last. 'Maybe that's why she was sent away, all the way south to Reykjavík.'

'Saw something?'

'That's right. The only window in the house that has a view over those damned cliffs is in her attic room. She was in there. They were playing hide-and-seek, and she left her sister outside. I reckon she went upstairs and was looking out of the window to see where her sister was hiding, and then she saw something she wasn't supposed to.'

'What makes you think so?' Ari Thór asked. 'Do you know anything that might support that idea?'

Thóra sat silent, apparently unsure how much information she should share with him. 'She hinted as much,' she said at last.

'Ásta?'

'Yes. Before she left here for good all those years ago. She blurted it out in anger – that she had to go because of what she'd seen. I asked her what she meant. "When you were *up in the attic?*" I said, and then I realised right away what she was implying. She nodded, but she didn't say anything else.'

'And what do you think she saw?' Ari Thór asked.

'Something dreadful,' Thóra replied reluctantly, with a weight to her words, as if they were being uttered after deep consideration.

'Such as what? Someone throwing a little girl off the cliff?'

'Exactly.'

'Who on earth would have wanted to do that?'

Thóra hesitated for the first time. She clearly appeared to have her own theory, but was debating with herself whether or not to share it with the police.

'Well, it doesn't make much difference,' she said after a moment. 'They're all dead now. I reckon her father was most likely the guilty one.'

'Her father?' Ari Thór could hardly believe what he was hearing. His thoughts immediately went to Kristín and the child she was carrying. Thóra's suggestion was beyond anything that he could understand 'What makes you think it was him?'

'Because he decided to send his daughter down south, wanted to let her forget. Or he wanted to let her begin a new life without him anywhere nearby. Who knows? After she left, he became more and more solitary. He had to be put in hospital in the end. He wasn't right in the head.' She put a hand to her forehead to lend emphasis to her words.

'How clearly do you remember that day – when Tinna died?' Ari Thór asked. He had his own doubts about whether or not these ancient events had any connection with the death that he and Tómas were there to investigate, but he wasn't willing to exclude anything. This whole case was odd, shrouded in bizarre mysteries.

'Very clearly, of course,' she said in a low voice. 'I was in the kitchen, tidying up after dinner, when I heard Reynir calling. Ásta had come to him, saying that Tinna was missing.'

'The kitchen up here in this apartment, or the one in the basement?'

'No, not down in the basement. At that time Óskar and I each had our own rooms up here in the main apartment. We were here all year round, you see. Reynir's father liked to have a housekeeper in the place. He was a gentleman of the old school, you know?'

Ari Thór nodded.

'And now you've been moved down to the basement,' he said adding a sharp edge to his voice, fishing for a response.

'That's life,' she said, and for the first time there was a hint of emotion in her voice. She coughed before continuing. 'Reynir wanted to change things,' she said with a wan smile. 'Anyway ... A search was organised for the little girl. It didn't take long to find her body on the rocks at the bottom of the cliff. It was a dreadful sight ... dreadful.'

'How long have you and your brother lived here?'

'About sixty years, I'd say. Óskar has been here longer than I have. I've stopped counting the years,' she said, a stony look on her face.

'That's a long time.' Ari Thór thought of his own twenty-eight years. Sixty years was practically a lifetime, and in some cases more than a lifetime. 'You say Óskar has lived here longer than you?'

'I moved to the south for a while, to study. This point and the bay, it's Óskar's territory. He knows it like the back of his hand and couldn't live anywhere else. Me ... well... You can get used to anything.' She said this in such a mournful tone that Ari Thór was at a loss for words, finding he had forgotten what he had intended to ask next. He glanced at Tómas, hoping for a lifeline, but Tómas sat without saying a thing, his face a mask of concentration.

Thóra herself finally broke the silence. 'I'm sorry. Maybe I was a little too forthright there. When you don't have long left to live, there seems to be little point dressing the facts up as anything else.'

Not long left to live? Ari Thór wasn't sure exactly how old she was – a year or two younger than Óskar, so probably sixty-five or sixty-six, he reckoned. Not many people of that age would put things in such strong terms, he was sure.

'So, sixty years you've been here? You have pretty much watched Reynir grow up,' Ari Thór said, wanting to suggest that she had been a surrogate mother to him, but leaving the idea unspoken.

'Since he was a small child, yes. But there have been lots of breaks. He spent a lot of time here, though. He often came here with his parents in the summer, while his grandfather was still alive. And Áki often let Óskar look after Reynir after his mother died. They were very different characters, the father and the son. Áki had no idea how to bring up a child and had little time for the boy,' she said, her fondness for Reynir shining through her words.

Ari Thór decided to steer the conversation in an unexpected direction. 'Reynir told me that you had heard a cry the night the two girls' mother lost her life.' He let the words drop, and then waited for Thóra's reaction.

'That's right,' she said gravely. 'I heard her scream. I'm sure of it. But nobody believed me.' She hesitated before continuing. 'It was in nobody's interest to believe me. If she had called out, then it was because she was pushed. That's an awkward explanation, isn't it?'

'And if she had been pushed…?' Ari Thór waited, hoping Thóra would finish his half-spoken question, but she remained quiet.

'Ásta was staying in her old room when she was here, wasn't she?' Tómas asked, unexpectedly breaking his own silence.

'Yes. Up in the attic.'

'Wasn't that difficult for her?'

'No, I don't think so. It was Reynir's suggestion. He thought it was the obvious arrangement. He asked me and Óskar to get the room ready for her. We'd been using it as a storeroom, so Óskar moved everything that was in there – dozens of boxes – into another room.' Her voice dropped. 'He took them all over to Tinna's room across the hall … It took me an age to scrub Ásta's room clean. There was so much dust in there that it wasn't habitable.'

'What kind of a girl was Ásta?' Tómas asked.

'Well, I hadn't seen her for a long time—'

'But you knew her years ago,' Tómas interrupted. 'Didn't you?'

'Of course.' Thóra paused. 'Ásta was determined, intense, stubborn. She didn't let anyone take liberties with her. Tinna was better-natured – sweet and obedient. They were very different but there was a strong resemblance between them – you could see straightaway that they were sisters. Ásta and Óskar got on well together, as I told you before,' she said and, once more, as she mentioned the fact, she hesitated. 'Ásta and Reynir were good friends too back then, even though there was such an age gap between them. Ásta was seven when she moved away, and Reynir was about twenty. They both found the sea enchanting, as I remember. At that time sailing was Reynir's main interest.' She smiled, apparently unconsciously, as she delved into the past. 'He spent the summer building himself a little boat … Or, rather, he got Arnór's father to do most of the actual work on it. Reynir has never been good with his hands. That boat was all Ásta could talk about; when it was ready she and Reynir were going to go sailing every morning.' Thóra smiled again, a look of sincerity on her face, now. 'That girl loved the water.'

Just as Ari Thór was about to bring Ásta's death up again, there was a knock on the door. It was Hanna. She told them that she and Mummi wanted to check the lighthouse but had found it locked.

'Do you have a key?' she asked them.

Tómas shook his head and looked enquiringly at Thóra.

'I don't have one,' she replied. 'Only Óskar and Arnór do.'

Ari Thór got to his feet and went along the passage to the living room, where Óskar and Reynir sat at either end of the sofa. He was sure that they had been sitting there in silence the whole time. A forlorn Christmas tree stood in one corner of the room, undecorated in spite of Christmas Eve being only a day away. This certainly wasn't the way Ari Thór had planned to spend the day leading up to the holiday.

'I need the key to the lighthouse,' he said, loudly and firmly.

'There are two,' Reynir said, answering straightaway. 'Arnór has one and Óskar has the other.'

Ari Thór glanced at Óskar. He stretched to reach for a stick and then got to his feet, limped out to the lobby and fetched a key ring from his coat pocket.

'There you go,' he said, handing Ari Thór the single key.

'Did that happen recently?' Ari Thór asked, pointing to the stick Óskar used for support.

'Six months or so ago,' Óskar mumbled. 'It's my knee.'

Ari Thór nodded, and decided, just as Tómas had, that an elderly man who walked with the aid of a stick was hardly able to commit murder easily.

He delivered the key to Hanna, who was waiting by the back door, and then returned to the office, where it was clear that Tómas had continued the conversation with Thóra.

'...not at all,' Ari Thór heard her say, as he walked in. Then she noticed him and fell silent.

'We were discussing the night Ásta died. Thóra was fast asleep and heard nothing,' Tómas said, and Thóra confirmed his words with a nod of her head.

'Óskar found the body,' she said. 'In the morning.'

'Was he searching for her?' Ari Thór asked.

'No. As far as we were aware, she was asleep upstairs. He's always out and about on the point, takes a walk in the morning and again in the evening.'

'With his bad knee?' Ari Thór asked, trying not to sound too suspicious.

'His knee isn't that bad, it just needs to be rested,' she said. 'He always walks along the shore down by the sea. He likes to clamber over the rocks to be near the water. Or I should say he used to like to do that. That was how he hurt himself, back in the spring. He's going to hurt himself badly one day. It'll be just as well if I go before him so I don't have to see it when it happens.'

Ari Thór felt uncomfortable asking her to explain, and she offered no further comment. He decided that sooner or later she would come back to it.

'You said just now that you have no theories about Ásta's death,' Tómas said.

'That's right,' she replied, but this time her hesitation was less well concealed.

'Nothing unusual you might have noticed? Nothing suspicious?' Tómas asked in an apparently offhand tone. Ari Thór knew, though, that Tómas's questions were at their most incisive when he adopted this manner.

'Nothing,' Thóra said, her eyes on the window, as if she longed to leave.

'Thanks,' Tómas said. 'That'll do for now.'

'She's hiding something,' Tómas said as soon as they were alone behind the closed door of the office. 'I got a definite feeling about it when we were talking about Ásta's death, while you were out of the room. I asked her much the same questions again, so you could see her reactions.'

'You're right,' Ari Thór agreed. 'There's something strange about her; you can't miss it. We should certainly talk to her again tomorrow. She definitely knows something more than she's letting on.'

# VIII

The face before them was tired and weather-beaten, but with surprisingly young eyes that had a distant look about them. Óskar sat downcast in the chair. He seemed to shiver in spite of his thick, blue rollneck sweater. The movement wasn't enough to be very obvious, but it caught Ari Thór's attention. Sitting in a room with two police officers, giving a statement as part of a murder investigation could be a trial for anyone, he thought. It was clear, though, that Óskar had no intention of letting anything slip accidentally, limiting his answers to their initial questions to monosyllables.

In an effort to bring Óskar out of his shell, Ari Thór decided to shift to new territory, to Óskar's home ground. 'I gather you're as knowledgeable as anyone can be about Kálfshamarsvík?' he asked with a small smile.

Óskar nodded, for the first time looking into Ari Thór's eyes.

'Is it true there was once a village here?' he asked. 'It's hard to believe it now.'

'Oh, there certainly was,' Óskar replied. 'There was a settlement here around 1900, a few houses on the point and round about. It was the bay that was the attraction, you see. The people here were fishermen. The buildings were turf, timber and stone, but now they're all gone. You should go for a walk around the point tomorrow, in the daylight; you can still see the ruins. The main areas have been marked with signs, for the visitors.'

Óskar had come to life now; Ari Thór's strategy had worked, so he continued along the same lines. 'What happened? Did the settlement just die out?'

'Not right away. There were more houses built after the turn of the century. There was even a school built here, and people used to gather there for dances. But life was no bed of roses in those years, and people were very poor. Some of them had smallholdings. By 1930 there were fourteen houses here – on the point and around it – about seventy or so people living here altogether, if I remember right.'

'Seventy people?' Ari Thór asked, taken by surprise.

'Something like that,' Óskar confirmed. 'According to the census from a couple of decades before that, there were even more. This place has always been a fine natural harbour, but conditions were tough. There's no fresh water out here on the point and the houses were heated by burning peat. The water and the peat had to be carried all the way here.' He fell silent for a moment. 'Anyway, the place began to decline and after 1940 there was nobody left.'

'Why was that?'

'People blamed the Depression and low prices for fish, and the fishing wasn't as good as it had been. There were lots of things that all added up ... Different ways of fishing, new methods. A good few people moved down the coast to Skagaströnd. That's the way it has always been. Settlements adjust to what nature has to offer. We're fishing people, and that's the way it should be. But now the country's gone to rack and ruin,' he added. 'And I know who's to blame!' He shook his head. The eyes that had been so distant were now alive with passion, although his voice remained low.

Ari Thór was unsure how to react, or if he should respond at all.

'Do you and your sister have roots in this area?' Tómas asked in a friendly tone. 'I see you know the history of the place inside out.'

'Not at all. Our mother came here when we were small, to work. The old man went abroad not long after Thóra was born. I'm two years older than she is, you see.'

'And you and Thóra decided to stay put when you grew up?'

'It's not that simple,' Óskar said, looking down at his palms.

'How so?' Tómas asked, a sympathetic look on his face.

'Thóra went to Reykjavík, years ago, to go to college – she's the clever one. But it didn't work out for her. She came home sick, a shadow of herself and it took a few years for her to get over it.' Óskar sighed.

'Sick?' Ari Thór asked. 'In what way?'

'Well…' Óskar began and glanced at Ari Thór with a look that said *don't ask me about this*. But Ari Thór waited patiently and finally, faced by the expectant silence, Óskar said, 'It's a sensitive matter; I don't really want to talk about it. You'd best talk to Thóra. Why does it really matter now, anyway?'

'This could be a murder we're investigating,' Tómas replied. 'Anything could be significant.'

Óskar hesitated before speaking again. 'She was addicted to drugs.'

Whatever reply Ari Thór had expected, it wasn't this one. 'She was into dope?' he asked, unable to prevent an unnecessary sharpness entering his voice.

'I wouldn't say that,' Óskar said in a slow, low mumble. 'It was the doctor. He prescribed her medicines because she was struggling to concentrate in her exams.'

'What kind of drugs?'

'Amphetamines.'

Ari Thór made a doubtful face.

'People were less strict about these things back then,' Óskar explained. 'It was a tragedy really. Thóra was just unlucky to be landed with that doctor. He was an old boy and he carried on prescribing amphetamines to his patients well into the sixties. I'm sure he'd been doing the same for years. Anyway, she couldn't cope with it and came back home. The withdrawal symptoms she suffered were terrible.' He shook his head as if to emphasise his point.

'She made a full recovery?' Ari Thór asked.

'Yes, but she never dared go back south to continue her studies, and I don't think she ever got over the disappointment. You could say the experience was the death of her,' he said, his voice dropping to a whisper.

'Death? What do you mean?' Tómas asked.

'She's had a distrust of doctors, ever since, and that's putting it mildly,' Óskar replied. He seemed agitated, but his voice remained low. 'Bordering on hatred, really. She flatly refuses to go to a doctor. Then she was complaining about being in pain for years but never did anything about it. When I finally convinced her to get help, there was nothing they could do. It's some damned cancer, deep inside her. The poor thing doesn't have long to live. Maybe a few months – a year, if she's lucky. She's refused any kind of treatment.'

Ari Thór was shocked. He hardly knew the woman, but it was uncomfortable to hear this about her. Now he saw their conversation with her in a new light.

'Don't let her know I told you all this,' said Óskar, a pained look on his face.

'That she's terminally ill?' Tómas asked.

'No, the stuff about the amphetamines. It's sort of a family secret. As for her illness, our friends in the area know she doesn't have long to live, even though we rarely mention it. That's the way life is.'

It was Tómas who came out with the question Ari Thór had been considering whether or not to ask.

'What was the name of the doctor who was responsible for all this?'

'Good grief, I don't remember,' Óskar said with a grim smile. 'I'm terrible at remembering names. All I can tell you is that he died years ago. Our mother made a fuss about it at the time, but she didn't get far. She lodged a formal complaint and we heard that it wasn't just Thóra who had suffered because of what he'd done.'

They were silent and Ari Thór felt the moment was right to bring things back to Ásta.

'Do you believe Ásta's death was accidental?'

'In all honesty, I don't know. Maybe … or maybe she jumped deliberately.'

'That's a possibility, of course,' Ari Thór agreed.

If that had been the case, what had gone through her mind on the way down? He recalled the photograph, those enticing eyes and the mysterious smile. There was something about Ásta that had an unnerving effect on him.

'What about Sæunn and Tinna?' Ari Thór asked, preferring not to talk about Ásta for the moment. 'Do you think they commited suicide as well?'

'Maybe Sæunn,' he said, his voice distant. 'You know what her name means, don't you? Someone who's drawn to the sea.'

Neither Tómas nor Ari Thór responded, so he continued awkwardly. 'I enjoy figuring out the meanings of names. Tómas denotes a twin,' he said, glancing at Tómas. 'And Ari? What do you think that means? There's even a Lake Ari out here on the headland.'

'Ari is an eagle,' Ari Thór answered, feeling as if he were taking an exam. 'That fits, doesn't it?'

'That's right. It's a lovely name. Just be careful not to fly too high,' Óskar said with a faint smile.

'Or too low,' Ari Thór replied. 'And what does Óskar signify?'

There was a short pause before he answered. 'An enemy,' he said and grinned suddenly, giving Ari Thór a sudden chill of discomfort.

'What happened to your knee?' he asked, settling himself deeper into his chair.

'It was those rocks,' Óskar said. 'I went for a swim in the sea and thought I'd try and climb up the point.'

'The same place they all died?'

'Close. You can't let yourself be too superstitious.'

'You swim in the sea often?' Tómas asked.

'I do. It gives you energy. It's not easy to swim these days, what with my injury, but I hope it'll recover soon, although now I'm no longer a youngster there's no guarantee. I still do what I can, though, and go for a dip without going too far from the shore.'

'Were you swimming the evening that Tinna, Ásta's sister, died?' Tómas asked.

'Yes, I was,' Óskar replied, the question apparently having taken him by surprise.

'And did you see anything?' Tómas asked sharply.

'No.'

It was difficult to tell from his one-syllable reply whether or not Óskar was lying. If he had anything to hide, then there had been a quarter of a century for him to ensure that it remained hidden.

'I don't believe there's anything supernatural about those deaths, though,' he added.

'Reynir told us about a place not far away that was haunted back in 1964. Furniture moving and broken crockery,' Tómas said.

'Phhh. I don't believe a word of ghost stories. But crockery has flown off the shelves around here,' he smiled.

'How so?' Tómas asked, glaring at him.

'There was a terrible earthquake, in 1963. I remember it as if it were yesterday. The house shook, pictures fell down, everything cascaded down off the shelves, and there were even cracks in the walls. It was winter, I remember. Mother and I were here alone. Thóra was studying down south. It was getting on for midnight, so we were fast asleep, when it happened. It shook us awake, all that turmoil. I remember we hurried out and it was almost morning before we dared go back inside.' Óskar seemed to come into his own when anything from the distant past was mentioned.

'I've heard about this earthquake in Siglufjördur,' Ari Thór said with a touch of pride at his knowledge of the town's history, 'and the impact it had there: the church bells started to ring and all the power went off.'

'Your sister said that Ásta had…' Tómas began, but then paused for thought. '…That she had been attached to you, if I can word it like that. You were good friends.'

'Well, yes. You could say that,' Óskar muttered. 'As far as there can be a friendship between a child and an adult. She was seven when she moved away, and I was around forty … forty-two.'

'Were the two of you also interested in sailing?' Ari Thór asked.

'What? Sailing?' Óskar said, looking at him in amazement before he realised what he was asking. 'Like Reynir and Ásta, is that what you mean?'

Ari Thór nodded.

'No, not at all. That was their hobby – Reynir's mostly. But Ásta was around him a lot and she was looking forward to going sailing when the boat was ready.'

'And did she?'

'No. Reynir finished the boat around the end of summer, and by then Ásta was gone. She moved away not long after Tinna died.'

'What sort of friendship did you have?' Tómas asked.

Óskar thought for a moment before answering. 'She could twist anyone around her little finger,' he said at last. 'She was fussy about her food and wouldn't touch a lot of what Thóra put on the table – and Thóra's a fine cook. So it turned into a habit for me to sneak something to her once she had gone to bed.' He smiled guiltily.

There was a sudden, determined knocking at the door, and Ari Thór started. It opened and Hanna put her head around it.

'Can I interrupt?' It was obvious from the look on her face that she had something important to say.

'Thank you, Óskar,' Tómas said. 'That'll do for now.'

Óskar got to his feet and limped out, supported by his stick. And, as he did, Ari Thór was gripped by the thought that he had forgotten to ask something, but he couldn't bring the errant question to mind.

## IX

Hanna told them that, at first sight, it looked as if there had been a struggle in the lighthouse. There were traces of blood on one of the doors inside, not far from the stairs, and it looked as if an attempt had been made to clean them off.

'If that's Ásta's blood,' Hanna said, in an even more serious tone, 'then it's possible she could have been pushed; she could have fallen and hit her head on the wall. There wasn't a great deal of blood, but a blow like that could have left her unconscious, or even have been fatal.'

Tómas spoke the words that had already gone through Ari Thór's mind: 'And if she was dead or unconscious, that would have made it easy to throw her off the cliff. The same place where her mother and sister lost their lives.'

Reynir had given them clear directions, so it didn't take Tómas and Ari Thór long to drive over to the farm where Arnór lived. The farmhouse itself was a two-storey building clad in corrugated iron sheets. It was showing its age, and the scruffy old pickup outside was the complete opposite of the luxury SUV by the house out on the point.

A boisterous dog welcomed them first, and then Arnór appeared, emerging from the house with slow steps as he greeted them.

'I've been expecting you,' he said. 'Arnór Heidarsson.'

They introduced themselves and followed him into the living room. There was considerably more Christmas spirit on display here than in

Reynir's house. Next to the television stood a small but smart Christmas tree, neatly decorated and strung with red and blue lights. Some parcels were already arranged beneath it, but they were few enough for Ari Thór to assume that there were no children in this house.

He had bought a pair of unassuming earrings and a book for Kristín. They had agreed to not spend too much on Christmas, preferring to save up for what they would need when the baby came.

The television was on, but the sound was turned down. A woman of roughly Arnór's age, or perhaps a little younger, sat at an old-fashioned dining table.

'My wife, Thórhalla,' he said.

She stood up and shook hands with them. There was a tired, concerned look on her face.

'I'm afraid we need to speak to your husband in private,' Tómas said, attempting to sound cheerful, although unable to hide the seriousness of the situation.

'I guessed that would be the case,' she said, her smile less than convincing. 'I'll go upstairs, sweetheart,' she said, turning to Arnór. There was little warmth in her tone.

Arnór gestured them to the chairs around the table.

Once they were seated, Tómas glanced at Ari Thór, as if suggesting he take the lead.

He needed no second invitation. 'Do you have a key to the lighthouse?' he asked, getting straight to the point.

The question appeared to take Arnór by surprise and he took his time to think it over, visibly nervous. 'Yes,' he replied at last. 'Óskar and I have keys,' he said. 'What do you think happened to Ásta? Was she ... Was she murdered?'

Ari Thór was not inclined to let him off that easily. 'Could you show us the key?'

He hesitated again. 'I ... Actually, no. I don't have it.'

Ari Thór waited, his eyes firmly on the unfortunate man who seemed to be trying to make up his mind whether or not to dig himself deeper into a pit of lies.

'I lent her the key,' he said finally, with a sigh.

'Her?'

'Ásta.'

'When?'

There was another pause as he hesitated again.

'Just before dinner … Her last day … The evening before she died, I mean.' He spoke with startling speed. 'She was standing there by the lighthouse and wanted to go inside, but the door was locked, of course. So she asked if I could lend her the key and I did. She wanted to take a look inside, after all these years.'

'Why didn't you tell the local police officers this when they were first here?'

Beads of sweat were showing on Arnór's forehead.

*And we're just getting started,* Ari Thór thought.

'I didn't think it mattered.'

'Everything matters,' Ari Thór said. That was something Tómas always said. He must have learned a few things from the old man.

'Did anyone see you?'

'What do you mean?' he asked in a halting, quavering voice, as if the question had a deeper significance.

'Is there anyone who could confirm that what you say actually happened – that Ásta asked for the key and that you gave it to her?'

'What? I see … No, nobody but Ásta,' he said. 'Does that matter?'

Ari Thór smiled. The thought had occurred to him that not much would be needed at this point to throw the man completely off balance. An unexpected smile would do the trick.

'Didn't she have the key on her?' Arnór asked, his desperation clear.

Ari Thór caught Tómas's eye and said, 'She had some keys on her, as far as we know. We assumed they were from down south. She was wearing a coat, with car keys and some other keys in the pocket.'

'You'll have to check,' Arnór yelped.

'So when did you sleep with her?' Ari Thór asked. He knew that he was pushing the boundaries now, maybe too far; the look on Tómas's face confirmed he thought the same.

Arnór appeared at a loss. 'What do you mean? When…?'

It was time for Tómas to make his presence felt. 'Apologies for the personal question,' he said, to Ari Thór's chagrin. 'But we need to know if you and Ásta … well, slept together. It'll be confirmed anyway when the samples have been analysed.'

Arnór stared at Tómas with a grave expression on his face, as if he was playing a game of poker in which the stakes were life or death, and he had to work out if he was being duped.

'No. I'm a married man; I don't sleep with other women.'

'You're a frequent visitor out there at Kálfshamarsvík?' Ari Thór asked.

'You could say that. Reynir doesn't have much time to see to maintenance and suchlike; he's far too busy making money. And poor old Óskar is getting on for seventy and he hurt himself back in the spring. I help him out with the lighthouse, although in theory he's the lighthouse keeper. Lighthouses are practically automatic these days, so it's not a big job.'

'And you get paid for all this?'

'Of course. Reynir can afford it; he's not short of money. I've lived here all my life and there's always been a lot of involvement between our two places. They're not far apart, after all.' He took a deep breath, as if getting to grips with the shock that the interview had given him. 'I was an only child, so it was good that there were other children out there at the point. Reynir's a few years older than me, but I was always welcome there. Then Ásta came…' He gave a smile that looked to be unconscious. 'She was three years younger than me. It was lonely once she moved away, but sometimes there were children who stayed out there over the summer.'

'Did you and Ásta talk for long?' Tómas asked.

'What?' Arnór asked, seemingly unsure of the question's meaning.

'By the lighthouse, when you gave her the key.'

'No,' he answered shortly. 'We sat there for a little while and mostly talked about the past.' There was a reluctance in his voice that bordered on regret.

'Where were you the night Ásta died?' Ari Thór asked, picking up the thread again.

'Right here, at home.' Arnór's voice grew louder. 'What sort of question is that?'

'You went home after the meal?'

'That's right. Home to bed.'

'I assume your wife…' Ari Thór fought to recall her name. '… Thórhalla, can confirm that?'

'Of course,' he said firmly. Maybe too firmly, Ari Thór thought.

'You remember when Ásta's sister died? Were you out at the point then as well?'

This time the answer was quick. 'Of course I remember it. How could anyone forget something like that? But I was nowhere near.'

'What do you think happened?'

'I don't know. I was ten years old at the time, and didn't get to hear much about it, apart from the obvious facts. My father used to be out at the point all the time, but he took care not to let me hear much about the accident. I suppose he didn't want me to have nightmares…' he added with a thin smile.

'An accident? You think it was an accident?' Ari Thór asked carefully.

'Of course it was. What else could it have been? You don't think a child would have taken a conscious decision to jump off the rocks?' He shook his head.

'Hardly,' Ari Thór said, keeping his own suspicions to himself for the moment. 'You must have been eight when their mother died.'

'That sounds about right.'

'Where were you that night?'

'What the hell are you insinuating?' Arnór snapped, his voice almost a shout. 'That I murdered a woman when I was eight years old, and then her two daughters afterwards, a quarter of a century apart? You're suggesting I threw them all off the cliff? I'm not having this,' he said and shot to his feet.

'Take it easy,' said Tómas, sitting solidly where he was. 'We aren't insinuating anything. Ásta's death was very similar to those of her mother and sister, so we're here to get to the truth. It may be linked to previous events on the point, or it may not be.'

Arnór sat down again. 'All the same, I'm not happy with these suggestions.'

'What kind of person was Ásta?' Ari Thór asked.

'I think I can say she was decisive. I only knew her as a child, but when we met again she didn't seem to have changed a lot. She kept people at a certain distance, I think, although I don't know whether she did it consciously or not. Maybe it was the distance in her eyes that made me think that – as if she was somewhere else, lost, even though she was standing right there looking at you. Do you know what I mean?'

'I think so,' Ari Thór said, the image from the photograph in his mind, her abstract expression. 'I've seen pictures of her.'

Arnór nodded.

'How was the meal? Did Ásta behave as you expected her to?'

Arnór smiled. 'That's a big question. How should she behave? I've no real idea. The dinner was fine, and I felt that she acted perfectly normally. Reynir had given her a room up in the attic, her old bedroom. Some people wouldn't have been able to handle that, but Ásta took it in her stride. I don't think she was easily upset.'

'Was your wife present at the meal?'

'Thórhalla? No. She has her friends and I have mine.'

'What did you talk about at the dinner?'

'I don't remember exactly. This and that.' He paused for thought. 'I recall that Ásta said she didn't miss the peace and quiet of the countryside, and that she had come to work on a thesis. I don't know if she was telling the truth, but at any rate, she said she wanted to make the most of having the countryside and the sea around her.'

He paused again, for a long while this time, seemingly deep

in thought. At last he looked Ari Thór square in the face. 'It's been rumoured that she saw her sister lose her life – that she she saw it happen from the attic window. And if Tinna's death wasn't an accident, then it may well be that Ásta saw someone push her off the edge.'

'Do you think that had anything to do with why she was here?' Ari Thór asked.

'Could be,' he replied thoughtfully. 'Maybe she intended to settle old scores, before it was too late.'

Ari Thór wondered if this statement needed further explanation, but Tómas spoke up before he had an opportunity to take it further.

'Do you know the view from the attic window? Have you ever taken a look down over the rocks from there?'

Now Arnór thought for a suspiciously long time before answering. 'Not that I recall. Maybe back in the old days. But I gather it's been used as a storeroom for years, and I've had no business going up there.'

'You didn't go up there with Ásta the evening before she died?' Tómas probed. 'After dinner?'

Arnór's anger again boiled over. 'No! I didn't go anywhere near her after dinner. I didn't sleep with her and I didn't kill her!'

Tómas stood up and Ari Thór followed his example.

'We need a brief word with your wife,' said Tómas firmly.

Arnór mumbled something under his breath and then called out her name. She appeared almost instantly, as if she had been listening close by.

'You want me to go upstairs?' Arnór asked with a sarcastic smile on his lips. 'I guess you want to ask her about my movements.'

'That would be ideal,' Ari Thór replied, although he was fully aware that there had been more than enough time for them to make their accounts match, so it would hardly make a difference.

Arnór left the room, and Thórhalla sat down, a sour smile on her face; she didn't ask them to take their seats again.

'As you're aware, we're investigating the death of Ásta Káradóttir,' Tómas said in a formal tone.

She nodded.

'Was Arnór home the night she died?'

'Yes,' she answered without hesitation. 'All night. He came home after having dinner out at the point.'

'Why didn't you go as well?'

'I don't enjoy that kind of gathering,' she said awkwardly. 'I prefer to stay at home. They gave up inviting me ages ago.'

'He was here all night, you say?'

'All night,' she repeated.

'Can you be certain? Were you awake all that time?'

'Well, no, of course not,' she said, clearly taken by surprise. 'But I think I'd have noticed if he had sneaked out. I'd have woken up.'

'How about him?' Ari Thór asked.

'Him? What do you mean?' she asked nervously.

'Would he have noticed if you had gone out?'

'Me? Why would I have…?'

Ari Thór caught Tómas's eye and then said: 'Thanks for your time.'

# X

It wasn't the illness – she had come to terms with that, as far as that was possible, but still Thóra was feeling a deep sadness. Ásta's terrible and unexpected death had brought a gloom to the point. It was a reminder that death, in all its guises, was always very close by.

Or maybe she was sad simply because she was missing the spirit of Christmas? Ásta had ruined everything by coming to Kálfshamarsvík; and by dying.

The night before Christmas Eve should have been a time for pure joy, just as it was in the childhood memories Thóra did her best to recapture every year. Her mother had always tried to make Christmas special, in spite of her difficult circumstances. The evening of the twenty-third was full of the final preparations for Christmas Eve: decorating the tree, wrapping the last few presents and then carefully placing them all under the tree, all while listening to the Christmas greetings on the national radio station. This was the night, too, before the last of the thirteen Icelandic yule lads came to town. As a little girl she would put her shoe near a window and hope for a nice gift from each yule lad. The last one, who would arrive on the morning of the twenty-fourth, was called Candle Beggar, so it was always a good idea to leave a candle for him.

This year Thóra had particularly looked forward to Christmas. She thought that this would be her last and that only an absolute miracle could let her see another.

Óskar was sitting at the piano, saying nothing. Every now and again he would pick out the tune that the young police officer had said was by Schubert. Why hadn't she ever asked him what the tune was? In spite of everything, she knew so little about her brother. What was it that kept him going? How had he been able to live here all this time without trying to leave, with each year much the same as the one before? Even each day was the same as every other one, damn it.

At least she had tried to do something different. That gave some meaning to her life, such as it was. Óskar, on the other hand, had wasted his, and he would just have to accept that.

But he was still as strong as an ox, while she was at death's door. He would outlive her, that was certain. How would he make use of his time after she'd gone? Probably by wandering in a daze from one day to the next, in bottom gear and on autopilot, continuing to squander his life.

Reynir was sitting on the sofa, a bottle of some ruinously expensive whisky at his elbow. She was sipping the red wine he had offered her. He had been brought up to have expensive tastes – if you could say that he'd been brought up at all. His mother had died young and his father had been away a great deal, and when he had been here, he had been distant.

Thóra had done her best to bring Reynir up herself, but there had been no thanks for her efforts. She shouldn't have expected any, she supposed.

The police were out there somewhere in the darkness, or, more likely, in the lighthouse. The two officers she had spoken to had actually left for the day, but as far as she knew, the other two were still there, in the lighthouse. The young woman had knocked and courteously informed them that they would need to investigate the lighthouse in detail and that they would be there well into the evening. She'd given no further explanation about what they were doing.

Languid Christmas music played in the living room, in direct competition with Óskar's tune on the piano. Thóra had spent some of the day decorating the tree, having collected the box of decorations from what had been Tinna's room in the attic. Going up there

still made Thóra shudder. There had been something particularly disturbing about the little girl's death; and it was as if all of them in the
house remained in the grip of those events, even all these years later.

There was far more that troubled Thóra, though. It upset her to
know there were so many secrets. She kept her silence on most of
them, of course, but she was sure she knew on whose consciences
they lay. And Óskar was so damned furtive; why on earth did he
always lock himself away during the day? There was no point asking
him, though. They respected each other's privacy too much for that.
And he'd never tell her, anyway.

She was feeling like she might have had too much of this red wine
– it seemed to have summoned a demon within her. She wanted to
break through the surface, dig down a little, conscious that she did
not have long to live, and that this might be her last chance to expose
the truth.

She put her glass down and began to hang a few more decorations on the tree. She had almost finished when there was a knock at
the door. Óskar's injured knee excused him from going, and Reynir
showed no sign of getting to his feet, so, as usual, she had to answer
it.

She had expected to see the young woman from the police at the
door, telling them that the investigation was complete, but instead
she found Arnór, standing there in the cold.

'Hello,' he said, stepping inside without waiting for an invitation.

'Arnór, my dear boy, come inside,' Reynir called from the living
room. 'Come and sit down.' He beckoned to Thóra and then to
Óskar. 'Why don't you two come and sit with us as well? We'll drink
to Ásta and her memory. She deserves that. It's terrible, absolutely
terrible, but we must stand together and look to the future.'

The four of them took their places in a semi-circle around the table,
Thóra with her glass of wine and the others sipping whisky, brought
together by the passing of someone none of them had known properly, Thóra mused, united in a vain attempt to mourn her memory.
Thóra was sure that she could see through the mendacity, certain

that each of them was occupied first and foremost with thoughts about himself.

'Thórhalla's gone to bed, but I couldn't get to sleep,' Arnór said, giving, unasked, a reason for his visit. 'It's not every day that you're grilled by the police and then try and close your eyes and get to sleep.' He took a gulp of whisky.

'Same here,' Reynir said. 'It's not something I'm used to.'

'They're still out there,' Thóra broke in, keen to see Arnór's reaction.

'What? Who are?'

'The police are still searching the lighthouse.'

'The lighthouse? Whatever for?' he asked in surprise.

Reynir beat her to a reply. 'No idea. Their investigation has hit a wall. The woman jumped off the edge, like her sister, and just as their mother did before them. It's something genetic and that's all there is to it,' he added with finality.

'Have they found anything in the lighthouse?' Arnór asked, visibly agitated.

'If they have, they're keeping it quiet,' Thóra said. 'They've been out there for a good while now, and I imagine they're searching every nook and cranny. So make of that what you will.' She paused, then asked, 'Did Ásta go out to the lighthouse?' She glanced at the three men but nobody seemed inclined to answer.

At last Arnór spoke. 'I lent her the lighthouse key,' he said shame-facedly. 'She said she'd like to take a look inside, and I couldn't see any reason why she shouldn't. I don't know if she did or not, though.'

'We were asked about exactly that,' Óskar said. 'If we had a key to the lighthouse. I let the police have my key.'

'Do you have yours?' Reynir asked, turning to Arnór.

'My key?' Arnór asked. 'Actually, no. Ásta didn't return it … she…'

'That could be unfortunate for you. I hope they found it on her,' Reynir said.

'I should hope so too!' Arnór said, breathing fast. 'This is a night-mare. You should have seen their faces. I'm just grateful that I wasn't locked up in a cell for the night.'

'Nobody's going to be locked up,' Reynir assured him. 'This investigation is a disgrace. We're practically hostages, all on account of a girl who came here to commit suicide.'

'They asked me about Sæunn and Tinna as well,' Thóra said. 'I can't help feeling that they want to link all these deaths together.'

'Link them? That's nonsense,' Reynir said. 'If there wasn't something in their genes, as I said before, something in the blood, then the explanation has to be that out here on this point there are sometimes forces that we don't understand.'

'Ghosts?' Óskar asked, staring at Reynir.

'Something supernatural,' Reynir replied.

Why had the boy started talking about ghosts all of a sudden? Thóra thought to herself.

'It's idiotic,' Óskar said. 'This is a beautiful, peaceful place. It's ridiculous that a man of your age should bring up ghost stories. All the bad luck this place has suffered has been caused by living people, directly or indirectly – consciously or unconsciously.'

'Are you suggesting someone threw Ásta off the edge?' Arnór asked.

'No, I don't mean that,' Óskar said. 'I think she simply did it herself, and maybe she came here for just that reason.'

Thóra sighed, tired in mind and body.

Óskar shot her a sideways glance. 'Are you all right, Thóra?'

'I'm just so tired.'

'It must be trying, all this,' Reynir said. 'Especially for someone in your condition.'

'In my condition, yes,' she said. 'There are things that come back to haunt you' – she snorted grimly at the irony of the word – 'thinking about old friends and the days gone by. I can't deny that Sæunn, Kári, Tinna and Ásta are very much on my mind, especially after what has happened here. And then there's Sara.' She spoke the last words in a low voice, quickly catching the eye of the person for whom they were intended.

And that person was unable to hide his fear, in spite of his best efforts.

She smiled and continued to unburden herself. 'Of course, if we're talking about Sæunn, we weren't alone here the night she died.'

She could see from Óskar's expression that he knew what she was driving at.

Reynir, on the other hand, was clearly taken by surprise. 'Weren't alone? The two of us were here, and Óskar, and of course Kári and the girls. Was there someone else?'

She nodded but didn't reply.

'I wasn't here,' Arnór said abruptly, 'if that's what you're implying. Isn't there anywhere a man can find some peace tonight?' he asked, obviously agitated.

'Relax, will you?' Reynir told him, topping up his glass. 'Nobody's suggesting that, are they?' he added with a look in Thóra's direction.

'Of course not. I didn't mean you, Arnór,' she assured him. 'And maybe some sleeping dogs should be left to lie.' She smiled again, enjoying the game. 'Some of them. Not all.'

She sipped her wine and surveyed the three men, trying to analyse the emotions each was displaying: fear, uncertainty, concern. Her eyes settled on her brother and she gazed at him for a long moment.

'There are some strange games of hide-and-seek being played here,' she said at last. 'Some people lock themselves away for half of the day with no explanation, for example. And I can perfectly understand why these policemen want to ask about the deaths of Sæunn and Tinna. Why didn't they do it before, is what I say. It goes without saying that there was something suspicious going on, but back then it was easier for everyone to tie up all the loose ends and say they committed suicide, or both had an accident. Don't rock the boat, keep everyone happy.' She looked at Reynir. 'Especially your father.'

Reynir made an obvious effort to remain calm. 'What do you mean? Dad would never have hurt a fly.'

'But your father was a powerful man, and a wealthy one too. People took care not to upset him. That's what Iceland used to be like, my boy.'

'That hasn't changed much!' Óskar snapped.

'Well … at least the police made an appearance this time, and they're clearly not here just for show, even though Reynir is such a big fish,' Thóra said pointedly.

'You're being very candid,' Reynir said with a forced smile, then looked at Óskar and Arnór. 'And I'm going to be the same. I'd like to ask you two gentlemen, which of you slept with Ásta?'

Óskar smiled, refusing to be shocked. 'That's a tasteless question,' he said. 'It's one that's better directed at Arnór than me, an old man with a wrecked knee, a worn-out body and a face that has seen better days.'

'Arnór?' Reynir probed, staring at him in a threatening manner.

'Why do you think that someone … slept with Ásta?' Thóra asked before Arnór could say anything.

'That's what the police implied. And I know it wasn't me, so that narrows it down.'

Arnór looked ready to get to his feet. 'All these insinuations … What's the meaning of it all?'

'I'm sorry, Arnór, but these are hardly insinuations,' Reynir said. 'Ásta was a cute girl, both then and now. You were around the same age, so it's not out of the question…'

'I'm a married man, Reynir,' he said firmly and took a big gulp of whisky.

'Yes, *I* know that. But did *she*? It's not as if you wear your wedding ring all the time, is it?'

Arnór was starting to sweat visibly. 'I work outside all the time, and I use my hands. It's not comfortable wearing it, and I wouldn't want to lose it somewhere in the grass.'

'Or in the sea,' Óskar muttered.

'Can't we talk about something other than … Ásta?' Arnór asked. 'We can't let this come between us. We've all known each other, well, all my life.' He tried to force a smile. 'We have to stand together.'

'You're quite right,' Reynir agreed. 'You can stay here with us tonight. Don't try to say no. We'll have a few more drinks and talk about the old days … the good old days. Let's try and forget this girl who's upset everything. And we can try and forget those wretched policemen too. How does that sound?'

Arnór nodded.

'That sounds good to me.'

## XI

As before, the three of them – Tómas, Ari Thór and Kristín – were the only guests in the hotel's dining room, although this close to midnight, it had become the bar. A middle-aged man in a red checked shirt stood behind the counter, casting an eye in their direction every now and then, anxious to close up for the night but unwilling to show his guests the door, especially when two of those guests were police officers.

Tómas had smoothly summed up the investigation so far, seemingly unconcerned that Kristín was at the table with them. She had hardly taken any part in the conversation, though, instead sipping lemonade while Tómas and Ari Thór treated themselves to beer.

'I have to say,' Tómas said thoughtfully, 'it doesn't look good for Arnór, poor lad. The girl was probably murdered in the lighthouse, with his key still in her pocket.'

Before leaving Thórhalla and Arnór, they had asked him for a description of the key. He'd said it was a single key on an unmarked red fob. On the way to Blönduós, Ari Thór made a call to Hanna to check what keys had been found on the body, and it appeared that the lighthouse key was indeed among them.

'If he had murdered her, wouldn't he have made sure to take the key?' Kristín asked, joining the conversation unexpectedly.

Tómas nodded his head and smiled in agreement. 'You'd think so. But we can't assume that someone who has just committed a murder, possibly in a fit of fury, is going to think logically. But maybe he is telling the truth … Maybe he lent her the key and didn't see her again after that.'

'You're working on the assumption that she was murdered in the lighthouse?' Kristín asked.

'It looks like that,' Ari Thór replied. 'The pair from forensics seem to think so.'

'So Ásta and her lover were having a tryst there?'

'You think so?' Tómas asked. He made a habit of answering questions with other questions, constantly in police mode, even on his third beer.

'Yes … bruises to the neck, sexual activity shortly before death. Isn't that what you said?'

'That's right,' Tómas said.

'Couldn't this have been a particularly rough sex game that went too far? Whoever it was dragged the body out to the cliff and pushed it off the edge to hide his trail, hoping it would be dealt with in a hurry as a suicide, an accident, just like the deaths of her sister and mother were?'

'It's a feasible angle on the case; no worse than any other,' Tómas smiled.

'And isn't this what we're all thinking?' Kristín asked, returning his smile.

'Not actively…' Tómas said a little awkwardly.

'Will we be able to go home for Christmas, as you promised?' Ari Thór asked, bailing Tómas out by changing the subject.

'I didn't promise that,' Tómas said slowly. 'But I expect it should work out. Hopefully we'll see Hanna and Mummi before we turn in.' He glanced at his watch. 'I asked them to stop by before going to their rooms. Then we'll start early and go back out to the point. If nothing crops up, then we should be able to take the afternoon off.'

The words 'if nothing crops up' were the ones that told Ari Thór that this case was far from closed, and that something was bound to crop up; Tómas's words had practically guaranteed that. He caught Kristín's eye, and saw from her expression that she was thinking the same. Nevertheless, he kept quiet, preferring to live in hope.

'Fine,' he said, hiding his doubts behind a cheerful facade. 'If the weather holds, then Kristín and I can go to Siglufjördur. You'll be going south?'

Tómas hesitated and then said, 'I expect so, although I can't be sure. Someone has to be around in case something … comes up.' He smiled but his expression lacked any trace of humour. 'It scores a few brownie points with upstairs – and with everyone else – to have to spend your Christmas in a hotel out in the country. It doesn't get much worse than that.'

'And on top of that they're playing Elvis behind the bar: "I'll Be Home for Christmas",' Ari Thór pointed out.

Tómas laughed. 'True enough…'

'You'll have to go home if you get a chance. Don't let your wife spend Christmas alone. I did that once, and believe me, it was a terrible mistake.'

He shifted closer to Kristín and put an arm around her. He looked into her eyes and she returned his gaze without any change of expression. They had made up long ago, and were even expecting a child, but there were some things that she clearly still thought were too sensitive to joke about.

'We'll see,' Tómas said in a low voice. 'The boy will be there so it's not as if she'll be alone.' As so often before, Ari Thór did not find it easy to interpret his tone and expression. 'But I'm amazed how willing you are to travel, considering the little one is on the way,' Tómas said, his words directed at Kristín.

'Willing to travel?' Kristín repeated.

'Yes … Back and forth in the dead of winter. Maybe you'd be best off spending Christmas in Blönduós.'

'We'll sort things out for ourselves,' Ari Thór said shortly, disliking what he saw as interference. He and Kristín had decided that neither her pregnancy nor the child would be allowed to dominate their existence. Kristín had coped well so far, with only rare bouts of nausea, although she tired easily and her mood swings were more extreme than Ari Thór had been used to.

He had often felt the child move inside her belly, kicking with all its energy. It was a strange feeling that brought everything sharply into focus – made it all very real. Ari Thór was far from certain that he was ready for his role as a father, even though he had wanted to become one. When they had decided to try to have a baby, the birth had seemed so far away, but now a definite kick from someone still in the womb who was looking to join the rest of the world brought the reality home to him.

They had not taken any decisions on what the child's name would be. Ari Thór had made a couple of attempts to start a discussion, but Kristín refused to talk about it until the child was born and its gender known. In his mind there was only one possible name if the child were a boy; Ari Thór Arason. It was his name, but more importantly it was his late father's name. He suspected that Kristín would not take kindly to the suggestion, though. There was always the possibility that it would be a girl, and although he would have liked to give the child his mother's name, for some reason he was more prepared to be flexible about that.

But he was sure that it was a boy. He had such a strong feeling, he was quite certain of it.

He was relieved that Kristín had travelled here with him. There was a comfort in being able to talk things over with her at the end of a long day. She was extremely clever, and often quicker than he was to work things out, but it was rare that he had the opportunity to discuss a challenging investigation with her. There had been a few interesting cases that had found their way to him since he had moved to the north – three major ones and one old, long-forgotten mystery – but it could hardly be said he was being kept very busy. Having been overlooked for the position of inspector in Siglufjör-dur, maybe it was now time to grab the opportunity and apply for a post with Tómas's department in Reykjavík. But could he ask Kristín to leave a good job at the hospital in Akureyri and move back to Reykjavík with him? If he had got the inspector's post, then it would be easier to justify staying, but police politics had ruined that for him.

'Wouldn't you be better off trying to figure out what kind of person Ásta was?' Kristín suggested, plucking Ari Thór out of his thoughts. He sat back and let Tómas answer.

'I'm struggling to get a handle on her. We know her life was one long tragedy. First she lost her mother, then her sister, and after that she was sent to live with an aunt, then she finally lost her father as well, although I understand his mind was already gone by that time. It seems fairly likely, too, that she saw someone throw her little sister, Tinna, off the cliff, even though I find it very hard to imagine how anyone could do that.'

'What do you mean?' Kristín asked. 'You think she saw it happen?'

'Yes, that's what the old lady, Thóra, says. Ásta told her she saw something from the attic window, and that's why she was sent away. From that room there's a view over the edge of the cliffs; it's the only window in the house that faces that way.'

'That's terrible,' Kristín said with a sigh. 'Absolutely terrible.'

'That's certainly true. Maybe it's why she seems never to have been able to stand on her own feet properly. She didn't get much of an education and she was badly off financially. Did you read through the case notes in the car, Ari Thór?'

Ari Thór thought of the folder he had brought in with him from the car and put on the floor below his chair. He longed to be rid of the damned thing, to forget all about Ásta, the portrait of her, that smile; at least until tomorrow. It seemed he had too much in common with her. He felt her pain, and would have loved to have been able to meet and comfort her; to tell her that it was possible to break away from the past – away from the fate of one's parents – to go further and do better, and to live a longer life.

He picked the folder up with an internal sigh. 'Yes, I had a quick read through it,' he said, handing it across the table to Tómas.

'Good grief, don't give it back to me,' said Tómas. 'I was immersed in it all day yesterday. You'll have to have a proper read through it tonight. You're so smart – I've faith in you.' He pushed the folder back towards Ari Thór.

At the same moment, Ari Thór heard footsteps and a chatter of conversation. He looked up to see Hanna stride into the dining room, with a glum Mummi hurrying behind her. Mummi looked as if he would rather be anywhere else but here at this moment; most likely he wanted to be in his own home.

'Good evening,' Hanna said brusquely, taking a seat next to Tómas.

Mummi remained awkwardly standing, as there were no more empty seats around the table.

'Fetch yourself a chair, man,' Hanna told him. 'We're not going to wait all night for you.'

'You're just in time,' Tómas said. 'I've almost finished this beer.'

Mummi pulled up a chair and sat down without a word, an uncomfortable expression on his face.

'So who's this young and very pregnant lady?' Hanna asked with a smile.

'I'm Kristín, Ari Thór's partner.'

'Pleased to meet you,' Hanna replied with a sideways look at Tómas. 'I suppose I'm free to speak even though we have a guest? At least, I can see the case notes are here for anyone to see.' She grinned, and Tómas nodded.

'I'll order you another beer first,' she said and looked enquiringly at Ari Thór, who shook his head and pointed at the half-full bottle in front of him.

Hanna tried, without success, to catch the eye of the barman. He seemed to be the same person who had been at reception when they checked in. In fact, he appeared to be everywhere in the hotel, and could well have been the manager too. He spoke slowly and was endlessly courteous in an old-fashioned kind of way.

Hanna gave up being polite and snapped her fingers with a crack that echoed around the room. The barman looked up quickly and came over with slow, easy steps, as impassive as ever.

'What can I do for you, miss?'

'Let's see,' she said, thinking it over. 'A beer for my friend here,' she decided, giving Tómas a pat on the shoulder and looking at Mummi. 'A glass of water for my talkative pal, and do you have a shot of sambuca for me?'

'Of course, miss. Coffee beans as well?'

'Now you're talking, my friend,' she said with a broad smile. 'Of course.'

Ari Thór could see from the look on Tómas's face that he was less than delighted with the way things were developing. But he said nothing. Not that there was much he could say: the four of them were off duty and, in any case, he had no authority over Hanna.

'It all seems clear enough,' Hanna began, once the barman had walked away. 'Or it looks that way for now. We'll send samples to Reykjavík for confirmation,' she went on, clearly satisfied, 'but it looks like someone attacked the poor girl in the lighthouse – that's what the blood spatter indicates. I don't know if she died in there or not, and wouldn't take bets on it. It looks like she took a heavy blow to the head, and the killer tried to hide his tracks by disposing of her over the cliff edge. It was a good move on his part, but Mummi and I aren't easily fooled. We've got a lad from the local force to go out there and keep watch on the lighthouse overnight to make sure nobody interferes with the crime scene. We took samples and pictures, of course, but it's as well to be sure. And I quite like the idea of that poor lad standing out there in the cold at the end of the world.'

'Are we looking at a rape case?' Tómas asked.

Ari Thór would have preferred to have asked about Kristín's theory – the idea of a sex game that got out of control – but was unable to put into words what she had suggested.

'Rape? Well we did find sperm residues upstairs, in the attic room, which suggests she had sex with someone there, but was murdered out in the lighthouse. Anyone would have to imagine that there has to be a link of some kind between the two incidents; and whoever she was with upstairs would have to be top of the suspect list. She could have been raped, or maybe it was consensual. She just felt like a quick one.' Hanna laughed.

'Hey, come on,' Ari Thór said, taking himself by surprise. He had not meant to wade in to defend Ásta's honour, but he found himself doing so all the same. 'We don't know anything about what happened before. Maybe it was someone she was in a relationship with, someone we don't know about. At any rate, it's most likely a person she was familiar with, and she knew all three men – Reynir, Arnór and Óskar – from way back. And, anyway, we ought to have some respect for someone who has just lost her life.' He looked down at his hands, hardly daring to catch Tómas's or Kristín's eyes after this outburst.

'Ari Thór is quite right,' Tómas added.

'Well, whatever. Take it easy,' Hanna said, unabashed. 'We'll find out who the guy was tomorrow. There were a few usable fingerprints in the room, and they appear to have done it against the wall, or started there, at least. We've been promised that they'll have analysed the samples before midday tomorrow.' She paused. 'And then I for one will be heading south. I can tell you I've no intention of spending Christmas here,' she added.

'And in the lighthouse? Any prints there?' Tómas asked.

'No, nothing that we could identify. The walls are coarse surfaces, which are hard to work with.'

The waiter arrived with a tray of drinks – beer and water, and a glass containing three coffee beans. He poured some clear spirit from a bottle over them, and then set light to the liquid.

'Thanks, I'll take it from here,' Hanna said, watching the flame flicker like a Christmas light in the December darkness, before putting it out by placing the palm of her hand over the glass. Then she lifted it, inhaling the fumes.

'Cheers,' she said, and knocked the contents back in one.

# XII

'Hanna's a lively one,' Kristín said when they were upstairs. She had made herself comfortable in bed, while Ari Thór was sitting at the little desk.

'You could say that,' he said, looking round.

'She reminds me of that singer…'

'She does,' Ari Thór smiled. 'So what did you do today?'

'Took it easy. I wasn't bursting with energy. I thought of going over to Saudárkrókur to see the old man. But I might go tomorrow instead.'

'On your own?'

'Yes, the roads are fine, and I need to have something to do. I'll be back by midday. I don't suppose for a moment that you'll be free tomorrow, so I expect we'll be spending Christmas here, which is fine with me. You're more of a one for Christmas than I am.'

'Don't be silly,' Ari Thór said mildly. 'We can stop off on the way back to Siglufjördur tomorrow. So, where did this passion for family history come from?'

'Let me do what I want, will you?' she snapped with sudden anger.

Ari Thór had learned to be wary of Kristín's mood changes. One moment she was as happy as could be, and the next there was the prospect of thunder on her face. He blamed the pregnancy and the fatigue that came with it.

'I want to know something about the past,' she said sullenly, 'even though you never say a word about your parents, and especially not your father.'

Ari Thór was silent. She had touched a nerve and she knew it. There was no point arguing about it.

'What was he like?' she pressed. 'What sort of father was he? I don't know anything…'

'He was good to me,' Ari Thór said quietly.

'I searched for information about his disappearance on the net a few months ago. You told me he was never found.' She paused. 'Do you think he committed suicide?' And she instantly looked as if she regretted having asked.

'I'd prefer not to talk about it,' Ari Thór replied.

'You don't want to know what happened to him…?'

'Talk about something else,' he said in a defiant tone of voice. 'We can discuss this later. I'm too wrapped up in this Kálfshamarsvík affair at the moment.'

He didn't want to lie, but neither was he inclined to tell the truth. He had never told Kristín, but back when they had only just started seeing each other, he had delved into the circumstances of his father's disappearance and found out the truth. As a result, he had decided to apply to the police – his efforts sparking a general interest in investigation. This job was something he could thank his father for; or, to look at it another way, he could blame him for it.

The story of his father's disappearance was something he was determined to keep to himself, for the moment, at least. Maybe one day he would tell her.

'Well … I want to find out about my great-grandfather, anyway' she said, her anger apparently having worn off. 'I find it fascinating, even if you don't. And tomorrow you'll be at work and I won't have anything else to do.'

She had clearly made up her mind, and Ari Thór reflected that this was Kristín all over. Once she had an idea in her head, she would focus on it and nothing could deter her. He knew that he was in no position to throw stones – not from his particular glasshouse – but sometimes she could be … well, a little too spiky.

'Why are you digging all this up, anyway? Does it make any difference to us?' he asked, knowing he sounded tired and irritable.

'Of course the past makes a difference. It shines a light on us.

Maybe it's the baby. It's a big step to bring new life into the world and be responsible for how someone grows up. We should know something about ourselves first.'

'Yeah, well,' Ari Thór muttered. 'Any more thoughts on a name?' he asked, one eye on the handsome swell of her belly.

'No, my love. You know I want to wait.'

'If it's a boy—'

She stopped him dead: 'Let's wait.'

'All right,' he conceded, but her retort left him annoyed, and he turned away to avoid an argument. Sometimes he wished that Kristín could be more easy-going and less unpredictable.

Unpredictable, just like Ásta, he thought, even though he had never met the dead woman. There was something about her that nagged at him – something in her picture, he thought, her expression and attractiveness. Somehow he'd seen in her expression, in the hint of a smile, some kind of warmth about her, combined with an element of mystery. The photograph was almost as mysterious as her behaviour had been.

He took the picture from the folder, and stared hard at it, before putting it away again and closing the file.

He stood up, removed his shirt, started to take off his trousers and turned to Kristín. 'How about we…?'

'What? Now?' she asked in surprise.

'It's safe for the baby, isn't it?'

'Yes.'

His clothes discarded, he gently pulled back the duvet covering her and smiled.

## XIII

Thóra was tired and after two glasses of wine – or was that three? – her head was starting to spin. She said goodnight to the men and went down the worn steps to the basement and her bedroom.

She felt dizzy. It was probably the wine, but she wondered if it also might be her body telling her that it was tired out. She knew her own body well, of course, after all these years, and couldn't escape the feeling that she didn't have long to go. The idea was not as bad as she had expected it would be.

An end, yes, in a way. But it might also be a new beginning.

She had always had faith, as her mother had before her. That could well have been the best thing – among the many – she had learned from her. In hard times, she took comfort in her faith; forgiveness, however, had always been a challenge.

She could harbour anger, and she was even capable of hatred. She had a hatred for that evil doctor who had given her that first dose of amphetamine. It could well be that he had done it with the best intentions, but all the same, he should have known better.

She realised now, that she had come all the way down to the basement still with half a glass of wine in her hand. That was probably just as well; and it was a fine wine, after all.

Now Christmas was almost upon her.

Whatever happened, she was relieved that she had one remaining Christmas – her last. She had no intention of allowing Ásta and the police to ruin this festive season for her; she was determined to enjoy this Christmas Eve to the full. She hoped that there would be a dusting of snow overnight. Waking up to snow in the morning would be a perfect start to the day.

She could expect one Christmas gift –that would be from Óskar, and she could be sure that as always, it would be a book. The two of them always kept up the old Icelandic tradition of exchanging books at Christmas. She had also bought a book for him, a biography, already wrapped in bright-red Christmas paper and tied with a ribbon. The pair of them had long been set in their ways.

Maybe Reynir had bought something for them as well, though. As far as she was aware, he planned to spend Christmas here with them. She had bought a book for him too, an autobiography of some business guru. She hoped he would like it.

Then her thoughts turned to Arnór. Maybe she should have bought him something? It was too late now to get him anything, and anyway, gift-giving wasn't a habit that had been established between them. She had always made sure to buy something for Arnór's father, Heidar, though. The thought of him gave her a warm feeling inside.

She had put away the parcels for Óskar and Reynir in the bedroom cupboard where she had also placed this year's crop of Christmas cards.

She lay on the bed with its snow-white cover, her wine glass on the bedside table, and took the cards with her, carefully opening each one and reading each message more than once.

There were only four of them, each with a short greeting, but she had a deep fondness for the few friends who had not forgotten her as the years passed.

She sat up in bed, put the cards aside and sipped her wine.

Then she turned off the bedside lamp, reclined back on the pillow, and gradually felt the fatigue leave her bones, as she savoured the darkness and the solitude, allowing herself to look forward to Christmas.

⊕

When she awoke, she was unsure what the time was. She found herself fighting for breath, opened her eyes and found she could see nothing. She tried to struggle, gasping for air, but everything was black. She felt powerless, paralysed by shock.

Was she dying? Was this how it happened?

Then she realised, to her horror, that there was more to it.

Someone was holding a pillow over her face.

She tried to call for help but the thick pillow swallowed her screams. In desperation, she fought back, stretching out both arms, and felt her hand clash with something. The wine glass.

She had been ready to die, sometimes almost waiting for death, but now that she felt it approaching at such a rapid pace, she was scared. More scared than she had ever been before. Death was imminent, but she wanted just one more day. One more hour. One more minute of breathing, seeing daylight.

She continued to struggle. But she knew deep inside that there was no point. She was weak and could not hope to resist the weight on her face, nor conquer someone's determination to end her life.

Of course, she knew who it was. She should have seen this coming.

The lack of oxygen started to have an effect. She knew she wouldn't last much longer, so she simply decided to give up. Why make things more difficult than they already were. She hoped that there was something better waiting for her.

She was conscious of her life draining away, felt the pricking of a tear, and at last conceded defeat.

# PART THREE
# INNOCENCE

# I

It was still night when Ari Thór awoke. He could sense a stillness to the air outside, and guessed that it must be around three or four in the morning.

The bedroom was uncomfortably cold, but this was not the reason he had woken up. He'd been trying to escape his dream and the disturbing emotions that came with it. Not for the first time, it had been about his father. His mother may have been there too, but that was beside the point. As he lay, blinking in the dark, he knew that it was the loneliness that had woken him up; the fear of solitude, the feeling that he managed to fend off during the day but that would sneak up on him at night. Without Kristín, he would be alone. He preferred not to dwell on the fact. His parents were both dead, as were his grandparents on both sides of the family, and he had been an only child. There were a few cousins here and there who were always friendly towards him, saying polite words and giving him hugs on the rare occasions they met, but there was nothing that showed they had any particular fondness for him. There was nobody who would be there for him if he needed comfort. Nobody would visit him in hospital if he were injured, and there was no family safety net if he were to fall into financial difficulties. He had no one he could go to for support.

Nobody but Kristín, of course. But their relationship was a powder keg, as he was fully aware. Even though they had known each other for a long time, if you counted up the days, weeks and months they had actually spent together it didn't amount to very much. All the same, she knew him better than anyone else did, and he couldn't afford to lose her.

She slept soundly at his side. He gazed at her. She was unbelievably beautiful, and in his eyes her pregnancy had only added to her beauty.

He had to stand up, stretch and drink some water. If he didn't move around a bit, he would not be able to get back to sleep – and he knew that with a long day ahead of him, he needed to sleep well.

He made his way soundlessly to the bathroom, turned the tap on a little way and took some sips of water. He had struggled to sleep when he had been a newcomer to Siglufjördur in the middle of a snowbound winter, but that problem had not returned for a good while. This time he wasn't sure what was wrong: a chilly and unfamiliar room, the pressure of the investigation, or just tension over approaching parenthood?

He turned off the tap and, before creeping back to bed, turned up the radiator a little.

It still took him a while to doze off, and he wondered again what was keeping him awake.

A phone was ringing. Ari Thór was certain, at first, that it was in his dream. But then it dawned on him that the sound was definitely real. He hurried to answer it, and heard Kristín stir as he did so.

He checked the time on the screen as he answered the call: eight-thirty.

Unsurprisingly it was Tómas on the line. 'Morning, my boy,' he said, and Ari Thór sensed immediately that something was wrong. His voice was sharp and he could hear him catching his breath.

'It's Thóra,' said Tómas, getting straight to the point. 'She's dead.'

'Dead?' Ari Thór rubbed the sleep from his eyes and made an effort to digest the news.

'Yes, damn it.'

'Her illness?'

'I hope it's that way, but we don't know for sure. Her brother found her this morning. She made a habit of being up between six and seven. He got her breakfast ready and then didn't get an answer when he knocked on her door.'

'Any marks on the body?'

'Not as far as I know. There's a doctor on the way; he might well be there by now. She was lying in bed, apparently. Died during the night. Under the circumstances, and until we know otherwise, we have to assume that this wasn't a natural death. We can't be too cautious. We're facing a tough situation here. I've called my boss…' He paused and sighed. 'Now they want to send me someone else – someone with more experience than you. I said it was out of the question and we could handle it. So there's a lot of pressure on us, now, if you catch my drift?'

Ari Thór mumbled his agreement as he spun the shower taps.

'We don't have long to get to the bottom of all this. It's only a matter of time before the media gets hold of the story. Two suspicious deaths in the same house in a matter of days. My instructions are clear: there has to be an arrest.'

'Absolutely,' Ari Thór agreed, still half asleep.

'So make a move. I'll see you in the lobby. I'm getting Hanna and Mummi up as well.'

'Fifteen minutes,' Ari Thór replied.

'You can have five,' Tómas snapped back and ended the call.

Ari Thór went back into the bedroom to Kristín. 'I have to run, sweetheart.'

'Of course,' she said, sitting up. 'See you this afternoon.'

'That's not certain now, I'm afraid,' he said, hesitating. 'There's been another fatality overnight: the woman who lived in the basement died in her sleep – or she may have been murdered, so…'

'So we'll be here for Christmas.'

'Let's not be too sure. We'll try and get home tonight. Let's see how things pan out over the day,' he said, and smiled.

'I think we both know there isn't much chance of that. I'll run over to Saudárkrókur later, and then we'll see if the hotel manager can rustle us up a Christmas dinner tonight.'

⊕

The snow began to fall as they drove northwards to Kálfshamarsvík, a beautiful white blanket settling over the landscape, giving it an appropriately seasonal covering. Ari Thór felt as if they could be driving either into a stunning postcard scene, or into the void. There was nothing here except a few farms and, of course, the house on the point. There was no village beyond Skagaströnd, nothing but nature covered in snow.

Christmas music blared from the police car's speakers, interspersed with phone interviews with Icelanders living in other countries who were comparing seasonal customs. Nobody thought to interview two police officers who were now expecting to spend Christmas in a hotel.

When Ari Thór and Tómas arrived at the point, the young police officer who had stood watch at the lighthouse overnight approached their car. He was clearly exhausted.

'I didn't see a thing,' was the first thing he said, his voice strained and nervous.

'Take it easy,' Tómas said with authority. 'She may well have died of natural causes. We'll soon find out. Were you out here by the lighthouse all night?'

'Yes. You can't see much of the house from there, and the doors all face in the other direction.'

'Would you have heard any traffic during the night?' Tómas asked calmly.

They were standing at the front of the house, with the snow falling softly around them. Ari Thór wanted to ask Tómas to continue the conversation indoors, but hesitated to interrupt him.

The young man thought for a moment. 'Yes, I'm fairly sure of it. There wasn't much that broke the silence last night, apart from the waves.'

'Are Reynir and Óskar both inside?' Tómas said, glancing at the house, which seemed to tower over them.

'Yes,' the police officer said haltingly. 'They're all three of them there.'

'Three? What do you mean? Who's the third one? Arnór?'

'That's right. Arnór. I gather he spent the night here.'

'Hell and damnation,' Tómas muttered. 'Keep an eye on them, and try to make sure, if you can, that they don't talk too much together, although it's too late to stop them now, I suppose. Ari Thór and I will check out the basement first.'

## II

The doctor, who'd come from Blönduós, was waiting for them in the basement flat.

'The only thing I can state for certain is that she's dead,' he said dispassionately. He was a tall, middle-aged man, his eyes hidden behind thick glasses. 'I presume you'll have a specialist carry out a post-mortem, and he'll be able to tell you more.'

'Was she your patient?' Tómas asked.

'She was. The people who live here generally come to Blönduós for all their health needs.'

'Does her death take you by surprise at all – knowing her condition?'

The doctor looked thoughtful and took his time before replying. 'Strictly speaking, a specialist in Reykjavík was handling her treatment, but the problem was that she had no interest at all in prolonging her own life. She didn't want all the side-effects that come with the medication she would have had to take. She only met the specialist once, and that was because I practically begged her to. I did my best to monitor her condition after that, but it was rare that she would agree to see me. Strange as it sounds, the truth is she suffered from some kind of phobia of doctors. She had already left it far too long before she came to see me, and as a result there was never any possibility that she could make a full recovery.' He paused. 'I saw her again in the autumn,' he continued, his tone grave. 'She seemed lively enough then. I would have given her another six months, maybe nine. However, I doubt that she would have had such a peaceful death as this. What I mean is that, in all likelihood, her condition would have deteriorated over an extended period of time – she would have become very sick. Unless it was her heart that gave out. I understand from Óskar that you were here yesterday interviewing people about the young woman's death. I couldn't rule out that that kind of stress could have pushed her over the edge.'

'Could she have been murdered?' Ari Thór asked bluntly.

'It's a possibility,' the doctor replied with no apparent surprise, in the same emotionless voice. 'There are no visible signs that would indicate that. I would say that she was definitely not strangled. If she was murdered, then it's possible that she could have been poisoned, or that she could have simply been suffocated.'

'Did Óskar say that he found the body?'

The doctor nodded and moved away from the bedside a little. Ari Thór noticed behind him an unmistakeable red stain on the white carpet: it looked like wine had been spilled there.

'Look,' he said, pointing it out to Tómas. 'Red wine?'

The doctor coughed. 'Well. I'll be on my way.'

Tómas thanked him for his time, and turned back to Ari Thór. 'No glass on the table. I'll check the kitchen,' he said.

He returned a moment later. 'There's an empty wine glass by the sink. She must have put it there herself. Hanna and Mummi are on the way, so we'll let them deal with it, but this could be an indication of an altercation during the night.'

'Or she could have just been clumsy,' Ari Thór said, almost against his own instincts. There was something about the stain that troubled him, something that told him she had been murdered, although he was unable to pin down precisely what brought him to that conclusion.

'What are you thinking?' Tómas asked sharply, as if he had been reading Ari Thór's thoughts.

'There's something going on in this house that we haven't figured out. Something is definitely lurking here, under the surface.'

'We'll leave Hanna and Mummi to do their work, and after that we'll have to look at her effects – documents and suchlike. But first we should speak to Óskar.'

⊕

They were once more using Reynir's office as a makeshift interview room, investigating a case that was becoming increasingly complex with every passing hour. Óskar sat in the same chair as he had the day before, wearing the same rollneck sweater. His hands shook and he appeared to have aged years overnight. Ari Thór was sure that he had been weeping. For most people this would be natural and unsurprising, but it somehow seemed unlikely in this strong, reticent, old-school type. Ari Thór wondered if he had misjudged the man.

It was warm in the office; the heating was turned up high. The curtains were drawn open but it had suddenly begun to snow so heavily that there was no visible horizon – everything was white, the snow reflecting light into the room on this Christmas Eve morning.

'Our commiserations,' Tómas said with sincerity. 'But you understand we have to ask you some questions.'

'Yes,' Óskar replied haltingly, as if his voice was about to crack. 'I understand that well enough.' He took a deep breath, reached a hand into his pocket, pulled out a handkerchief and blew his nose. 'I'm sorry. I still haven't taken this on board. It was so sudden. Of course she was ill, but she had been quite lively recently. I was sure that she had a few months left, maybe a year – or even two. I had no idea it would happen so soon.'

Ari Thór caught Tómas's eye, and a glance told him that he was free to step onto more dangerous ground.

'Is it conceivable that her illness was not the cause of her death?' he asked carefully.

'What do you mean?' Óskar spoke slowly, as if not understanding immediately what Ari Thór was implying.

'There are indications that Ásta might have been murdered—' Ari Thór began, but Óskar interrupted him.

'Is that definite?' he asked in astonishment.

'It's one possible explanation, for the moment at least,' Ari Thór said, after a pause. 'And, considering what happened out here on the point a few days ago – when Ásta died – I'm sure you can appreciate that, when someone else loses their life so soon after, we have to examine all possibilities.'

'What the hell?' Óskar retorted, his voice still low. 'Surely you don't think that someone murdered my sister?'

'We can't rule it out.'

'We also found some evidence of a possible altercation,' Ari Thór said, concerned, though, that he might be giving too much detail away. Tómas, however, didn't intervene.

'An altercation?' Óskar repeated.

'Do you think you would have been aware of anything like that happening in the apartment?' asked Ari Thór.

Óskar thought for a moment. 'Probably not. Our bedrooms are at opposite ends of the basement, and we always close our doors at night. It's an old habit. Maybe it says something about us, but when you share a place with someone other than a spouse, your bedroom becomes a refuge. That's the way it was in the old days as well, when we lived in the apartment upstairs.'

Ari Thór decided to use this opportunity to explore another line of questioning; he wanted answers to the thoughts he had been turning over in his mind since the previous day.

'Was that normal at that time … for the staff to share their living space with the house's owners? Was that a typical arrangement back then?'

'I'm not sure you'd have seen the same situation anywhere else, even back then, so I'm not surprised you ask,' Óskar said. 'You'll have seen that the main apartment is on two levels. At that time the owners' rooms were on the upper floor. Reynir's grandfather didn't use the place all year round. Thóra, our mother and I were in the attic to begin with, but when Kári and his family came here, we were given space downstairs. That's the same level as the kitchen, so it was convenient, as Thóra did all the cooking. Back then Reynir had taken over the basement, otherwise we'd have undoubtedly been moved down there. When Reynir's father started breeding horses, I looked after all that business. But now it's Arnór's responsibility.' He paused, taking a deep breath. 'Anyway, the cohabitation – if we can call it that – was fine. We were like a sort of family. In fact, it was the only family that Thóra and I ever had. That was fine with me. I don't ask for much and I love the place. I'll die here, sooner or later. I think Thóra would have liked her life to go in other directions, but this is how things worked out.'

'If someone did harm her,' Ari Thór said cautiously, 'how would that person have got into the basement?'

'The outside doors to the house are rarely locked,' Óskar said falteringly. 'And the stairs lead down from this floor and to the base-ment. There aren't any locks on the doors between the floors … You're not implying that Arnór or Reynir sneaked downstairs in the night to…'

'Of course that is a possibility. But it's not the only one,' Ari Thór said.

Óskar showed no sign that he understood what Ari Thór was implying.

'Why do you think that Ásta was murdered?' he asked unexpectedly.

Now it was Tómas's turn to speak. 'We can't comment about that at the moment.'

Óskar glanced out of the window and Ari Thór instinctively fol-lowed his gaze. He saw that the Christmas Eve snow was still falling, but not as intensely as a moment ago. Under any other circumstances it would have been no bad thing to spend Christmas Eve in such a beautiful place – in this fine old house on a magnificent headland, close to the striking lighthouse and the twisted columns of basalt, with picture-postcard snow falling. Here, in the middle of nowhere, far away from any village, they were so close to nature in all its stunning fierceness, yet they were inside a warm and comfortable home. It would have been a wonderful place for a cosy Christmas break with Kristín.

'I had a letter from her,' Óskar said, almost under his breath. 'Maybe I should have told you yesterday.'

'A letter? From Ásta?' Tómas asked sharply. 'When?'

'Ages ago. Almost twenty years,' Óskar said. 'But I kept it. I had to go to Reykjavík for some reason, and I decided that I'd finally go and visit Kári, her father, who was in hospital there. We'd lost all contact with him after he moved away from Kálfshamarsvík, and he was already a sick man by then. I don't know what his illness was called, at first it was just some kind of nervous breakdown, but later on he was in a world of his own. The poor man had suffered some terrible trauma. I managed to find out where he was and went to see him during visiting hours one Sunday afternoon. He was in a psychiatric ward, naturally, but he wasn't considered dangerous to anyone, so he could receive visitors. It was a shock to see him, though. He was so distant, I hardly recognised him, and he said practically nothing that made any sense. He was sedated, most likely. I tried to talk to him about how things used to be, but his eyes were just completely blank. He had a room of his own, and it was a sunny day, so it was nice and bright, but even so it was such a gloomy, grey place. That's how I remember it, anyway. There was a photograph of his wife and daughters on his bedside table. And now they are all gone.'

'Wasn't Ásta in Reykjavík at that time? That must have been some kind of comfort to both of them,' Ari Thór suggested.

'You'd have thought so,' Óskar replied. 'But the staff told me how good it was to see Kári getting a visitor, as nobody had come to see him for a long time. I asked, didn't his daughter come to see him regularly, but they said that she'd only come once and hadn't stayed long even then.'

'It's hard to believe,' Ari Thór said, almost to himself. Was his mental image of the dead woman all wrong? 'So Ásta wrote to you, you said?'

'That's right. I wrote to her first, you see, just after I came back up here. I didn't feel it was right to visit her when I was in Reykjavík. She had been taken in by her aunt, and I didn't want to just drop in and disturb them.'

'What was your reason for writing to her?' Ari Thór asked.

'Well, I wanted to know how she was, first of all, but also to encourage her to visit her father. I don't have my letter, so I don't recall exactly what was in it.'

'And what did she say in reply?'

'Nothing unusual. I could fetch it and you can see?'

Tómas got to his feet. 'That's OK, but I'll go with you. We have to take care not to disturb the forensic team down there.'

Tómas left the office door ajar and Ari Thór knew that Arnór and Reynir were sitting in the next room, waiting to be called. They made no sound, though, and he couldn't escape the feeling that this old house's native tongue was silence.

While he waited his thoughts turned to Kristín. She was undoubtedly on the way to Saudárkrókur by now. She could have won prizes for stubbornness; it was certainly not an aspect of her character that had mellowed during her pregnancy. He wanted to call her, but didn't want to distract her while she was driving.

A moment later, Tómas was back. 'No problem to get to the basement,' he muttered to Ari Thór. 'Like he said, there's no lock on the door leading there, so any one of those three could have sneaked into Thóra's room last night.'

Óskar limped into the room a few moments after Tómas, leaning heavily on his stick. 'Well, here's the letter. I suppose I've been sentimental, keeping it.'

Tómas took the letter from him and sat in the chair behind the desk – the chair he seemed to have taken ownership of. He laid the letter flat on the desk so that Ari Thór, sitting at his side, could read it as well. It was written in red biro on lined paper – probably torn from an exercise book – the handwriting regular and neat, with each letter sloping to the right. It was like the hand of a schoolchild who had not yet given up on taking care with their writing.

*Dear Óskar.*
*Thank you for your letter.*
   *It would be fun to visit you and maybe look out over the bay*

*again. I hope Reynir was able to finish his boat. But now I'm here in*
*Reykjavík, I don't think I'll be allowed to come and see you. I don't*
*like my aunt and she doesn't like me, so I'm sure she won't let me*
*have a holiday. She wants to send me to college because that's what*
*my father asked her to do. I don't know whether I want to go or not.*
*I'm going to start work as soon as I can, though. That's what I really*
*want to do.*

*She made me go to visit Dad with her once. I'm not going again,*
*though.*

*Say hello to everyone for me and tell them I hope they're all well.*
*Don't write to me again, please. I don't think I'll know what to write*
*back.*

*Ásta*

Ari Thór looked up at Óskar once he had finished reading.

'Odd, isn't it?' said the old man. 'She was twelve or thirteen when
she wrote that. After that I didn't hear from her again, not until she
turned up here unannounced before Christmas.'

'Can we keep hold of the letter so we can get it photocopied?'
asked Ari Thór. 'I'll make sure you get the original back.'

'Well, yeah. I suppose so,' Óskar said with noticeable reluctance.
He seemed to be attached to the letter.

'If your sister…' Ari Thór began, but hesitated before starting his
sentence again. 'If your sister's death was not natural, do you have
any idea why someone might have wanted to harm her?'

'And why right now?' Tómas added. 'In the middle of an investigation, with the police everywhere. There was even a police officer
out by the lighthouse all night. Did something happen after we
left?'

Óskar took his time to think it over. 'We all sat and talked, and
that's about all there is to it,' he said shortly.

'We all?'

'Reynir, Thóra and I. Then Arnór turned up, said he couldn't sleep, which was understandable. He seemed to be quite upset, said he had lent Ásta the key to the lighthouse and that the key was now lost.'

'What else did you talk about?' Ari Thór asked. 'Did Thóra say anything significant?'

Again Óskar took his time before answering. 'Yes, now that you mention it, she did. She reminded me that the night Sæunn died we weren't the only people in the house.'

'Well, that's obvious, isn't it? Sæunn's husband and her daughters were here as well, weren't they – Kári, Ásta and Tinna?' Ari Thór couldn't disguise his irritation; he was determined to avoid wasting any time, and hoping against all his instincts that he and Kristín would be able to get home by evening.

'She didn't mean them,' Óskar said in a flat tone.

Ari Thór glanced at Tómas. 'Who was she referring to, then?' he asked bluntly. 'Is it someone we haven't heard about before?'

'We're not investigating Sæunn's death,' Tómas added gently, his words directed at Óskar. 'But if you know who it was it might help. It could be important.'

Óskar remained silent, but Ari Thór noticed that his hands shook even more than before.

'I couldn't say for certain,' Óskar said at last, 'but I can guess.' His voice was low, as he didn't want to break his sister's confidence.

Tómas and Ari Thór waited.

'My guess is that it was Heidar,' Óskar said with a sigh.

'Heidar?' Ari Thór asked as he wondered for a moment who Óskar meant. 'Arnór's father?'

'That's right.'

'And what would he have been doing here in the middle of the night?' Tómas asked.

'You can figure that out for yourselves,' Óskar retorted.

'Were he and Thóra … a couple?' Ari Thór asked.

'A couple? No, nothing like that. Heidar was a married man. But let's say they got on well together. He'd show up here, late at night, whenever there was an opportunity. That's to say, if his wife was away and there weren't too many people around.'

'So he was cheating on his wife?' Tómas asked in astonishment, as if this took him by surprise. Ari Thór knew, though, that Tómas himself would never indulge in such behaviour.

'It runs in the family,' Óskar replied, his voice cold.

'Meaning what, exactly?' Tómas asked.

'His son's a chip off the old block.'

'What makes you say that?' Tómas said, probing further.

'I hear stories – gossip, you know. And you can't avoid seeing that his marriage to Thórhalla isn't exactly a happy one. They might have been happy together at one time, but that's all over now. They don't have children and it's just the money that keeps them together.'

'What money?'

'Thórhalla's money. Heidar was a good farmer but he wasn't smart when it came to money, and Arnór was close to losing the farm. He was lucky enough to marry a girl from a well-off family, and they've made some good investments. Apparently, they want to start attracting tourists for the summer. They're planning to build chalets and offer horse-riding and all sorts. Arnór even said something about running trips along a ghost trail in the area – all connected to those ghost stories that Reynir told you about. It's all rubbish, but people will do anything to try and make money when times are hard.'

'Do you think that Heidar had anything to do with Sæunn's death? Is that what your sister could have been hinting at?' Tómas asked, his brow furrowed.

'I don't think so,' Óskar replied. 'But you never know…'

'What do you mean by that?' Ari Thór asked.

'Thóra was deeply fond of Heidar, I know that much. If he hadn't been a married man when they got to know each other, then I don't doubt that she could have seen herself as Heidar's wife. I couldn't say whether or not her love – and I think we can say she was in love with him – was fully reciprocated. As I said before, one woman wasn't enough for Heidar; probably two weren't enough, for that matter.'

He sighed. 'My sister didn't have a happy life, as you'll have realised by now. She had always been keen to further her education, but, as I've already told you, her studies ended suddenly. And I'm sure she dreamed of having a family of her own, or a husband at least. When she finally found the right man, he was already taken.'

'It can't have been easy for her to carry on an affair with a married man,' Ari Thór said, thinking that Thóra had seemed a respectable elderly woman. He didn't expect an answer, but got one all the same.

'Thóra was tougher than you think,' said Óskar. 'She could be formidable and knew how to look after herself. Of course, it wasn't easy, falling for a married man like that. But I assure you she didn't feel the slightest twinge of conscience having him come and visit her now and then.' He smiled. 'If Heidar had been involved in Sæunn's death, then Thóra would undoubtedly have known about it, and she would have been prepared to keep quiet about it, too.'

'How come she saw fit to allude to him last night, do you think, even if it was just a hint?' Tómas asked.

'She was a little tipsy. She didn't have much of a head for drink,' Óskar said with another smile. 'I think she was just feeling a little mischievous, wanted to spark a little curiosity or sow some doubt. She dropped some strong hints that there was something mysterious about Sæunn's death and that it had all been covered up to keep Reynir's family happy.' Óskar's tone turned sharp now. 'You know as well as I do that his father was a wealthy and influential man who could be as bloody-minded as hell ... and he was well connected in political circles, too. He could live with the fact that a woman had committed suicide on his land, or had died as the result of an accident, but he'd never have allowed a murder enquiry to take place.'

'Was anything else mentioned last night that we ought to know about?' Tómas said, one eye on the clock.

Time wasn't working in their favour, and Ari Thór was sure that he knew exactly what Tómas was thinking, that it would be best to take all the statements as quickly as possible and try to make as much progress as they could while there was still something left of Christmas Eve. Once Christmas began, the investigation would slow down, regardless of what they chose to do. Any support from Reykjavík would be at an absolute minimum and they might not be able to resume until two or three days after the holiday.

'Yes and no,' Óskar replied right away, and it was clear from his manner there was something he wanted to get off his chest. 'All of a sudden she mentioned someone called Sara.'

'Sara? Who on earth is that?' Tómas demanded.

Óskar sat quietly for a moment before replying. 'I can't say for certain who she meant…'

'Who's this Sara?' Tómas snapped, his patience now running out. 'Come on, out with it.'

Tómas's harsh tone took Óskar by surprise, but he finally blurted out an answer.

'My guess is that she's a girl who was here one summer, a long time ago.'

'When?' Ari Thór asked, taking over from Tómas.

'I can't be sure, not exactly. There were a few youngsters who used to come here for the summer. That was Thóra's department.'

'Was that before Ásta moved here?'

'Before? No. It was after Ásta and Kári moved away. There was some kind of subsidy from the government for it – we had young-sters here for the summer for a few years, normally two or three of them. The money went towards our wages – Thóra's and mine. But I can't remember who was here and when,' he said, sounding flustered.

'Did anything unusual happen while this Sara was here? Did she stand out for any reason?'

'Not that I recall, but I had nothing to do with the children. Maybe I felt I'd had my fingers burned once already, having made friends with Ásta,' he said, and paused before continuing. 'Look, I was fond of the girl. I found it difficult to deal with when she was sent south to Reykjavík.'

Ari Thór found himself sympathising a little with Óskar, but decided it was best to keep the conversation centred around Sara rather than Ásta.

'How old was this Sara?'

'They were all much of an age – eight to twelve or thereabouts. I don't remember much about her other than the name. I remember names but tend to forget faces,' he said. 'Especially recently,' he added.

'Do you remember her full name?' Tómas asked.

'Not a chance,' he said. 'And it could be that Thóra meant some other Sara, I suppose.'

Tómas rose to his feet. 'We'll check it out. Thanks for telling us. You'll be around all day, won't you?'

'Well, yes. I always go to church at six on Christmas Eve, the one at Hof, not far from here. Thóra and I always used to go,' he said, in a voice laden with regret. 'Reynir said that he might come with me.'

Tómas nodded. 'No doubt we'll need to speak to you again before then.'

Óskar was on his feet when Ari Thór remembered the wine stain – it was something that had been bothering him since he'd first seen it.

'You said Thóra had been a little tipsy last night, didn't you?'

'Yes, I did,' he replied suspiciously.

'What was she drinking?'

'Red wine.'

'Did she take a glass with her when she went downstairs to bed?'

'She could have, yes,' Óskar said, pausing as he thought back. 'She turned in some time before the rest of us, so I don't remember exactly.'

'One more question,' Ari Thór said thoughtfully. 'If she had spilled red wine on the white carpet in the bedroom, would she have left the stain overnight?'

'Definitely not. Thóra wasn't the housekeeper in name only. She took her work seriously and had a solution for everything. I seem to remember her putting white wine on a red wine stain once, weird as that may sound, and it worked. But why do you ask?'

# III

The interview with Óskar didn't go on for much longer. Ari Thór went to the other room to fetch Reynir, and Arnór approached him.

'Do you need to speak to me?' he asked cautiously.

'That's the idea, yes.'

'Then could I go next? I need to get home … I wasn't going to be here this long, you see. But there was that fine whisky, so I couldn't turn down Reynir's offer to stay.'

'You were drinking into the night, then?'

'Well, yes. Reynir and I stayed up for a while,' Arnór stammered.

'Maybe it would be best if I drive you home; that way we can talk on the way. And we can't be sure the booze is out of your system yet.'

Arnór seemed ready to protest, but decided against it and sat down. Ari Thór asked Reynir to come with him.

Tómas was in the middle of a phone conversation in the office, so they stood for a moment outside the door.

'There's no peace with you guys here,' Reynir said lightly, but Ari Thór detected a serious note to what he said. 'My office taken over for days on end. I can't get anything done.'

'Really? Were you supposed to be working today?'

'There are no days off in my business. The US markets will be open well into our evening, and I have interests to look after there as well as in other places,' he said pompously.

'We've plenty on our plates as well,' retorted Ari Thór.

'Aren't you making a mountain out of a molehill?' Reynir asked. 'A sick elderly woman dies in her sleep, and the police are here in force. All that's missing is the sirens.'

Ari Thór had to admit to himself that there was every chance Reynir was right, but he was certain there was something suspicious about this death. There had been no opportunity for Thóra to deal with the stain on the carpet, but all the same, someone had taken away the wine glass, maybe to try to hide anything that might indicate a struggle. The attempt had not been well thought out, however; it had probably been done in the heat of the moment.

The door swung open before Ari Thór had time to reply.

'Come in,' Tómas said in his thundering voice.

He looked tired. This second fatality, and hopefully the last, seemed to be tormenting him.

'Was that the wife?' Ari Thór asked amiably, in a low voice. It wasn't so much because he was interested in the answer as to lift the sombre mood.

'No,' Tómas answered gruffly, as if it had been a ridiculous question. 'I had a word with a colleague down south – one of my team, I mean. Asked him to check if there's a ministry that holds a list of children who might have been here, since the state paid a subsidy for them.' He glanced at the clock. 'I hope he can get hold of someone by midday, before people start to disappear on holiday. We're pressed for time.'

Ari Thór noticed that Reynir was following their conversation with interest. Tómas obviously noticed this too.

'Do you recall someone called Sara?' he asked. 'She was here a long time ago – came to spend the summer?'

'Sara…' Reynir echoed thoughtfully. 'I remember that Thóra had some youngsters up here every summer for a few years. It brought some cash into the household, otherwise we wouldn't have done it. But I couldn't recall any names, even if my life depended on it.' He gave them a friendly smile. 'What's her connection to the case?'

This time Tómas was keeping the reins of the conversation firmly in his own hands. 'Thóra mentioned her yesterday.'

'Did she, now?' Reynir asked.

'She mentioned the name Sara. And Óskar remembered a girl by that name who had been here.'

'Well, I don't remember that, but drink plays tricks with your memory, and I'd had a few yesterday,' Reynir said cheerfully. 'But I can understand why Óskar might remember her.'

'What do you mean by that?' Tómas asked.

'I've sometimes wondered about the friendship between him and Ásta…'

'And what would you base such an assertion on?' Tómas said, his expression serious.

'Nothing in particular. But I can hardly be the only one who has asked themselves the same question.'

'Do you know of anyone else called Sara who has a connection to this house?'

Reynir thought before replying. 'The honest truth is that there's nobody of that name who comes to mind.'

'Your mother – what was her name?'

'Emilía,' he replied shortly, as if he had nothing more to say about her.

Ari Thór knew Tómas well enough to be confident that such an abrupt reply would only elicit more questions.

'When did she pass away?'

'A long time ago. 1970.'

'And Thóra took over the maternal role, to some extent,' Tómas said, speaking slowly.

'I may have said she took my mother's place,' Reynir said firmly. 'But it's not something you should take too literally. She was always good to me, though, and taught me a lot about life. I suppose she must have been twenty-four or twenty-five when my mother died. I was six and of course I always saw her as being extremely grown-up.' He laughed, as if at his own wit, but it was empty, embarrassing laughter.

'How did your mother lose her life?'

He took a deep breath before replying. 'A riding accident.'

'And she was killed instantly?'

'Yes. A broken neck.'

'Were there any suspicious circumstances around her death? I mean, might there have been anything dubious about it?' Tómas asked.

Reynir sat up, leaned forwards and raised his voice. 'I think we've had quite enough of these insinuations. It's as if nobody can die in this area without there being something suspicious about it. It was just an accident – a bloody accident. My mother was an experienced horsewoman, but that kind of thing can happen to anyone.'

'And you're a horseman yourself?'

'Well, I own a lot of horses. I'm probably the most important horse breeder in the district. My mother loved them and my father saw an opportunity there to make some money. And he did – like he did with everything. But Arnór handles all that for me now. He has also started offering top-notch horse-riding trips around the countryside, for tourists, you know…' A note of unease was creeping into his voice.

'You didn't answer my question,' Tómas remarked, his tone casual.

'If I'm much of a horseman?' Reynir smiled. 'That I'm not. I haven't ridden a horse in years – not since my mother died. Actually, I was never happy that my father kept that part of his business going. It's something he should have sold years ago, and in money terms it doesn't matter to me one way or the other.' He seemed even more ill at ease now.

'So why don't you get rid of the horses now? It must be up to you now that your father's no longer with us.'

'I'd like to, but I don't want to pull the rug from under Arnór and Thórhalla. I couldn't do that to them.'

Now it was Ari Thór's turn to break into the conversation. 'Speaking of Arnór … You knew his father, Heidar, didn't you? Was he a frequent visitor here?'

'A frequent visitor?' Reynir repeated. 'What do you mean by that? He was always welcome, just as Arnór is, but he never worked for us. He had his own farm to run. I didn't know him especially well. He was from another generation, if you see what I mean.'

'Were he and your father friends?' Ari Thór continued.

Reynir snorted. 'My father didn't have many friends,' he said, as if this were a sore point. 'He was too busy. He only kept in touch with people he thought could be useful to him.'

The next question that seemed logical to Ari Thór to ask was about the relationship between the father and son. However, he held back from asking it. He wouldn't have wanted to answer that kind of question himself, and as far as the case was concerned, he could hardly justify treading on such dangerously personal ground. He reminded himself, too, that Reynir was under no suspicion of any wrongdoing, at least as far as their current investigation was concerned.

'I gather Heidar and Thóra were close,' Reynir added unexpectedly, interrupting Ari Thór's thoughts.

'How close?' Ari Thór asked, watching carefully for Reynir's reactions.

'How would I know?' Reynir muttered. 'I suppose you're aware that Heidar was a married man. But, well … all the same, the apple doesn't fall far from the tree.'

Ari Thór decided to change tack a little, letting these last words go unremarked. 'I understand that Thóra hinted last night that at the time of the investigation into Sæunn's death, it was effectively rubber-stamped as a suicide, so as not to upset your father. Would you agree with that?'

'Of course not, damn it,' Reynir retorted angrily. 'Thóra could be poisonous when she was in the mood. There's nothing behind what she said, though, and anyway, she'd had more than enough to drink.' He sighed, appearing to contain himself. When he continued, he seemed to choose his words with greater care. 'We're all under pressure, as I'm sure you can appreciate. I asked Óskar and Arnór which of them had slept with Ásta, which, I admit, was extremely tasteless on my part.'

'You said that there was nothing behind what she said. Did anything come up that you remember in particular?'

'Well, since you're asking…' he said, after a pause, a perplexed expression on his face. 'She said that someone had locked himself away during the day without giving any reason for it. I think she spoke about playing hide-and-seek. I didn't understand what on earth she was talking about, but I know she wasn't aiming this at me. I shut myself away in the office occasionally when I have to work, but there's nothing suspicious about that. No, I think she was dropping a hint about her brother. Not that I have a clue what he might be hiding.'

Ari Thór had the strong feeling now that the friendship between the four people who had sat drinking together the previous night did not run to any great depth. Each of them had taken every opportunity to deflect suspicion onto one of the others, both in connection with the recent deaths and those in the past. And Thóra – the dead woman herself – had been no less guilty than the others in this poisonous game.

They had just finished with Reynir when Hanna came to tell them that the initial examination of the basement was complete and an ambulance had taken the body away. She added that Tómas and Ari Thór were now free to take a look at the lighthouse if they wanted.

Ari Thór had suggested to Tómas that they should drive Arnór home and question him on the way. Tómas agreed to his idea, but first he wanted to look over the lighthouse. Arnór was rather disgruntled at being kept waiting longer and threatened to set off home on foot.

'Do what you like. You're a free man,' Tómas told him. 'We appreciate that you have things to do.' In themselves his words were perfectly courteous, but Ari Thór saw that Tómas was communicating a clear message: a man with nothing to hide would not be in a hurry to get away.

Arnór scowled and stayed where he was.

The snow seemed to have stopped for the time being, but the day was still heavily overcast, and there was every likelihood that there would be a further snowfall. Óskar offered to show them the way to the lighthouse, and to take them to the notorious cliff edge on the way. Tómas accepted the offer graciously, but said that only he and Ari Thór would go inside the lighthouse.

'That's fine with me,' Óskar said. 'I've seen the lighthouse more times that you can imagine; I've no reason to go up there today. In any case, with my bad knee I can't manage the steps.'

They followed him into the bitter cold outside and took the path that led around the corner of the house.

'As you can see, the house is built in a hollow in the middle of the point, so there's no view from it over the cliffs, except from the attic window, and we can only just see the lighthouse,' Óskar said, limping up the slope with the two police officers at his heels. Behind the house was a patch of grass bordered by stunted trees of a type hardy enough to withstand the conditions on the stormy headland.

'You look after the garden, do you?' Ari Thór asked Óskar.

'The garden? No, not me. Thóra was the head gardener in the family,' he said, his voice cracking with emotion and his words coming with clear difficulty. 'I don't suppose it'll be tended now that she's no longer with us…'

As if to change the subject, he pointed to the remains of an old building behind the back garden. 'This is where the school used to be, the one I told you about. These are the most complete ruins here. Time hasn't been kind to the rest of the old settlement. It's difficult to imagine that there was once a sort of village here; there's almost nothing left of the turf houses.'

They continued slowly, at the speed of a man with a damaged knee.

'And here are the cliffs,' Óskar said and muttered under his breath: 'Those dreadful cliffs.'

Ari Thór stepped warily towards the edge. The rocks had been made slippery by the falling snow, but he was confident he could keep his balance. He had seen higher cliffs, but there was something unsettling about the sheer drop here, about looking down and seeing what awaited anyone unlucky enough to lose their footing … the sharp edges of the basalt columns, the boulders lining the shore, the dark sea. The cold wind from the north reminded Ari Thór of where he was; this was the edge of the habitable world.

He thought of Sæunn and her daughters, Tinna and Ásta, and wondered if there could be something about this unearthly but magnificent place that he couldn't fathom, but that drew those three to it. He shook himself, trying to rid his mind of any such thoughts and bring it back down to earth. It was Sæunn's disturbed mind that had made her take her own life, and pure chance that it had happened here. The fact that Tinna and Ásta had gone over the edge of the same cliff had to be connected to that first fatality. That was the only logical explanation; Ari Thór was determined to be guided only by cold, hard facts.

He turned to gaze at the lighthouse. It was a simple, dignified building and somehow it seemed to be waiting for them. What had taken Ásta up there? Had she been murdered there, as all the clues indicated?

*Who did you go to meet in the lighthouse, Ásta?*

He turned back and took a small step further across the wet rocks, and leaned forwards to look down. For a split second, just as he gazed into the waves below, he had the mad urge to jump. He knew that he would never act on that impulse, and took a step back. But as he did, he slipped, and felt, all of a sudden, as if he was losing his footing. He didn't have the time to call for help, and had to use all his energy to stop himself falling.

He tried to pull himself back, using his arms to keep his balance, holding his breath and feeling his heart hammering in his chest, thinking what would happen if he lost his balance; could he possibly survive?

Finally he managed to shift his weight far enough that he fell backwards in an uncomfortable heap.

The relief was indescribable. His thoughts went to the unborn child who had almost lost its father.

He heard Tómas calling to him. 'For God's sake don't have an accident, young man!' His voice was sharp but full of concern.

Ari Thór got to his feet; he was uninjured.

'It's all right. I not hurt,' he said, his voice shaking. The wind whistled in his ears and he was sure he could hear the gulls calling in the distance. He looked around as he tried to get his bearings, gazing out over the bay of Kálfshamarsvík, taking in its majestic basalt columns.

'Let's get to the lighthouse,' he said finally.

They pressed ahead and, as they approached the white-painted tower, he looked back. From here he could see the jagged cliffs where he had almost come to grief.

'It's seventy years since it was commissioned,' Óskar said. 'That makes it older than me, so that's quite something.'

'It's impressive,' Tómas said, taking the key from his pocket. 'How high is it?'

'The tower itself is around thirteen metres, and the lantern room at the top – that's where the light itself is – makes another three metres,' Óskar replied. 'I'll just wait here,' he added.

'Yes. Please do,' Tómas said, unlocking the door and pulling it open.

Ari Thór glanced upwards. An inverted cross had been cut into the stonework above the entrance. He was far from religious, and God had abandoned him when he had lost his parents. The decision he'd made to study theology – long ago now, before he became a policeman – had perhaps been an attempt to try to find some kind of faith.

Ari Thór had to stoop to pass through the doorway and when he straightened up again he found himself in a cavernous space with steps that spiralled high up the walls. He was sure it was colder inside the building than out, somehow.

Tómas shut the door behind them. Ari Thór felt uncomfortable, as if he wanted to open the door again and walk back outside.

'So this is where the poor girl was murdered,' Tómas said, his voice echoing so much that Ari Thór had to listen carefully to make out his words.

'That's not certain yet,' Ari Thór said, almost against his own better judgement.

'Well, it looks likely to me. From here it's not far to the cliffs; it wouldn't be hard to drag a body there and pitch it over. And both are out of sight of the house, more or less.'

'Except for the attic, of course.'

'And the only person who was staying up there was the deceased,' Tómas observed.

The inside of the lighthouse was empty. Like the outside, the walls were painted white and opposite the door were narrow, elongated windows glazed with thick glass that let in light but offered no view. Brooms and shovels were propped up by the stairs. There were shelves on two walls and there was a wooden bench below the windows. Ari Thór looked up and saw more steps, landings and windows. The space reached ever upwards; this was no place for anyone suffering from vertigo.

Hanna had told Tómas that the bloodstains had been located on the wall at the foot of the steps. Tómas walked over there now.

'Whoever the killer was, he came here with Ásta for some reason,' Tómas said, more to himself than to Ari Thór. 'The two of them argued, and, without thinking about the consequences, the killer threw Ásta against the wall.' He paused for a second. 'That would fit, wouldn't it?' He looked over at Ari Thór.

'It's a scenario we can't rule out,' he replied thoughtfully.

Tómas took a couple of steps upwards.

'You're going up?' Ari Thór asked in surprise.

'Of course. Even if it's just out of curiosity. The building is quite famous, you know, because of its design. It's been photographed many times,' he said, and continued up to the first landing.

Ari Thór hurried after him. The stairs seemed sturdy enough, but the handrail was disturbingly low, as if it was just there for show. One false step could be an expensive mistake.

He heard Tómas say something, but the words were lost in a muddle of echoes.

Tómas stopped, turned and looked down to Ari Thór. 'I said, it's fantastic. Don't you think?'

Ari Thór was less impressed, but nevertheless nodded his agreement. He continued upwards to the next landing, by which time Tómas was already out of sight.

At last, Ari Thór was standing on the third landing. He couldn't help looking down into the depths below. It was a good ten-metre drop to a concrete floor, and with nothing much more than an inadequate handrail between life and death. He felt dizzy, and turned to look at at the ice-cold walls behind him. He felt beads of perspiration break out on his forehead. He had never been afraid of heights, but now he felt overwhelmed. The incident at the edge of the cliff had clearly troubled him.

He stood still for a while trying to calm himself down.

Tómas's voice echoed indistinctly downwards. 'Aren't you coming?' he thought he heard Tómas call out.

Ari Thór called back that he was, although the words were unlikely to reach their destination with any clarity. He mopped the moisture from his brow and gingerly climbed the last set of steps to find a landing with an electrical fuse board, batteries and two more sets of steps leading upwards.

'At last,' Tómas grinned. 'It looks like these steps lead up to the lantern room, so shouldn't we go up and see the view? The other steps probably go out to the balcony. It's damned cold and windy out there, so I don't think we'll try that.'

He set off and Ari Thór saw him squeezing himself through a narrow trap door that, if he'd been carrying any more weight around his midriff, would not have let him through. Ari Thór followed behind. His vertigo was gone, but he felt no less uncomfortable in this tiny room, even with the views all around him, in every direction. The wide bay of Húnaflói, the coastline of the Strands beyond it and the majestic mountains inland could all clearly be seen, reminding Ari Thór how grand the terrain was, but also how cruel nature could be. The sea was unforgiving and the mountains could be perilous for those who didn't fully respect them.

The house on the headland was also clear, as were the treacherous cliffs.

They didn't stay long in the lantern room. Ari Thór followed Tómas's example, going backwards down the first set of steep steps and holding on tight to the handrail, feeling deeply relieved when he made it all the way back down.

He was surprised to see Óskar had waited for them outside the lighthouse. He seemed to be frozen to the spot, his back to the light-house, staring out over the rocks. He was not immediately aware of them.

'Well, then,' Ari Thór said in a loud voice.

Óskar started and looked round at Ari Thór. There was such an expression of pain and sorrow on his face that Ari Thór again felt a pang of sympathy for the old man. He longed to ask Óskar what thoughts or memories were having this effect on him.

'Impressed with the lighthouse? It's a magnificent building,' he said, his gaze still distant.

'It certainly is,' Tómas agreed.

Slowly and carefully, as before, they followed Óskar back to the house.

At the door, he turned quickly to face them, his face dark. 'If someone did Thóra harm, you promise me you'll find the bastard,' he said in a measured voice. 'I can't believe it was either Arnór or Reynir. I've known them both for years. But if one of them killed her…'

He had no need to say any more. The hatred shone from his eyes. Then he looked away and with slow steps, went into the house.

'Take care you don't reverse into the pond,' Arnór warned from the back seat of the police car.

It was a strange place for an interview, not that there was anything normal about this investigation taking place in a remote corner of northern Iceland, on Christmas Eve.

'What pond?' Tómas demanded, braking hard and looking around.

Arnór pointed. 'There's a little pond here on the headland, but it's hard to see at the moment. It's iced over and you can't see it for snow, but I think you are fairly safe, you'd have to go a good way before you were in the water.'

Tómas snorted, put the car into reverse and bumped them over the rutted track and out onto the main road.

'I nearly came to grief there once,' Arnór said. 'That was years ago. I was just a kid. The ice broke under my feet, but I was saved, fortunately.'

'Who by?' Ari Thór asked.

'Reynir wasn't far away and heard me calling for help. He was there in a flash and pulled me onto dry land.'

'Are you close friends?'

'Me and Reynir?' Arnór asked, and the silence that followed served as an answer. 'We've known each other forever,' he said eventually, 'and we get on just fine. But there's a ten-year age gap between us, so we were never childhood playmates or friends. And on top of that, he's always had a home down south as well.'

Ari Thór glanced over his shoulder at Arnór. The man appeared to be personable, trustworthy and pleasant. The two other men out here – both Óskar and Reynir – had hinted that Arnór had been unfaithful to his wife, but was there anything to support those rumours? Had Arnór been the one who had slept with Ásta?

'Why did you go out to the point last night?' Ari Thór asked.

'Any death is a shock to the system, isn't it? And it didn't help being caught up in a police investigation. I thought I'd feel better if I went to see them all and talk things over. And that's what happened. After a couple of drinks, Reynir asked if I'd like to stay, and I accepted.'

'So our visit yesterday upset you?' Ari Thór suggested, trying to sound relaxed, hoping to keep the conversation on a friendly footing. Arnór seemed more willing to open up when there was no great pressure on him.

'You could say that. I felt terrible because I had lent her the key to the lighthouse. I told them that last night. Reynir and Óskar must think I'm at the top of the suspect list,' he said with a note of hope in his voice, as if he wanted Ari Thór and Tómas to assure him that this wasn't the case.

Instead there was a painful silence, which Tómas eventually broke. 'We think we've found the key,' he said.

'Where?' Arnór demanded.

'Ásta had a key on her that fits the description: a single key on a red fob.'

'Thank God,' Arnór muttered.

*You're not out of the woods yet,* Ari Thór wanted to tell him.

'Did you notice anything unusual yesterday evening,' Tómas asked, 'or during the night?'

'During the night?'

'Answer the question, will you?' Tómas told him, with more abruptness than was necessary.

'I slept like a log, in one of the spare rooms in the main apartment. But I can say that people at the house were unusually sharp last night – brutally honest. Everyone's on edge because of this.'

'How so?' Ari Thór asked gently. 'Can you give me an example?'

'Óskar got angry when Reynir started making connections between ghosts and the deaths on the cliffs. That seemed to upset him. And Thóra seemed to think there was a guest in the house the night Sæunn died, years back.'

'Did she say anything else about that?' Ari Thór asked.

'I said that it hadn't been me,' Arnór said with a nervous laugh. 'She said I wasn't the one she was referring to.'

'Do you know who she meant?'

There was a second's hesitation before Arnór answered. So when he said a quiet 'no', Ari Thór knew he was lying.

'You're sure?' he asked, not inclined to give up.

There was no reply this time, so Ari Thór persisted. 'Do you think she meant your father?'

Ari Thór half expected Arnór to take the suggestion badly, so his reply took him by surprise.

'I wouldn't rule it out,' Arnór said in a low voice.

'Do you have anything to back that up?'

'Not exactly. I suspect he was with Thóra that night, based on what was said yesterday. And I think my mother was aware that his friendship with Thóra went deeper than he wanted her to think. That's what I figured out for myself as I was growing up, at least. But it all turned out well enough for them – my parents I mean. They never parted company. But I have to say it was always a little strange being around Thóra and knowing about it.'

Ari Thór was not entirely sure that he could accept Arnór's version of how marriage should work out, but he kept it to himself.

'Then Thóra mentioned some woman,' Arnór continued. 'I wasn't sure who she meant, and I don't even remember the name.'

'Sara?'

'Sara. Yes, that could be it.'

'Any idea who she was talking about?' Ari Thór asked.

'To tell you the truth, no. Maybe some old friend? It doesn't have to be anything suspicious.'

Before Ari Thór could ask his next question Tómas's phone rang. Tómas glanced at the phone, hesitated for a moment then answered it.

'Yes ... yes. Still up north and we'll be here for a while,' he said, speaking in a low voice. 'I'm not sure ... Of course I'll do my best to be there tonight ... Of course, sweetheart ... Three and a half hours to town. Fine, I'll speak to you later.'

He dropped the phone back in his pocket and coughed. 'Sorry about that.'

'No problem,' Arnór said politely.

Tómas turned the car off the road and they followed the short track to the farmhouse they'd visited the previous day.

'What do you think about the idea,' Ari Thór began, as they drew to a halt, 'that Reynir's father may have obstructed the investigation into Sæunn's death, and maybe also Tinna's?'

Arnór's answer came straight back. 'I wouldn't be surprised. He was that kind of man, and he had a reputation to protect. Nobody wants to see his back yard turned into the scene of a murder investigation.'

'We hear you're planning on setting up a tourism business – building chalets et cetera. Do you think this case might harm your plans?' Ari Thór asked.

'Good grief, no. We're aiming it at foreigners, and they're hardly going to hear about a couple of policemen spending a few days investigating a fatality.'

'Exactly,' Tómas said slowly. 'So long as you didn't commit a murder, then everything should be fine.'

His voice was as cold as ice. Ari Thór was taken by surprise, as was Arnór, who did not even try to brush the comment off. 'What's that supposed to mean? Am I still a suspect?' he said.

Tómas did not reply, letting the ensuing silence last for a moment, before glancing in the mirror and making eye contact with Arnór. 'Did Reynir ask you if you were the one who slept with Ásta?'

'Yes, he did,' Arnór said casually, drawing a deep breath. 'I'd forgotten that. He asked me and Óskar. He wasn't being entirely serious, I think.'

'And what answer did you give him?' Tómas asked. 'Did you sleep with her?'

Arnór's patience finally snapped – which was probably Tómas's intention, to push him off balance. Ari Thór felt that his own preferred strategy would have been to keep Arnór inside his comfort zone, to ensure that he remained at ease as far as possible, and to hope that he would let something slip.

'I already answered that yesterday,' he snapped back, his anger obvious.

'So you're sticking with your original story?' Tómas said in a formal tone, not raising his voice to match Arnór's.

'Original story? It's the truth, plain and simple. Can I go now?'

'Of course,' Tómas said politely. 'Thank you for your help.'

Arnór swung the door open and got out of the car.

He was already halfway to the house when Tómas rolled down the window and called out to him.

Arnór stopped and looked back. 'What?' he demanded.

'I won't see you again before Christmas, so I just wanted to wish you a happy Christmas.'

'What? Yeah … Happy Christmas,' Arnór muttered and strode away.

## VI

'Was I too hard on the boy?' Tómas asked, switching on the radio and letting Christmas music fill the car. 'There, let's have a little seasonal spirit, it's about time.'

Ari Thór was unsure whether or not Tómas expected an answer to his question. 'Maybe,' he said, all the same. 'It was interesting to see his reaction. He's a pleasant enough person on the surface, but he has a short fuse.'

'That's exactly what I thought. We'll get to the bottom of it all, don't worry. But maybe I should have been more cautious. I've had enough of this case, now, though – especially today, of all days. That call I took was from my wife. My son was supposed to be having dinner with with us this evening. But his girlfriend has invited him to have grouse with her family, and he says he couldn't tell her no…' He lapsed into silence for a moment. 'The upshot is that my wife will be alone for Christmas if I don't make tracks. So, let's take a look at Thóra's room again and then call it a day.'

'That sounds good to me.'

Ari Thór took out his phone and called Kristín. It took a few rings for her to answer.

'Hi,' she said cheerfully.

'Hi, how is it going? We're almost done here, so we should have time to get back to Siglufjördur tonight.'

'That's great. I've just found the old guy's house in Saudárkrókur. He must be pretty fit for his age, if he's still living in his own house. Anyway, we'll see if this turns out to be a wild-goose chase. Even if his family knew my great-grandfather, that doesn't mean he'll know anything about him.'

'Well, good luck, my love.'

'How are you getting on?'

'We're making progress, slowly…' Ari Thór replied. If their progress was quicker, he thought, maybe he would even have accepted spending Christmas at the hotel. 'How are the roads over there?'

'Oh, not too bad,' Kristín said. 'There's been some snow and there are patches of ice here and there.'

Ari Thór felt a stab of concern in his belly. 'Please be careful, won't you?'

'Of course I will. I'll see you in Blönduós in an hour or two. It's only a forty-minute drive, or so.'

'Fine,' Ari Thór said, ending the call.

The music from the radio filled the ensuing silence. There was little to be said. They had done what they could, and the case had practically come to a dead end. Ari Thór's thoughts moved to the evening to come. He glanced at the clock. They might just make it home in time to cook their Christmas ham. The earrings and a book were waiting for Kristín. He wondered if he should have bought her something else? It was a little late in the day now to do any better, though. And he wasn't about to buy her some last-minute gift from a petrol station.

They had pulled into the turnoff to the headland and the house when Tómas's phone rang again. He slowed down and answered it. It was a short conversation, Tómas's side of it consisting of monosyllables. Ari Thór saw how his brow darkened with each passing second.

'Can you wait there for us?' Tómas said finally. 'Make sure nobody goes down to the basement before we've had a chance to check Thóra's things.'

With the conversation over, Tómas stopped the car, and, to Ari Thór's surprise, manoeuvred it round on the narrow gravel track, so that they were going back the way they came – it was no easy task, but he managed it.

It wasn't until he was driving at full speed, away from Kálfshamarsvík, that Tómas explained why.

'The bastard lied to us,' he said in a steady voice, the underlying anger unmistakeable.

Ari Thór had learned from experience that Tómas was almost always good-tempered. But, while he was inclined to forgive most things, being lied to always sparked his fury.

'Who did?'

'Arnór, of course. That was Hanna with the results of the fingerprints. It seems he left some in Ásta's room.'

'And this is the man who said he hadn't been up there for years, if I remember correctly.'

'Exactly,' Tómas said. 'And if he's said that, he's bound to have told us more lies too. My bet is that he did sleep with her, and that's what we're going to find out now. No more kid gloves.' He paused, gripping the wheel tightly, clearly seething with anger. 'You know what all his lies have brought him?'

Ari Thór sat silent, knowing that Tómas would answer his own question.

'Christmas Eve in a cell,' he said at last.

## VII

Thórhalla opened the door with a look on her face that combined apprehension and resignation; it seemed she knew what was coming.

'You want to see Arnór?' she asked, before either of them had said a word.

Tómas nodded.

'I'll fetch him,' she said, her voice cracking.

Arnór appeared in the doorway a moment later, with Thórhalla standing behind him.

'We need you to come with us to the station to make a statement,' Tómas said, his voice even deeper than usual. 'Your status is that of a suspect in the investigation into the deaths of Ásta Káradóttir and Thóra Óskarsdóttir. You are not obliged to comment. You have the right to a lawyer before making a statement, and if necessary we can appoint your defence.'

Arnór stood stock still for a moment, taken completely by surprise. Tómas waited patiently while he gathered his wits. Ari Thór kept his eyes on Thórhalla; she did not appear to be too perturbed by what was happening.

Arnór's face had gone white.

'Good God,' he said finally and dropped into a chair in the hall; he took a deep breath and reached for his shoes. He slipped them on, stood up and put on a black down coat.

'I don't need a lawyer. I haven't murdered anyone,' he said and looked at his wife. 'It's some mistake. A terrible mistake.'

She gave him a warm smile. 'I know, my love.'

'Come along,' Tómas instructed, and set off for the car. Arnór followed as if he were being led.

Ari Thór, taking a seat in the car after Tómas and Arnór, glanced at the house before they drove off towards the road. His eyes met Thórhalla's cold gaze.

Arnór sat at a table in the Blönduós police station, sipping water from a plastic cup, still wearing his black coat. It was chilly in the police station, but not enough to warrant this outdoor winter clothing.

'Are you sure you don't want a lawyer?' Tómas asked gently.

'Absolutely sure,' Arnór stammered, and in that moment Ari Thór was gripped by the feeling that they had arrested the wrong man, in spite of the wealth of evidence that linked him to the case. Ásta had had sex in her bedroom with someone shortly before her death; his fingerprints had been found there, even though he denied having set foot in the room. Time would tell whether or not the semen samples found there would prove to be his. That was if he hadn't already confessed by then. Another fact that sat awkwardly for him was that he had loaned Ásta the key to the lighthouse – the place where she had presumably been murdered. There were also the rumours that he was unfaithful to his wife. And the final piece of the puzzle was that he had been a guest at Kálfshamarsvík on the night of Thóra's death. Perhaps the simple truth was that he portrayed himself as a convincingly sympathetic character, while really he was devoid of any morals. Ari Thór had encountered people such as this before, and had almost been taken in.

'You told us yesterday that it's been years since you last went up into the attic and saw the view from Ásta's room,' Tómas said.

The silence that followed was long.

Finally, Arnór replied: 'Yes…' he said slowly, his eyes flashing from side to side.

'It that still your version of events?' Tómas asked in a harsh tone.

Arnór said nothing.

'We found your fingerprints there, and I suspect you may have left a few other traces of yourself as well. So I'll give you one more opportunity to answer the question we've asked you twice already. If you lie again, then we're finished here and we'll see each other after Christmas. So, did you sleep with Ásta?'

Arnór did not answer immediately, but stared down at the table and into the half-empty cup of water, avoiding Tómas's and Ari Thór's eyes.

'Yes … but I didn't kill her!' he said, practically overcome.

'That's for us to decide,' Tómas said quietly.

'You have to believe it,' he said, a tremor in his voice. 'I'm no murderer.'

'Then tell us the truth. What happened, exactly?'

'She asked me for the key to the lighthouse, just as I told you. I've no idea why she wanted to go in there, and I didn't go with her,' he said and paused to catch his breath. 'I dropped the key in to her after dinner that night – the night before she died. It was late, so I went in the back door where you can go straight up to the attic. I didn't want to disturb the others in the house, you see.'

'Did you go there so you could cheat on your wife?' Ari Thór broke in.

'No…' Arnór said, hesitating. 'Or…'

'Telling lies isn't going to help you,' Tómas said sharply.

'Yeah, I suppose I was hoping something might happen. There was a bit of a spark between me and Ásta.'

'She didn't know you're married?'

'No. Well, I don't think so. I hardly ever wear my wedding ring, and I didn't mention Thórhalla when I was talking to Ásta – I made sure of that – and no one talked about her at dinner either.' His voice wavered.

'So this was all carefully thought out?' Tómas suggested, with clear disdain.

'You need to understand that it's not exactly a happy marriage,' he said, breathing hard. 'We work well together. We're building up the tourism business, so a divorce isn't exactly on the cards, not right away, anyway. But, well … we're not close in any other way, not anymore…'

Tómas nodded. 'We hear it's her money that keeps the marriage afloat. Is that true?'

The question took Arnór by surprise. 'What? No, I wouldn't say that. She had money of her own, but we tied it up in investments. Some of it has been lost, now, so we're pinning our hopes on the tourists. And there's a sort of arrangement between us – a tacit agreement – that we can go … and, well, meet other people.'

'And does she do that as actively as you?' Tómas asked, keeping a firm hold on the reins of the interrogation.

'I don't think so,' he blurted out. 'I mean … I wouldn't know,' he added.

'Is this something you've discussed between you?'

'No, not exactly.'

'Do you think she knew you had gone to meet Ásta that night?'

'Definitely not. I went out quietly when she had gone to sleep. She turns in early and she's a heavy sleeper.'

'What time was it?'

'I'm not sure. Eleven? I don't remember.'

'So you met Ásta?'

'Yeah, and it was … what I'd expected.'

'We found semen traces not far from the wall where we also found your fingerprints,' Tómas said.

'We did it against the wall. We couldn't use her old bed … it creaked too much, or so she said.'

'And then things became violent, and you grabbed her by the throat? We found injuries on her body, bruising to the neck,' Tómas said, slowly and calmly.

'Hell, no!' Arnór yelled. 'That wasn't how it was! Those injuries had nothing to do with me,' he said, utterly dismayed.

'You have to admit that it doesn't look good for you,' Tómas said, still in the same serious tone.

'Do you need to tell my wife about this?'

'That's one thing you can be certain we'll do,' Tómas told him. 'We'll need to see if she can shine any light on the events of that night. That can't be a big issue, surely? Don't you have a ... "tacit agreement" ... about sleeping around?' Tómas's disgust at Arnór's adultery was clear.

Arnór made no reply, so Tómas continued. 'How long did you stay with Ásta?'

'I don't know exactly. An hour, and hour and a half, maybe.'

'And you went straight home?'

'Yes.'

'Can your wife confirm that?'

'She was fast asleep.'

'That's a shame,' Tómas said. He paused and straightened up. 'Shall I let you hear my theory?'

Tómas left a long silence, more to build up emphasis, Ari Thór felt, than as an opportunity for Arnór to reply.

'She never asked you for the key to the lighthouse. You certainly came back that night to have sex with her, and you may well have arranged it with her in advance. Once the fun was over up in the attic, the pair of you decided to make an old dream a reality by doing it in the lighthouse. Not that I can imagine it's all that exciting – it's a strange, cold place. You had the key to the lighthouse with you. Ásta opened the door with it and dropped it in her own pocket. And that's when things started to get heavy – maybe with her consent. Young people get up to all sorts of strange things these days. Anyway, things went too far – maybe she blacked out, or maybe you slammed her against the wall. And that's when she lost her life. Then, instead of shouldering the responsibility for what you had done, under cover of darkness, you carried the body to the edge of the cliff and pushed it off. You hoped that the whole thing would be dealt with simply – that everyone would be satisfied with the explanation that this young woman had come back to the place where she had spent part of her childhood in order to take her own life, just as her sister and mother had done.' Tómas leaned back in his chair and waited for a response.

'That's bullshit, from start to finish,' Arnór said, still deeply agitated. 'I told you the truth. Ásta was alive and well when I left her up in the attic, and I didn't see again.'

'And Thóra? When did you last see her?'

'The evening before she died, of course. You're not going to pin that on me. The woman died in her sleep. She was very ill.'

'Well, that's your opinion,' Tómas said. 'We're keeping you here until tomorrow. We need to decide whether or not to seek court approval to keep you in prison for a few days more while we continue with the investigation.'

Arnór looked thunderstruck. 'I'm innocent! You're not going to lock me up for cheating on my wife.'

Tómas was on his feet.

'Surely you're not going to keep me in here overnight?' Arnór protested. 'It's Christmas Eve!' There was a childish misery in his voice.

'I'm sorry, but that's the way it is,' Tómas said. 'Is there anything you haven't told us? Anything that could point us in the right direction, if, as you say, you really are innocent?'

Arnór thought for a moment. 'There is something. I was sworn to keep it a secret, so I've kept to myself. I don't even think it has any bearing on all this, but I suppose it's as well to tell you.'

'Go on, let's hear it,' Tómas said, sitting down again.

'I had this from my father – he was the one who asked me to keep it quiet.' Arnór sighed, and drank what was left in his cup. 'We've already discussed how my father and Thóra were ... close, if I can put it like that, and she told him a few things. She had spoken at some point to Kári, Ásta's father, about Sæunn's death. Sæunn had suffered from depression for a long time; it was one of the reasons they decided to move out to the countryside – a way of changing their environment. But once they were here, things only got worse, and one night she ran outside and was going to throw herself off the cliff. Kári followed her, caught up with her at the edge of the cliff and was able to grab her. He tried to hold her back, but she was too strong for him. She went over the edge and died.'

'So Sæunn's death *was* suicide?' Ari Thór asked.

'According to Kári's account of what happened. But my father did say that Thóra had her own doubts about the truth of the story. She felt that Kári might have … embroidered … his role in it. I don't suppose we'll ever know what the real truth is. But I don't believe that what my father heard from Thóra was untrue. She had no reason to lie to him…'

'I don't think any of this helps you,' Tómas said after a pause. 'But I appreciate that you've finally told us. It's important for us to be able to see the big picture, even though we're not investigating those deaths.'

Arnór said nothing in reply, so Tómas stood up again and said with finality: 'You'll be taken to Akureyri tonight, and tomorrow we'll see what the situation looks like.'

## VIII

'This list was emailed from down south,' said the Blönduós station inspector, handing Tómas a printed sheet. 'Youngsters who stayed out at Kálfshamarsvík.'

'Aha,' Tómas said, taking a quick look over the list and handing it to Ari Thór. 'I didn't think they'd get it to us today. It's not a lot of use to us, now that I reckon we have the right man.' He caught Ari Thór's eye. 'What do you think?'

For a moment it occurred to Ari Thór to agree with Tómas, but it was against his own better judgement. And while he didn't like to disagree with his superior in front of the inspector – an officer neither of them knew – he decided to not let that stop him. This was simply too important.

'I think he's innocent.'

'Innocent?' Tómas said in apparent astonishment. 'He lied to us again and again; he didn't tell us the truth until we had solid proof. And I'm sure he's lying about the things we can't prove yet too – like going out to the lighthouse, for instance.'

'So you want to keep him in isolation over Christmas?' Ari Thór said. He felt some sympathy for the poor man, but was relieved that the decision was Tómas's.

'Absolutely. This is going to be worth a few brownie points – an arrest on the second day of the investigation. And, considering the circumstances, nobody's going to give us a rap over the knuckles for locking him up. In fact,' Tómas went on, more solemnly now, 'anything else would be plain irresponsible. I'll speak to the prosecutor in Akureyri and see if we have enough evidence to request a further period of custody. Then I was thinking of making tracks for home and coming back up here tomorrow. We'll let the lad spend a night in the cells. That might even encourage him to come clean.'

Ari Thór was taken aback by Tómas's attitude. He seemed so different from the measured, careful investigator Ari Thór had previously worked with. Why was he so keen to prove himself? And did he think that Arnór's arrest alone demonstrated that he had done everything he could? Or maybe it was simply that he couldn't face disappointing his wife by leaving her alone on Christmas Eve? He had certainly gone to great lengths to keep his marriage afloat – even resigning from his position as Siglufjördur's senior police officer, selling up and moving to Reykjavík.

'That's fine as far as I'm concerned,' Ari Thór said, keeping his thoughts to himself. 'Shall I follow up on this Sara angle?'

'What? No, not unless you feel like it. We'll try and nail Arnór for Ásta's murder. I'm starting to think that Thóra's death was natural.'

The Blönduós inspector looked awkward as he stood in front of them, taking no part in the conversation.

'In spite of the wine stain?' Ari Thór asked sharply.

'The wine? Yes, in spite of that. Right, there are two things I want you to do: speak to Arnór's wife and take a look at Thóra's things. Apart from that, I think we're good to go.' Tómas turned to the inspector. 'Do you have a car you could lend my colleague for the afternoon? I'll be going south in mine.'

Ari Thór sat in the borrowed car and went through the list of young people who'd stayed out at the point. There were thirty-three, and only one Sara; Sara Margrét Thrastardóttir. Ah, but there was another at the bottom of the list, a sort-of Sara, at least: Elín Sara Stefánsdóttir. It shouldn't take long to have a word with them both.

Tómas was a hard worker, perceptive and he had a knack of making things happen – but, in Ari Thór's opinion, he sometimes allowed himself to take the easy way out, concentrating on the most straightforward solution rather than the more difficult one.

Ari Thór went back into the police station and typed the two names into the national registry and then the phone directory. He quickly found both women. The names were exactly the same as on the list, and both were unique. One had been born in 1979, the other in 1980, which fitted perfectly; the women would have been the right kind of age to have spent a summer at Kálfshamarsvík around 1990.

He went back out to the car and set off towards the farm to meet Thórhalla. As he drove he called Sara Margrét's number. She answered on the fourth ring. The voice on the line was warm, and surprised, as if she were asking herself who could be calling her on Christmas Eve.

'Hello? Is that Sara?' asked Ari Thór. 'Sara Margrét Thrastardóttir?' It was awkward to start a conversation this way, but he had to be sure he had found the right person.

'Yes,' she replied, albeit with a note of hesitation.

'I'm sorry to disturb you. My name's Ari Thór Arason. I'm a police officer,' he said, deciding that there was no reason to make things more complicated by mentioning that he was based in Siglufjördur.

'The police?' she asked, and there was no doubt that she was gripped by sudden concern.

'It's nothing serious,' he said quickly, although that wasn't exactly true. 'I need to ask you a few questions in connection with an investigation here in the north.'

'An investigation up in the north?' Sara Margrét answered, clearly taken aback.

'Yes. It's in connection with a fatality at Kálfshamarsvík.' There was no response. 'Just north of Skagaströnd and Blönduós,' he added by way of further explanation.

'I don't understand. How is this supposed to have anything to do with me?' she asked.

'I understand you spent some time there when you were a child. Do you remember when that was?'

'In the country? In Kálfs– … what did you say the name of the place was?'

'Kálfshamarsvík.'

'I've never been there,' she said firmly. 'I never spent time in the country when I was a child.'

'You're sure?'

'Of course I'm sure.'

'Your name is on a list of children who were there; each child got a state subsidy to be there,' Ari Thór said. 'Could you have maybe been there for a short time? A couple of days, maybe?'

'What is this bullshit? My name's on some list?' she demanded, clearly upset. 'I don't know anything about this place and I was never sent to spend time in the country, not even for a short while.'

Her replies left Ari Thór at a loss. 'Could it be someone with the same name?' he suggested.

'As far as I know I'm the only one in Iceland with this name.'

'In that case I apologise for the disturbance, have a Merry Christmas.'

'What? Oh yes, of course. And you.'

She put the phone down.

*What the hell?* he wondered. Had he been given the wrong list?

When Elín Sara answered her phone, she seemed as astonished as the other Sara to receive a call from the police on Christmas Eve.

'We're investigating a fatality in Kálfshamarsvík,' Ari Thór explained, 'up here in the north.'

'You mean the woman who jumped off the cliff?' she asked right away.

This took Ari Thór by surprise; he thought they'd kept things discreet. The only reports had been that the body of a woman from Reykjavík had been found on the rocks at Kálfshamarsvík. The media had assumed that it had been suicide, and they generally kept their coverage of such cases low-key. That would probably change now, though, he mused, once news of Thóra's death and Arnór's arrest became known.

'That's right. A young woman lost her life up here a few days ago.'

Elín Sara said nothing.

'Did you by any chance spend time at Kálfshamarsvík when you were younger?' Ari Thór asked, half expecting a 'no'; his faith in the list was already dampened, but at least she seemed to know of the place.

She was silent for a moment and finally answered with an abrupt 'yes'.

'When was that? Do you remember?'

'It was 1988. I was nine years old.'

'OK, thanks. I just have a few questions, for you, Elín. Or are you normally called Sara?'

'I'm Sara,' she replied.

So this had to be the girl Thóra had mentioned, he thought.

'Do you remember Thóra Óskarsdóttir?'

'Yes, I do,' she said quietly. 'Why do you ask?'

'She died last night, I'm afraid.'

'So,' Sara replied in a startlingly cold voice. 'What does that have to do with me?' There was no anger or upset in her voice, she came across as distant and uninterested.

'She mentioned you last night.'

'She mentioned *me*?' She was clearly surprised by this news.

'Yes,' he said, waiting for a further response.

'What did she say?' Elín Sara asked finally.

'She said she had been thinking of you,' Ari Thór said. 'I understand that she said you had been much in her thoughts.'

'Much in her thoughts?' she repeated in a low voice. 'Did she say anything else?'

'Not as far as I know. Do you have any idea why she might have said that?'

There was a long pause. Then, 'No, I can't imagine why she'd say such a thing.' But her tone was unconvincing.

'Who was there the summer that you were?' Ari Thór asked.

She hesitated again before speaking. 'Well, there was Thóra, of course. Her brother as well, and Reynir. Do they still live there?'

'They do,' Ari Thór confirmed. 'Óskar and Reynir. Were there any other regular visitors out there on the headland? Maybe people from the farms in the district?'

'Yes, there was a boy who came sometimes, but I don't remember his name.'

'Arnór?'

'Arnór? Could be. I know his father was more often there.'

'Were you and Thóra close? Did you get on well?'

'No, we didn't,' Elín Sara answered sharply.

'And was there any further contact between you after that summer? Have you met again recently?'

'No, I never spoke to her again,' she said. 'After that summer, I mean.'

'Did anything unusual happen? Anything that could have preyed on Thóra's mind all those years?'

'No,' she said. It was another abrupt answer.

Ari Thór paused, and was about to end the call – he had done what he could, after all – when Elín Sara asked a question of her own.

'Did she jump, this woman?'

'Her name was Ásta,' Ari Thór replied. 'She was around your age. We're still investigating what happened.'

'Do you know why she did it?' Elín Sara asked. 'Why she took her own life?'

'As I say, it's under investigation. At the moment we can't say exactly what happened,' he said formally, surprised at her interest. 'But please get in touch if there's anything that comes to mind. Would you do that?'

He gave her his phone number and she mumbled something that Ari Thór took as agreement.

Once the conversation was over, he called the inspector at the Blönduós station and asked him to find some more phone numbers for the names on the list. He chose the more unusual names – ones that would be more likely to return the right person. By the end of the call with the inspector he had what he thought were eight promising mobile numbers.

In the time it took to reach Arnór and Thórhalla's farmhouse, he had made all his calls and had reached five people. He told them all who he was and that he was simply calling to check out whether they had stayed at Kálfshamarsvík. Two of them remembered it, and one had even been there the same summer as Sara, but didn't recall anything remarkable happening.

'It was so cold there, even though it was summer,' was his abiding memory.

The other three people declined to confirm that they had ever stayed at Kálfshamarsvík; they said they had never even heard of the place.

He found it difficult to believe that all three were lying to a police officer in response to a relatively straightforward question. There was always the possibility that he had reached the wrong people, he supposed. But if they *were* the right names, and none of them were lying, how had they found their way onto this list?

## IX

It was warm, without being overpoweringly so, inside the farmhouse. An old standard lamp, along with the Christmas tree lights, cast a pleasant light around the living room. Now that Christmas had been postponed, however, there was no comforting aroma of cooking, no ham in the oven or smoked lamb simmering on the hob. Thórhalla appeared to have been expecting Ari Thór, or someone from the police, at least, and she asked him in straightaway, offering him a seat on the sofa. What struck Ari Thór most about the living room was the absence of books. There were a few photos and landscape paintings on the walls, and small figurines and other decorations on the shelves, but not a single book. An old record player brought some comfort – suggesting that there might at least be music in this house; however, there were no records in sight.

'There's hot cocoa if you'd like some,' she said, apparently bearing no grudge against the man who had led her husband out, practically in handcuffs, on Christmas Eve.

Ari Thór accepted a cup, although it didn't live up to her description: it was cocoa, but it wasn't exactly hot. The chocolate flavour was powerful though, reminding him of past Christmases he had spent with his parents. It summoned childhood memories that he would prefer not to recall right now.

'He didn't do it,' was the first thing Thórhalla said. 'He didn't kill that woman.'

'What makes you so sure?' Ari Thór asked calmly.

'I know Arnór and I know he'd never do anything like that. Is he coming home tonight?'

'Unfortunately, I think that's unlikely.'

She nodded, presumably having expected his answer. 'They slept together, didn't they?'

Ari Thór refrained from replying, hoping that Thórhalla would continue.

'I know he sneaked out that night. He thinks I sleep through it, but I always know when he's up and about. And I know what he's been doing. I can smell his girlfriends on him when he crawls back into bed. I only pretend to be asleep.'

Her openness took Ari Thór by surprise. 'Did you know he had gone to meet Ásta?' He decided not to point out that she had lied to them before.

'No. Arnór hadn't even told me that she was staying out at the point. It's obvious now why he didn't.'

'And you put up with all this?' Ari Thór asked, recognising immediately that the question was inappropriate, and nothing to do with the investigation.

'Sometimes I've had enough and…' She seemed almost to have spoken without thinking, her voice disturbingly sharp. She stopped herself mid-sentence. 'It's no concern of yours what I put up with,' she said heavily. But then added, in a softer tone, 'He's always been like this. He's never been able to withstand the temptation of pretty girls. Having no children of our own hasn't helped. We're nowhere near setting off for the divorce courts, though. I think we've both figured out that we're not in love and perhaps never were. But we're good friends and business partners. So it could be worse.'

'Do you remember what time he went out that night? And when he came home?'

'As far as I remember, he left around eleven and he wasn't long, an hour or so. I remember noticing that he was quicker than usual. His girlfriends are normally in Blönduós or Skagaströnd, or further away. It occurred to me that he might have had a genuine errand to run, just for once. But that wasn't the case, as we know now,' she said, and gave him a reluctant smile.

Was she covering for her husband? Was this all one big lie? Could this be a carefully rehearsed play with her the actor and him the sole member of the audience? She had certainly gone to some lengths to convince Ari Thór that she didn't love her husband, that he had cheated on her numerous times, and that she really had no reason to lie on his behalf. On top of that, she had done her best to give him an alibi, although it wasn't a particularly strong one, even with the weight of her confidence behind it. Arnór could have driven out to the point, had sex with Ásta in the attic, taken her out to the lighthouse, murdered her there, dumped the body off the edge of the cliff and driven home all in the space of an hour. Ari Thór did have to admit to himself, though, that the man would have been hard-pressed to manage all that.

'He's a good man, in spite of everything,' she added. 'And he's no killer.'

⊕

As he pulled up at Kálfshamarsvík, Ari Thór checked the time. He was concerned that he was taking too long in his investigations, and that Kristín would be waiting for him. His plan was to check Thóra's room, which he was sure would not take long, then speak to Óskar and Reynir to get answers to a few more questions. He was sure that Arnór was not the right man – uncomfortably so – and he felt guilty that Arnór would be spending Christmas in a cell.

He found a local police officer in the basement, the same one who had spent the night watching the lighthouse.

'I was asked to make sure nobody came down here,' he said glumly, undoubtedly wishing he could be anywhere but here, especially on Christmas Eve. 'Do you need me here much longer?'

'No, not now, thanks,' Ari Thór said. 'I'll take over.'

There was a knock at the basement door. Ari Thór looked round; the door was ajar and he saw Reynir looking through the gap.

'How's it going?' he asked jovially, coming inside.

'We arrested Arnór.' There was little point keeping it quiet. 'We need to talk things over with him in more depth.'

'I can't say I'm surprised. I guessed it was him who slept with Ásta. But I didn't know he had a violent streak. Not that it's always easy to judge these things.'

'We can't say for sure that Ásta was murdered,' Ari Thór said with determination. 'And neither can we be certain that Arnór was responsible.'

'But you arrested him, you said?'

*It wasn't my decision,* was what Ari Thór longed to say.

'You spoke to Ásta after dinner, the evening before she died,' he said instead. 'That's right, isn't it?'

Reynir hesitated for a second. 'Yes, that's right. I told you that already.'

'Do you remember what time that was?'

'No, I don't,' he said, the question appearing to irritate him. 'We've already been through this, haven't we?'

'Was it before or after midnight?'

'Before. I'm pretty sure of that.'

It was possible, therefore, that Reynir's account could tie in with Arnór's and Thórhalla's. On the other hand, were it in his interest to lie, his claim was still imprecise enough to fit with that, too. Had Ásta gone downstairs after dinner, chatted to Reynir, and then gone up to the attic, where Arnór had then visited her? It was a possibility. Had she then gone out to the lighthouse and been assaulted there? Did someone go with her, or had someone been lying in wait for her there?

'How's Óskar?' Ari Thór asked.

'The poor old boy's not too bad. He's upstairs. Thóra's death has come as a huge shock, even though he must have known she didn't have long to live, as we all did,' Reynir said. 'Are you trying to pin Thóra's death on Arnór?' he added carefully. 'Her illness caused her death, surely.'

'We're looking into all possibilities. I'll come upstairs in a while. I need a word with Óskar before I'm on my way.'

Reynir nodded, and seemed to understand that his presence in the basement was no longer required. 'You can find me in my office, if you need me,' he said, and left.

Ari Thór turned and entered Thóra's bedroom, and as he did, the red wine stain on the carpet immediately caught his eye, reminding him that things were far from settled, and there was a good chance that Tómas had arrested the wrong man. There was nothing to connect Arnór to Thóra's death, other than the unfortunate fact that he had spent the night in the house.

It occurred to Ari Thór that, if Thóra really had been murdered, the wine could have splashed on the attacker. But this seemed unlikely, as the bedside table was on the opposite side of the room from the door. Surely the murderer would have taken the shortest route to the bed…

The room was a spartan place, with one window set high in the wall. The bedside table was empty and, opening the drawer in it, he found only some painkillers. There were four Christmas cards lying on the bed. Ari Thór read them all, aware that he was intruding into someone's personal effects, but that could hardly be avoided. It was unlikely that Christmas cards would contain any particular secrets. The senders' names were unfamiliar and the messages were impersonal and short. Merry Christmas, best wishes, and so on. It was the number that attracted Ari Thór's attention, though. Wouldn't a woman of her age have gathered more friends over the course of her life, and therefore received more cards at Christmas? Although, to go by what her brother and Reynir had told them, she was troubled, so perhaps she wasn't the most sociable of people and found it difficult to maintain friendships.

A low wooden cupboard stood against one wall. One door was unlocked and the other locked, although the key was in the lock. Perhaps it was simply a courteous reminder to the others in the house that this was private and they should keep out.

The unlocked side revealed some worn paperbacks – all novels and all of them in Icelandic. On the lower shelf were two Christmas packages in bright-red wrapping paper that looked likely to be books; one was labelled for Reynir and the other for Óskar.

Ari Thór turned the key in the locked side. There was nothing in here but a tattered brown envelope. It contained a dozen or more Christmas cards, two handwritten letters and some clippings from old newspapers. None of the Christmas cards was signed, although, judging by the handwriting, they all appeared to have been sent by the same person. The messages contained in them were short, personal and intimate. The two letters were both signed, though, and the handwriting was undoubtedly the same as on the cards. They were from Heidar, Arnór's father. Ari Thór scanned the letters rapidly; one was dated 1985, the other five years before that. They were old-fashioned love letters, courteously romantic. Both were sent from Reykjavík. Heidar had presumably been travelling there and had made the most of the opportunity to write to her.

The newspaper cuttings Thóra had kept were obituaries of two men: one of them Heidar. He had died in 2000 at the age of sixty-four. Thórhalla had written a short appreciation of her father-in-law. At first sight it was affectionate in tone, but when read with greater care there was a certain distance and coldness in the words. Work colleagues and school friends also provided their contributions and Áki Reynisson, Reynir's father, said his farewell in a few words to what he called a 'good man', calling him 'a trusted friend, a good husband and father,' as well as 'a regular visitor to our house in the country'. Thóra had written nothing about her lover.

The other man had died in 1989 at an advanced age – he was born in 1901. The name – Sölvi Árnason – was unfamiliar to Ari Thór, and at first he didn't make the connection with Thóra. The picture only began to come together when he read that the man had been a general practitioner until the late 1960s. Ari Thór read through the plaudits: 'A man of fine character and professional standards' who had 'dedicated himself to improving the lives of others'. He had passed away at 'a great age after an unblemished career'.

There was no word of his shortcomings, which had undoubtedly been the reason why Thóra had kept these cuttings. There was no mention of him having been accused of prescribing young students amphetamines when he should have been aware of the dangers of the drugs. The picture of him that accompanied the obituary was the very image of a trustworthy man of medicine 'of fine character and professional standards': it showed a kindly-looking elderly man with thin grey hair, narrow glasses and a friendly look on his face. His only son, Sölvi Sölvason, had been born in 1934, which put him close to eighty now, assuming he was still alive.

Reynir was back in the master of the house's seat, occupying the leather chair behind the desk in his office. Ari Thór handed him the bright-red package without a word.

'A Christmas present?' Reynir said in astonishment. 'That's very thoughtful of you,' he chuckled.

Ari Thór stood still, waiting for Reynir to look at the tag.

'From Thóra?' he said in surprise. 'For me?'

'Didn't you expect to get anything?'

'Certainly not,' he replied in apparent sincerity.

'Did you buy anything for her?'

'No. Nothing. I never have.'

Ari Thór remained silent, waiting.

'Am I supposed to open it?'

'That's what I'm here for,' Ari Thór replied. 'I want to know what's inside.'

'Well, fair enough.' Reynir ripped the paper off to reveal a book, just as Ari Thór had suspected.

'Oh, I've already read it,' Reynir said. 'It's not too bad.'

'What book is it?'

'It's an autobiography of someone I know. Experiences from a life in business, or, rather, him going on about what a great guy he is. He's never really achieved that much, but he uses a smart PR agency. It would have been a different story if I'd written it.' He put the book aside, placing it on the edge of the desk.

'You said Óskar's here? I'd like to have a word with him,' Ari Thór said.

'The old boy's in the kitchen.'

'What's going to happen to him?' Ari Thór asked lightly. 'Are you going to keep him on?'

Reynir glanced at the door. Ari Thór had left it slightly open; he turned around and pushed it shut.

'I don't have the heart to throw him out,' said Reynir quietly, 'but I'm concerned that he's likely to become needy now. I'm considering asking him to take on some of the work his sister did, for the same salary, of course – he's not going to be much use for anything else. I've kept him on these last few years almost out of charity.'

'Let's hope it works out,' Ari Thór said, his hand on the door handle. 'Thanks for taking the time to talk.'

'Do you need to take the book with you?' Reynir asked. 'It can hardly be evidence can it?'

The book was still in its cellophane wrapper, so Thóra could not have written any personal message in it. Nothing that might have been helpful for the case.

'No, it's no use to us,' Ari Thór said, quietly pleased that Reynir had asked. Maybe he had been fond of the old lady, after all, and wanted to keep the last thing she had planned to give him.

Óskar stared into a cup of coffee that sat in front of him on the kitchen table.

'Hello,' Ari Thór said quietly.

Óskar started and looked up. 'Oh, hello,' he replied, trying to look alert. His eyes went straight to the package in Ari Thór's hands and he appeared to put two and two together right away.

'I was wondering where the present ...' he began, before his voice cracked. He drew a deep breath before continuing. 'I'd wondered where the present from Thóra was. She always gave me something at Christmas, and I'd always have something for her. That's the book from her, isn't it?'

Ari Thór nodded.

'I thought I recognised the paper. We've been using it for a few years. One roll lasts a long time when you don't have many friends,' he said, and tried to squeeze out a smile. 'I bought her a book as well. Some novel that the lad in the Co-op said was at the top of the bestseller list. She would always sit down with a book on Christmas Eve and read well into the night, a habit that never changed. Always so peaceful and satisfied. She'd been through plenty of adversity over the years, so it always gladdened my heart to see her happy at Christmas. That's when everything was right with the world, even if it was just for one night.'

Ari Thór handed him the parcel. Óskar placed it on the table and thanked him, even though he had done nothing that called for gratitude.

'I have to ask you to open it now,' Ari Thór said hesitatingly, after they had sat in silence for a moment.

'Now?' The expression on Óskar's face was horrified. 'Surely you don't mind if I keep it until later?'

It crossed Ari Thór's mind that enough was enough. But he couldn't just let this go. The investigation had to take priority. He would be unable to forgive himself if the package revealed something important.

'Unfortunately not,' he said.

'Oh, well.' Óskar nodded in acceptance. 'It's probably some biography.' He handled the parcel carefully, cautiously removing the paper. 'Yes, that's right. I've seen this one advertised and wanted to read it.'

Óskar sat in silence for a moment, taking off the cellophane wrapper and flipping through the pages. Ari Thór could see that his eyes were filling with tears. The old man turned away, dabbing at them.

Ari Thór felt uncomfortable, having made Óskar open his present right away. Unsure of what to do, he waited, giving Óskar time to collect himself.

'I wanted to show you this as well,' he said, placing Doctor Sölvi Árnason's obituary on the kitchen table.

Óskar peered at the picture and said, 'That's him, the bastard.' There was no respect in his voice. 'Sölvi, that was his name, right enough. I'd forgotten that, but I remember the picture. Thóra showed me the obituary when he died. I racked my brains to work out how an ordinary man, who looked so decent, could do such a thing to a young girl. I don't doubt that he meant well, but he wasn't capable of doing his job. What would I know, though?' He paused before continuing. 'I can tell you that Thóra was glad he was dead. I remember it clearly, the way she reacted. It was unusual for her, disturbing, even, but understandable all the same. The man as good as destroyed her life. But imagine holding on to that hatred all that time...' He fumbled in his pocket for his reading glasses and peered at the text. 'Yes, 1989. More than twenty years ago. The man was well into old age when he died.' He looked down at the yellowing cutting again. 'He was almost ninety, but she still hated him...'

'She was unforgiving,' Ari Thór said, at a loss as to how to contribute to the conversation.

'More than just unforgiving,' Óskar said.

'He had a son. Do you know if he and Thóra had any contact?'

'I don't imagine they did,' he said. Then his expression changed and he looked up and stared into Ari Thór's eyes, as if the horrible possibility they'd suggested to him before had finally hit home. 'My sister's death – do you suspect someone is responsible for it in some way?'

Ari Thór sensed that Óskar wouldn't be able to bear it if that were the case. Especially if Arnór and Reynir were suspects: both were close acquaintances, and the latter provided his living.

'We don't know yet,' Ari Thór replied in all sincerity. 'Did Reynir tell you that Arnór has been arrested?'

It was immediately obvious from Óskar's look of astonishment that he hadn't. 'Because of Thóra?' he asked quickly.

'No, we're primarily exploring his relationship with Ásta. But we're keeping everything open for the moment. We'll have to wait and see.'

Óskar buried his face in his hands, hung his head and sighed as if all the burdens of the world were resting on his shoulders.

'Is there anything I can do?' he asked at last, in a low voice.

'Tell me something,' Ari Thór said, taking a seat at the kitchen table. 'Reynir mentioned that your sister had talked last night about some kind of hide-and-seek, that someone made a habit of shutting themselves away. Do you have an idea what she meant?'

Óskar was silent for a long while, as if searching for the right words. 'I should have said something to you this morning,' he said at last, his drawn face showing that his words were weighing heavily on him. 'It's nothing to do with your investigation, which is why I said nothing. She meant me.'

'Really?'

'Thóra and I lived comfortably together for so long mainly because we didn't each have our noses in the other's business. We had our own lives and this little quirk of mine is nothing special – nothing to be ashamed of. It's an interest, if we can call it that, and I wanted to keep it to myself. I've been studying the financial crash here in Iceland, you see,' he said with a quizzical look.

'The Crash?' Ari Thór asked in amazement. 'How?'

'I've put time into reading the papers, listening to the news, trying to dig deeper, trying to form an opinion on those who were responsible for it – the ones who gambled with other people's money.'

'Do you think Reynir was one of them?'

'Well, he wasn't one of those who bankrupted the country. I gather that he runs his business fairly responsibly.'

'So how does this connect to the hide-and-seek that Thóra spoke about?' Ari Thór asked, feeling like his patience was running out.

'I've been listening to a radio programme – on a station based in Reykjavík. People call in and say what they think is wrong with society, and of course they talk about the Crash. I always listen when

I can, and that's when I shut myself away, because…' He looked down shamefacedly. 'Because I call in to the radio show as well and say what I think. I have the same rights as everyone else, don't I?'

'Well, yes,' Ari Thór said.

'I didn't want to involve other people here in what's become a sort of hobby, you see? Sometimes you have to keep things to yourself.'

'I agree.' Ari Thór paused, aware of the time and that he needed to get going soon. 'Can I ask you one more thing…'

'Yes?'

'About Sara.'

'Sara, yes. Of course,' Óskar said, a wide-eyed questioning look on his face.

'You said you had youngsters stay here over a few years, if I recall correctly.'

'That's right.'

'How many years?'

'Only a few. Three or four years, maybe.'

'How many youngsters were there altogether? Ten? Twelve?'

'I don't remember,' Óskar said, seeming to have little interest in the matter. 'That sounds about right, more or less.'

'We received this list from the ministry this morning,' Ari Thór said and took the folded sheet of paper from his pocket, placed it on the table and pushed it towards Óskar. 'There are thirty-three names. I've spoken to some of these people and they say they were never guests here. Only a few said they'd actually been here.'

Óskar didn't look at the list, and he averted his eyes from Ari Thór's gaze too. His hands began to tremble and he clenched his fists as if to stop them. He was still wearing that same blue roll-neck sweater. Would he dress up for the Christmas mass? Ari Thór wondered.

'I don't know what to say,' Óskar mumbled at last.

'I can wait,' Ari Thór said coolly. He knew he would have no problem breaking down Óskar's resistance, especially now. He suspected that this was a harmless man who wouldn't stand his ground too fiercely. Ari Thór almost enjoyed the feeling of seeing how easy it would be, then felt a slight pang of conscience, but didn't let it trouble him too much.

'I can't … I can't really talk about this now,' Óskar said, his voice tremulous.

'Why not?'

There was a short silence. 'Because of Thóra,' Óskar whispered. 'You mustn't ask me about this. Not now,' he begged.

'You have to understand that we can't let the investigation be held up without good reason. We need to have everything clear.'

'This is nothing to do with Thóra's death, and certainly not Ásta's.'

'I have to decide that for myself,' Ari Thór said solemnly.

'I just can't talk about this. She's only just gone.'

Ari Thór sat in silence. Óskar was no longer able to stop his hands trembling. He seemed about to mutter something, but didn't. At last he looked at Ari Thór with a haunted, desperate cast to his face. The last of his defences had fallen.

'She meant well, my sister. She always meant well. The system had let her down, you see, and she thought she was owed,' he whispered.

'Owed what?'

'Well, money. I found out by chance. She denied it at first, but that was useless. And then she tried to justify it. She found out that first summer how easy it was to get these grants – all you had to do was send in a list of names and wait for the payment. The next year she added a few names, which she took from the children's pages in the papers. If some nine-year-old had sent in a story to the paper, then she would say they stayed here, and they wouldn't know a thing about it. Then the next year she went a little further and added a few more. For a couple of summers we didn't have any children at all here, although the names that were on the grant application form said we did.' He cleared his throat. 'You understand that I had nothing to do with this. It was Thóra's idea, she did it all and pocketed the cash. We've never been all that well paid here. And did Thóra get any compensation from the government because of that business with the doctor – a doctor on the state payroll – who ruined her chances of studying? Not a penny! Not a single penny!' His voice was rising now.

'So she decided to swindle money out of the government?' Ari Thór asked, keeping his own voice calm.

'Swindle? I wouldn't put it like that,' Óskar said. 'Of course, she knew what she was doing was wrong, claiming money for kids who never stayed here. But she was resourceful, my sister, and she had a sense of justice.'

Ari Thór smiled.

'Are you going to take this any further?'

'It's probably beyond the statute of limitations,' Ari Thór said, without answering the question directly. 'But Sara, was she genuinely here? Or just on paper?'

'She was one who was here. I haven't been lying to you about her. But I don't know why she seems to have been on Thóra's mind.'

Ari Thór stood up, and suddenly remembered the question he had forgotten to ask the day before. 'While I remember…'

Óskar looked up.

'Reynir mentioned yesterday, just after we arrived, that he doesn't have a computer in his office. I thought you were about to say something about that, and I was going to ask you about it when there was a chance. I gather that Reynir works all the time, since the markets never sleep, so it seems odd that he doesn't have a computer.'

'Well…' Óskar began slowly, '…I didn't want to say anything bad about Reynir in front of you, but that's not right. He always has his laptop with him.'

'Always?'

'Good grief, yes. He never stops. He's glued to it.'

'When did you see it last?'

'I'm not exactly sure.'

'Did he have it before Christmas? After Ásta's death?'

'Yes, I'm sure he did.'

Ari Thór thanked Óskar and hurried back to Reynir's office, knocking and opening the door without waiting for an answer.

Reynir seemed to take the unexpected intrusion well. He smiled at Ari Thór. 'Did you forget something?' he asked casually.

'Where's the computer? Your laptop?'

Presumably expecting the question, Reynir took it in his stride. 'It was stolen. Damned bad luck.'

'Did you lie to us the other day?' Ari Thór asked, suddenly angry.

'Lie to you?' Reynir remained unruffled. 'Not at all. I said I didn't have a computer, and that was true. Why would I lie to you about something so trivial?'

'Where was it stolen, and when?'

'In Blönduós or Skagaströnd, the day after Ásta died. It was on the back seat of the car. I forgot to lock it, which was completely stupid of me.' He smiled. 'I didn't notice it was gone until I was home.'

'I assume you reported it to the police immediately.'

'No, I didn't. Careless, I know. But I don't keep anything important on the laptop itself. That's all securely stored in the cloud, so I haven't lost any business secrets, and, to be honest, I'm not worried about the price of a laptop. I'll buy another one when I go to Reykjavík after Christmas.'

'Let me know if it shows up,' Ari Thór said, and left without another word.

# X

Ari Thór sat in the patrol car, looking out over the bay of Kálf-shamarsvík, with the inspector from the Blönduós station on the phone, searching the databases for a number for Sölvi, the doctor's son.

Ari Thór wondered if Tómas had maybe come to the right conclusions – that Thóra's death had been the natural culmination of a long illness, and that Arnór had murdered Ásta during a tryst that had gone badly wrong.

'Here it is,' the inspector said. 'Sölvi Sölvason, born 1934, lives on Hringbraut.' He read out the number.

Once again Ari Thór tried to justify to himself that he was doing the right thing, disturbing strangers just a few hours before the Christmas celebrations were due to start.

Sölvi answered the phone promptly. Ari Thór introduced himself and got straight to the point.

'I need to ask you a few questions about your father.'

'My father? Yes, of course. May I ask why?'

Judging purely by the man's voice, Ari Thór would not have imagined that he was close to eighty.

'We're investigating the death of an elderly woman up here in the north. Her name was Thóra Óskarsdóttir. She had been a patient of your father's at one point, a long time ago.'

'I'm not familiar with the name.'

'She felt she had unfinished business with him, or so I gather. It seems he prescribed amphetamines for her while she was studying, and that had some unfortunate consequences.'

'Ah, she was one of them, was she?' Sölvi asked.

'You know about this?'

'Yes, I know my father got into some trouble over this kind of thing a long while ago. It was standard practice back then, though. And he was of the old school – a bit of a dinosaur, I suppose. He didn't adapt easily to new ways of doing things. But he meant nobody any harm. It's hardly a crime not to keep up with new developments, to refuse to accept change, is it?'

There was no indication in Sölvi's voice that he expected an answer to his question, and Ari Thór wasn't inclined to give him one. 'Did they ever meet after that?' he asked instead.

'No, I don't think so. She tried to squeeze some money out of him, but Dad held on to his cash. Then she tried to sue him, if I remember correctly, but nothing came of that. But it was a burden for my father, as I recall.'

'For her as well, I understand,' Ari Thór said.

'Her? The woman, yes … well.'

'Thanks for talking to me, and have a good Christmas.'

Ari Thór ended the call and then phoned Tómas. He was still on the road to Reykjavík and said that he had spoken to the prosecutor in Akureyri, who had agreed, reluctantly, to examine the case and decide whether or not there were grounds for keeping Arnór in custody for a longer period. 'He wasn't overjoyed at having to work right now,' Tómas said.

Ari Thór described what he had discovered: Thóra's extortion, the laptop, the doctor's obituaries. He almost felt ashamed that he was pointing out to Tómas that there were still a lot of loose ends to the case; it was as if he was hinting, indirectly, that Tómas had been too hasty in putting Arnór behind bars.

There was a silence at the other end of the line when he'd finished. He could sense that Tómas was far from delighted by his narrative.

'You want me to turn round?' Tómas said eventually. 'All right, I'll come back.' It was clear from his expectant silence, though, that he was waiting for Ari Thór to tell him there was no need.

Ari Thór decided to humour him, almost against his better judgement. 'I can handle it,' he said, reflecting that it was Christmas and there was little else they could do. He had turned over every conceivable stone, and if there were any more, then he would have to dig deep for them. But that could wait until after Christmas.

His phone rang almost as soon as he had hung up. He was sure it was Kristín, impatiently waiting for him in Blönduós.

'Ari …' He heard her breathing hard and fast, knowing instantly that something was wrong. 'Ari …' she repeated breathlessly. 'I think the baby's coming. The baby…'

## XI

It was as if the words passed him by, as if he refused to believe them. Then his heart lurched, he started the car before saying anything and set off faster than was wise along the potholed road, if it could be called a road.

'Are you all right? Where are you? I'm on the way.'

'I've already called an ambulance and they'll be here before you,' she said, and he remembered that she was always the more practical one, with no patience for undue sentiment. 'They can't be far away,' she continued. 'I've tried to call you again and again, but the line was engaged the whole time.'

'Where are you?' he repeated. 'Are you all right?'

'The car slid on the ice on the mountain, on the Thverárfjall road. The car skidded, but it's nothing serious.' Her words came quickly, between rapid breaths. 'I was a little shocked,' she added, and now he was sure she was holding back tears.

'Stay calm,' he told her, trying to hold his own car on the road. There was snow fluttering down – enough to slow him down but by no means a blizzard.

He did his best to help Kristín remain relaxed, without knowing if his words were having any effect. It wasn't as if he had ever become a father over the phone before.

⊕

The child was born on the mountain, in Kristín's car. Ari Thór listened to everything over the phone as it happened, and was finally given a message by one of the paramedics that everything was fine. Kristín was in the ambulance and he should go straight to the hospital in Blönduós. He didn't even get a chance to ask if it was a boy or a girl – not that it mattered to him.

He soon caught up with the ambulance and followed it to the hospital, so he was there as Kristín emerged and he saw the baby for the first time, carefully wrapped up.

Everything that had taken place at Kálfshamarsvík vanished from his thoughts as he smiled at the baby, its eyes open as the little boy or girl took in the big world around it. Then he turned to Kristín. She gave him a weak smile back, the baby still cradled in her arms. She looked exhausted, and as he moved closer to kiss her cheek, she whispered to him.

'It's a boy.'

'Congratulations, my love,' he whispered back.

The boy was put into Ari Thór's arms for the first time only when they were inside the hospital. It was all so unreal – the tiny fingers that held onto one of his so tightly; the fact that he was a father with responsibility for another individual in the same way that his parents had taken responsibility for him. He was determined to watch over his son for longer than his own parents had been there for him.

'He's fine, even if he's a little early,' said the doctor who had delivered the baby, or at least who had been present, the boy having been well on the way by the time the ambulance had arrived.

'Would you like to dress him?' the doctor suggested, pointing Ari Thór towards some clothes that someone – a nurse maybe – had laid out on the bed. He and Kristín had not brought with them any of the baby clothes they had already bought.

Ari Thór hesitated. But he told himself to try, although he hardly dared move with the baby in his arms, and wasn't even sure that he would be able to put clothes on such a delicate little creature. As he fumbled to dress his son for the first time, he realised that life would never be the same again.

While Ari Thór did his best to get his son into a tiny green

Babygro – with more success than he had expected – he heard Kristín taking the opportunity to call her parents with the happy news. He wondered if there was anyone he should call; and the first mixed feelings intruded into his cloud of happiness. He had no parents and no siblings, just a few relatives he had little contact with. Should he tell Tómas, maybe? Could his older colleague be the one who was at the top of the list? Was Tómas in reality his closest friend? It had been months before he had even got round to telling him that he and Kristín were expecting a child.

He could hear that Kristín's conversation with her parents was an emotional one, which was exactly as it should be, he mused. Kristín spent some time convincing them that there was no reason for them to take the first available flight to Iceland, which wouldn't be until the day after Christmas, anyway. Her father worked as an adviser in the financial sector, and her mother was an architect, and they now lived in Norway, having moved there when the Crash resulted in them both losing their jobs. Kristín had often warned Ari Thór that, once their grandchild was born, they would find a reason to move back. Whenever she'd spoken to them in recent months, they'd asked apparently offhand questions about whether or not the employment market back home in Iceland was improving, so she was convinced that their homecoming plan was already in motion.

'Looking good,' Kristín said, once the conversation was over. The little boy was dressed for the first time, in a green Babygro that fitted him nicely. 'Mum and Dad will be here after Christmas, so it looks like we'll have two days to ourselves before the circus starts.'

She gave him a heartfelt smile, but Ari Thór could see that she missed her parents. And although she always bore it well, she had more than once mentioned her concerns about the difficulties of embarking on family life without having anyone close by for support. She didn't want them to be all alone.

Ari Thór felt it was best to wait for a while before discussing the boy's name. He was reluctant to spoil this wonderful moment by starting a dispute, and it had also occurred to him that the child's name was less important to him than he had thought it would be. It had become a trivial thing all of a sudden. Perhaps the boy would get his late grandfather's name – or perhaps not. It didn't seem to matter.

He thought for a second about how old his father would have been, if he had lived: he would have been fifty-two, soon to be fifty-three. The newborn boy would never get to meet his paternal grandfather, or his paternal grandmother; both had been dead for fifteen years. But at this moment, as Ari Thór held his own newborn son close to his chest, he felt his own father was nearby – so prominent was he in his thoughts.

Towards six that evening, mother and son were sleeping peacefully, tired out by the tough day. Ari Thór sat at the end of the bed and surreptitiously took a few pictures using Kristín's phone.

She opened her eyes and smiled.

'How are you, my love?' he asked.

'Fine. Just fine. But exhausted. This is going to be a strange Christmas.'

'Not exactly what we expected; we don't even get the Blönduós hotel Christmas that we'd been talking about,' he said.

'This is just perfect,' she said, the fatigue obvious in her voice.

'Your present, or all the presents … they can wait until tonight.'

'We ought to get something for him as well,' Kristín said.

'You're right. I wasn't ready for this. I can't imagine that there's a shop anywhere open now. We'll just give him your book, and write something in there for him. His first Christmas present.'

'My book?' she asked and realised what he meant. 'Oh, of course, you'll have bought me a book? Thank you.' She stretched to take his hand. 'Hopefully something suitable for a child…'

'A novel, not a children's book, of course, but it'll do. The poor boy … having his birthday on Christmas Eve. I hope people don't think they can get away with only giving him one present a year for the rest of his life.'

'It was unbelievable, Ari Thór,' she said. 'The birth. I'd never imagined the pain of it...'

'You were unlucky this time,' Ari Thór said without thinking; and then realised that he'd implied there would be more children to come. He had always longed for siblings of his own and saw himself as having at least two children – although the size of their family was something they had never discussed.

Kristín nodded and Ari Thór made an effort to change the subject. 'How did it go with the old man? What terrible secrets did you find out about your great-grandfather?'

'I told you last night about his daughter, remember?'

Ari Thór shook his head and felt a pang of guilt. 'Not really.'

'Well,' Kristín smiled. 'What seems to have happened was that Great-Grandad went to Saudárkrókur one winter when the weather was bad, leaving his family behind. While he was away his wife was taken ill and she died shortly afterwards, before he returned. Their daughter, my grandfather's sister, had no way of getting a doctor and she did everything she could to keep her mother alive until her father returned. It turned out badly. She had to watch as her mother died. It seems she always blamed her father for that – not that he was guilty.'

Something about the short tale caught Ari Thór's attention, something that was tantalisingly out of reach.

'Why wasn't he at home?' he asked after a moment's silence. 'What took him to Saudárkrókur?'

'That's what's so remarkable,' Kristín replied. 'He had volunteered to take some kind of medicine there. There was a seriously ill child who needed medicine that was only available in Blönduós. Someone had already agreed to take it from one town to the next. Then the weather took a turn for the worse and this person didn't dare travel any further. He stopped off at Great-Grandad's place on the way and turned back to Blönduós as quickly as he could. So my great-grandfather offered to make the trip himself – in the depths of winter, simply to help some family he didn't know. It turned out to be a fateful decision. The old man I met in Saudárkrókur knew the story well. The child the medicine was for was his elder brother. My great-grandfather saved his life by bringing the medicine in time. The old man said his family thought Great-Grandad was practically a saint for doing it.'

Ari Thór's thoughts remained with the first part of the story. Kristín had said that her great-grandfather's daughter had watched her mother die before her eyes and blamed her father for it, despite his innocence.

'Excuse me, my love. I need to call Tómas.'

'What? Now? To tell him about the baby?'

'Yes … Well, yes and no. You don't mind?'

'Of course not. I'm going to try and get some more sleep. But don't you think it's remarkable that this man meant so well and it turned out so badly for him? It's so unfair.'

'Deeply unfair. But at least I know you come from good people,' he said, smiling at her, stroking her cheek and taking a look at the little child asleep in his mother's arms. Then he went out into the corridor to call Tómas.

'Well, I'll be damned!' shouted Tómas down the phone as he gave him the big news. 'Congratulations, my boy, I'm delighted for you. You must be walking on air.'

'That's about the shape of it,' Ari Thór replied, truthfully. He was still trying to appreciate the fact that he had a son, and that this child was asleep in a hospital ward. There had been a few months to get used to the idea, but all the same, nothing had prepared him for this dizzy, elated feeling.

'You're in Reykjavík?' he asked.

'Yes, I'm home now,' Tómas answered. 'My wife was glad to see me. It would have been a lonely Christmas on her own.'

'I have a theory I want you to hear – about the case.'

'Really, you're still thinking about that? You never stop, do you? Oh, well. Fire away.'

'As we know, Ásta's attic room is the only one that has a view over the cliff edge.'

'That's right,' Tómas said slowly.

'And, when she was a child, she told Thóra that she had to leave because of what she had seen from up there, correct?'

'Yes, that's what Thóra told us, at least.'

'So quite a few people have accepted that she witnessed her sister's death – or even saw someone push her over the edge. Do you also remember what Arnór told us? He said Kári told Thóra the story of what had happened when Sæunn herself went over the cliff edge – she'd simply run out during the night and tried to throw herself off. Kári claimed he had tried to stop her but failed?'

'Yes, I remember all this. What are you trying to tell me?'

'And finally,' Ari Thór continued, 'this morning we got to see that old letter Ásta wrote to Óskar when she was twelve. From that it seems she avoided visiting her father in hospital. Anyway, Kristín said something, which has nothing to do with all this, but has got me thinking. Could we have misunderstood the whole thing? And not just us, but Thóra as well, and everyone else involved? Could it be that Ásta did actually see something from the attic window; but it wasn't her sister's death that she witnessed, it was her mother's? And could she have lived her entire life in the belief that Kári threw her off?'

## XII

'Well, I'll be damned,' Tómas said for the second time in the space of a few minutes. 'So what age was Ásta when her mother died?'

'Just five years old,' Ari Thór answered, without needing to think about it. He had the main points of the case at his fingertips.

'Good grief, imagine the effect that must have had on a small child. Five years old, and seeing something like that…'

'Exactly. It was bad enough if she saw her mother lose her life in such a terrible manner, but to live with the idea that her father had been the one who pushed her over…' Ari Thór sighed. 'Then she was sent to Reykjavík after her sister's death. It could be that her father really was trying to prevent the same fate befalling her; but maybe she thought it was so he could get rid of her so she wouldn't tell anyone what she had seen. Perhaps, then, she nursed a grudge against him for a long time; if we go by the letter she sent to Óskar it certainly sounds like it. And perhaps she believed, to the end of her life, that her father had been responsible for her mother's death – that he had pushed her off the cliff edge. When, in fact, he was trying to save her.'

'It's an interesting theory, but it doesn't let Arnór off the hook,' Tómas said.

'I'm aware of that.'

'If anything, I'm even more convinced that he murdered her.'

'Really?' Ari Thór asked in surprise.

'Yes, because it eliminates the theory that someone else murdered her – that that someone, whoever it was, also killed Tinna, and wanted Ásta dead, thinking she'd come back to tell the truth.

If what Ásta *actually* saw was her mother's death, that whole theory falls apart.'

Ari Thór thought for a moment.

'That's true. But we've all been assuming that Ásta knew something about Tinna's death. If that person – the person who killed Tinna – thought the same, and wanted to be sure Ásta didn't expose them, then...'

'I can hardly believe that idea,' Tómas said. 'You wait and see ... Arnór is as guilty as hell. He'll confess tomorrow after a night in the cells. That normally does the trick.'

Ari Thór stayed out in the corridor after speaking to Tómas, deciding to give Kristín the opportunity to sleep.

He was telling himself that this was the right, fatherly, thing to do, when his phone rang unexpectedly. It wasn't a number he recognised, but he decided to answer it anyway. It had to be important for someone to be calling him at this time, with Christmas about to begin.

'Ari Thór,' he said shortly.

'Yes, hello, Ari Thór.' It was a woman's voice, a familiar one. 'It's Sara again ... Elín Sara. We spoke this morning.' Her voice was halting, as if she was not sure that this was a conversation she wanted to be part of. 'I'm sorry to call you so late, I'm sure you're at home waiting for your Christmas dinner...'

That was far from the reality of his situation, but he was feeling courteous and amicable, so he replied that she was not disturbing him. As he spoke he had the growing feeling that there had to be something significant on her mind – some facet of the case that could cast a new light on the investigation.

'I've been thinking things over since we spoke this morning ... and I maybe wasn't completely open with you,' she said, a noticeable tremor in her voice. 'It was a shock to think about that place again, even though it's not somewhere I could ever forget. And I was very surprised that Thóra even mentioned my name after all these years. I've borne a grudge against her for so long, you see; not that that's going to change … but it's a relief to know it preyed on her mind.'

'Did she do something to you?' Ari Thór asked cautiously, confused by what he was hearing.

'Thóra? No, it's not what she did exactly,' she said slowly, 'more what she didn't do. She should have reacted differently. Her behaviour was dreadful.' There was a long pause. 'I had a breakdown you see … retreated into my shell and never said a word about it, not to anyone, for all these years. And then you called and I've been thinking that this is maybe the opportunity I've been been waiting for; an opportunity to tell the story … and I think it would do me good.'

Elín Sara fell silent. Ari Thór took a seat on one of the yellow plastic chairs that lined the hospital corridor; it proved to be as uncomfortable as it looked. 'What happened?' he asked.

She waited before replying; it was clearly difficult for her to talk about this. 'Of course, I should have done something at the time, even though Thóra let me down. But I was just nine, a child. But I still had the sense to get away.'

Ari Thór wanted to repeat his question, but held back, careful not to apply too much pressure.

'He took me up to the lighthouse, to show me around. That was quite exciting. I didn't realise it at the time, but I know now that he chose exactly the right moment, when nobody would see us. It wouldn't have mattered anyway because once we were inside the lighthouse he locked the door behind us. I remember it so clearly; it was so horrible. But I never said anything.'

Ari Thór could imagine the scene vividly. He had felt deeply uncomfortable in the lighthouse himself.

'We didn't even go up the steps. He made his move right there inside the doorway.' She fell silent, drew a deep breath and struggled to continue. 'I've never had to put this into words before, and I don't know if I trust myself to. But he took off his trousers, and his underpants…' she said, and lapsed into silence again. 'You understand…'

Ari Thór would have preferred not to hear any more; he felt overwhelmed by revulsion.

'He didn't touch me – but that doesn't make it any less bad. I've never…' she said, then repeated the word for emphasis, '…*never* got over it. I tried to tell Thóra right away that evening and I remember her immediate reaction. "You're lying, child," she said as easy as you like. Like she didn't even care. But I didn't give up, and I could see that eventually she believed what I was saying. And you know what she said?'

'No,' Ari Thór said.

'"Life can be unfair." That was what she said, the evil old bitch!' Elín Sara's anger burst out. '"Life can be unfair!" I couldn't stand any more. I called my parents and asked them to collect me. I never told them why. I could never talk about it to anyone, not until now, to you. It's a relief, I can tell you. Of course, I should have done something about this when I was old enough – dragged the bastard to court. But the more time passed, the less I wanted to talk about it. I just wanted to forget about it.'

There was a silence again.

There was one remaining question that demanded an answer. Ari Thór realised that, deep inside, he hoped the person in question was Arnór. That way Tómas would have arrested the right man, although on dubious grounds.

'Who was it? The person who treated you like this?' he asked at last, listening hard for the answer.

'It was Reynir, of course. And to add insult to injury, he's there in the papers all the time, with that smile across his face, Mr Perfect. I remember that smile so well. But to me it means something else. Something revolting.'

# XIII

Ari Thór looked in on Kristín and the baby and saw that they were both fast asleep. He hated to leave them, but this was a job that he had to complete. He asked the nurse to give Kristín a message when she woke up, then rushed out to the patrol car he still had on loan from the local station and drove out to Kálfshamarsvík, as fast as he dared, and sometimes faster. The road was icy and it was snowing, so the conditions weren't perfect for speedy driving.

All the pieces were starting to fit together. Reynir had not abused just one girl, he was sure of it. Ásta must have endured the same experience and kept quiet about it, just as Elín Sara had done. The reason Ásta had returned was to seek revenge; or even to squeeze some money out of him, which seemed likely as she had been in financial difficulties. Ásta's death had shaken Thóra; it had brought all her old suspicions back to the surface – she knew what Reynir had done to Sara.

If Reynir had done the same to Ásta, and maybe Tinna, had he therefore been responsible for murdering them?

After a few glasses of wine, Thóra had dared to mention Sara's name. Reynir had been shocked, and wasn't prepared to take the risk that she would say more. So, he must have smothered her during the night. No doubt he justified it to himself, telling himself her days were numbered anyway.

Yes, it was all coming together.

It was dark at the point when Ari Thór arrived. The lighthouse was bright, but there were no lights on in the house, and Reynir's 4×4 was nowhere to be seen.

Ari Thór jumped out of the car, jogged to the gate and spent a frustratingly long time opening it, then hurried on towards the darkened house. He hammered on the door, but there was no response. He tried the door and found that it was unlocked. Going inside, he called out, looking around all the rooms, but the house seemed empty.

Then he realised that it was getting on for seven o'clock, and that Óskar had mentioned that he and his sister usually went to church at six on Christmas Eve. Óskar had even mentioned the name of the church, but Ari Thór couldn't remember it. He called the Blönduós inspector's mobile number, forgetting to apologise for calling him while the Christmas festivities were in full swing, and not even wishing him a merry Christmas. He simply gave his name and got straight to the point.

'Where do the Kálfshamarsvík people go to church?'

'Probably at Hof,' the inspector replied in a relaxed voice.

*Hof, that sounds right*, Ari Thór thought.

'It's a special place,' the inspector continued amiably. 'There was a priest there who was once convicted of witchcraft … a long time ago, of course.'

'Thanks,' Ari Thór said, in an attempt to stem the flow of information. 'How do I get there?'

'Where are you?'

'Out at Kálfshamarsvík.'

'Drive back towards Skagaströnd, and after ten minutes you should see it on your left. You can't miss it. But what are you doing out there…?'

Ari Thór ended the call without replying and turned the car around. He drove in silence, as fast as he could, while taking care to keep the car on the road. It was still snowing, and the enveloping darkness made the trip quite treacherous. Some brightness was reflected from the snow though, and he found the church fairly easily – it was well lit and there were several cars parked outside.

Ari Thór pulled up next to a tired tractor that looked like it would have been bright red when it was new, but whose best days were far behind it. He went quickly up the steps leading to the church, the warm hum of a Christmas hymn drifting out into the cold. The church was neat and painted white, the red of its roof showing through a layer of snow.

He stood for a moment beneath two crosses by the entrance, hesitating to interrupt the service. He opened the door cautiously and looked inside. Reynir was sitting near the back of the church, next to the nave, Óskar at his side.

The priest looked down the aisle directly at Ari Thór, but the other churchgoers paid him no attention, not until he walked forwards, tapped Reynir on the shoulder and whispered in his ear.

'Can I have a word with you outside? Now, please.'

Reynir got to his feet, astonishment – or was it fear? – on his face. A mutter passed through the congregation while the choir did its best to continue with the hymn – not entirely successfully.

Ari Thór led Reynir out into the lightly falling snow. He had meant to direct him to the patrol car, when Óskar unexpectedly appeared on the steps behind them. For once he was not wearing the usual blue rollneck; he had replaced it with a grey suit, a white shirt and a green-striped tie. As usual he held a stick in his hand.

'What on earth is going on?' Óskar demanded, with more determination and energy than Ari Thór had expected of him.

Ari Thór stopped, as did Reynir.

'I need a word with Reynir.'

'About what?'

Ari Thór sighed. 'Some new information has come to light. I have some more questions to ask.'

'How dare you haul me out of a service on Christmas Eve?' Reynir hissed at Ari Thór, clearly deciding that attack was the best form of defence. 'I've let you get away with all kinds of liberties, but this goes too far. I'll be making a complaint first thing tomorrow.'

Arrogant to the end, Ari Thór thought. Well, Óskar may as well find out what kind of a man he was.

'It's all over, Reynir,' Ari Thór snapped back. 'Sara – Elín Sara – called me this evening and told me the whole story. The silence has been broken. How long did you expect you'd be able to keep all this secret?'

It was obvious that Reynir was taken unawares by this, that Ari Thór had hit his mark. But he seemed determined to maintain the pretence. 'What are you talking about, boy? I don't know any Sara. And that's all I have to say.' He began to walk back to the church.

Ari Thór caught hold of Reynir's arm. 'You're going nowhere.'

'Sara? The girl who stayed with us?' Óskar asked.

'That's the one,' Ari Thór replied, wiping flakes of snow from his eyes.

'Did she call you?' Óskar continued.

'Don't encourage this stupidity, Óskar,' Reynir said sharply, as if he were giving an order to a subordinate.

'I was in touch with her earlier today and she didn't want to say anything. But then she called me again this evening and told me the whole story – she described exactly how Reynir had treated her.'

Reynir stood as if frozen.

'He got her to go to the lighthouse with him, locked the door behind him … and sexually abused her.'

'What the hell?' Óskar shouted. 'Is this true, Reynir? Is this true?'

Reynir looked at Ari Thór and then at Óskar, his face expressionless, as if the matter had nothing to do with him. 'Of course not. It's a pack of lies.'

'The girl, Sara, told Thóra, but Thóra wouldn't help her. And I can imagine that this mistake plagued Thóra to her dying day,' Ari Thór said.

'What the hell?' Óskar said, and then swore, glaring at Reynir. 'She always looked out for you. She looked on you as her son, the son she never had. And you always treated her so badly.'

'I owed her nothing,' Reynir said. 'She was an employee, and she never replaced my mother. If that's what she thought, then she was even weirder than I had imagined.'

'How dare you speak like that about my sister?' Óskar said through gritted teeth, apparently forgetting that he depended on this man for his living. Reynir said nothing and Óskar continued. 'What sort of man are you? Abusing a little girl? Was that why Ásta turned up here before Christmas? Did you abuse her too? Did she want to get her own back?' Óskar demanded, striking out with his stick and raising his voice. 'Answer me!'

Reynir still said nothing.

'My God,' Óskar said. 'What would your mother have said about all of this?'

'Leave my mother out of it,' Reynir retorted, stung into replying, his voice less harsh than it had been.

Óskar took a couple of steps towards Reynir and pushed him hard, sending him flying backwards.

'Were you fiddling with Ásta back then?' he snarled, moving closer to the helpless man on the ground and placing a foot on his throat, menace on his face. 'Were you? Tell me the truth!'

Faced with Óskar's unexpected fury, Reynir looked terrified. Ari Thór remembered him saying that Óskar was as strong as an ox.

Ari Thór was ready to intervene, but held himself back. He knew he should step in to separate them and take Reynir away to be questioned, but he wanted to see how the altercation between Reynir and Óskar would be resolved. Although he knew better, he decided to wait, something told him there was more to discover.

'I want the truth!' Óskar repeated.

Reynir looked ready to speak, but was struggling to breathe. Óskar lifted his foot.

'I never touched Ásta!' gasped Reynir. 'Never! I left her alone. I swear it … she was too aggressive. Tinna was so much easier…'

'You bastard,' Óskar spat. 'What did you do to Tinna?'

'I never touched them!' Reynir said.

Óskar stepped back, letting Reynir sit up a little.

'We found the computer,' Ari Thór lied, the reason Reynir had 'lost' it suddenly occurring to him.

'What? You found it?'

'You didn't want us to see the pictures, did you?'

'I've stopped…' he blurted out. 'They were just pictures off the internet!'

*Hell*, thought Ari Thór. His suspicion was right.

'Yeah, I understand,' Ari Thór said, trying to make the most of Reynir's weakness. 'I think I have it worked out.'

'I'm not a bad person … you have to understand that I never touched them,' Reynir said, staggering to his feet.

'And Ásta's death was an accident?'

'She was going to blackmail me for millions. She said that she'd decided to do it once my father was dead, now that everything was mine.' He paused. 'She didn't realise that there isn't much left. The old man had a better nose for business than I do. I took a couple of decisions that weren't all that smart, I guess.'

'And what happened that night?' Ari Thór demanded.

The snowflakes continued to flutter to earth, but they didn't seem to bother Reynir. They reminded Ari Thór of the fact that this was, after all, Christmas Eve. They were serene, majestic and impartial, these tiny sparkling crystals; it didn't bother them that one of the people outside of the church might be a murderer.

'She knocked on my door late that night, pretty drunk, and asked if I'd go with her out to the lighthouse. I didn't understand what was going on, so I went with her.' He sighed. 'I shouldn't have done that. She probably knew where I had taken Tinna.'

'Where you had taken Tinna?' Óskar broke in.

'Yeah … out to the lighthouse…' The old arrogance was gone. Reynir seemed relieved, as if his confession was accompanied by some kind of absolution. 'She made all kinds of threats, said she had proof. I think she was bluffing, but I lost my temper. I knew that if it all came out I wouldn't just lose the business, but my reputation as well. I'd end up with nothing. I lashed out, but I didn't intend to kill her!'

He sobbed, but it was impossible to see for the snow if there were tears in his eyes.

'What happened?' Ari Thór asked calmly.

'I caught her by the throat, gave her a shake and somehow her head hit the wall. It was an accident! I never meant to kill her,' he repeated.

'Why did you throw her off the cliff?'

'What was I supposed to do? She was dead, lying there on the cold floor in the lighthouse in the middle of the night. I thought of the cliffs right away. It wasn't all that crazy an idea that she'd take her own life in the place where her mother and sister died. I hoped it would be dealt with as a suicide ... but it didn't work out like that...'

'You made a point of talking about ghosts around here, didn't you, hinting at all kinds of supernatural stuff. That was deliberate, wasn't it?' Ari Thór asked. 'All part of weaving more of a mystery around these three deaths.'

'You could say that,' Reynir muttered.

'Now I remember something you said the night Thóra died,' Óskar said in a fury. 'That Ásta had been a cute girl – both now and then. She was seven when you saw her last. You're beneath contempt.'

'And what about Thóra?' Ari Thór asked. 'Why did she have to die? Was that because she mentioned Sara?'

'Thóra caught my eye just as she mentioned Sara's name. She clearly knew what had happened, and I was sure she wouldn't let it lie. She must have wanted to settle old scores before it was too late. I couldn't take that risk. But she had so little time left it was an act of mercy on my part to give her an easy way out instead of a lingering death,' he said. Ari Thór knew he'd been right when he thought that Reynir would justify killing Thóra like this.

Óskar tried again to get to Reynir, but this time Ari Thór did hold him back. 'Take it easy,' he told him.

'You bastard!' Óskar spat. 'You murdered my sister! How could you do that?' He leaned forwards and hung his head, exhausted.

'She seems to have resisted,' Ari Thór said to Reynir. 'As the spilled wine showed.'

'Yes, she did, to begin with. Then it seemed to me that she just gave up, accepted what was happening.'

'And am I right in thinking that you pushed little Tinna off the cliff?' Ari Thór asked cautiously.

Reynir stared wide-eyed at Ari Thór, as if asking for mercy. 'Absolutely not! I didn't touch her! Not in that way … Are you crazy? It would never occur to me to murder a child. That must have been an accident. I'd never do anything like that, never.'

Ari Thór's instinct was to believe Reynir, although he could have drawn the line at admitting to such a crime. But Óskar spoke up, his words meant for Reynir.

'I hope you burn in hell, you bastard,' he swore. Then he turned to Ari Thór. 'I'm going to come clean. I've kept quiet for too long. As far as I'm concerned, the blame for Tinna's death can be laid at Reynir's door. So I'm not telling you this to save his skin, but to put an end to this secret once and for all. It's long overdue.'

'What do you mean?' Ari Thór asked sharply. Could it be that this amiable man had a terrible crime on his own conscience? Could he have murdered the little girl?

'Reynir didn't murder Tinna.'

'How do you know?'

'I sort of saw what happened. I was swimming, some way from the shore, but I never said anything, couldn't bring myself to. Perhaps it doesn't make much of a difference now. The truth always comes out in the end, doesn't it?'

'This was an accident?' Ari Thór asked. He had a disturbing suspicion in his mind, a theory he had not previously considered but which now had become the most likely explanation. He desperately wanted to be wrong, and he hoped that Óskar would show that he was.

'No, it was no accident,' he said and sighed. 'I think Ásta pushed her off.'

'Ásta pushed her own sister off the cliff?'

'Yes, that's what I think happened. Ásta wasn't like other children, especially after her mother died.'

'After she witnessed her mother's death, maybe?' Ari Thór added, thinking of his new theory.

'You think that's what happened? It would certainly explain a few things. Ásta was cold, distant – almost emotionless. But we got on well together. I was fond of her. But after her sister died, I was able to figure her out more easily. She was cunning and absorbed in her own world. I said to you this morning – without thinking – that I had been burned by that friendship. I saw the two of them on the cliffs, that day, when I was swimming. Nobody else was anywhere close by. I'm sure they were just playing, and then all of a sudden Tinna wasn't there. I thought she must have gone inside, so I didn't hurry back to the shore. Then when I heard that Tinna had fallen from cliffs, I knew what must have happened. I could see it in Ásta's face. She lied to everyone, said she had been nowhere near the cliffs.'

His image of Ásta had been shattered. Ari Thór could still see that enigmatic smile and the distant eyes. Was this the girl who had murdered her little sister at only seven years old?

'Why on earth did she do it?' Ari Thór asked.

Reynir seemed to have come to his senses, his voice back to its former strength. 'I can guess,' he said. 'There's something she said to me long ago, not long after her sister's death.'

'What was that?' Ari Thór demanded, maybe too eagerly.

'She said that now we'd be able to go sailing in the summer; that Tinna was gone so she would never be able to tell tales about me to their father … and I'd always be around to take Ásta out to sea. She was fascinated by the boat that I was building back then, you see. I had promised her that we could go sailing every day once the boat was finished. At the time that promise was all she spoke of. Perhaps … perhaps she thought she needed to get rid of Tinna to make sure her dream wasn't spoiled.'

Ari Thór turned to Óskar. 'Why didn't you say something at the time? Why didn't you explain what had happened to Tinna,' he asked. He knew well why Reynir had stayed silent, about the boat and his promise to Ásta; he'd wanted to keep his own secrets well out of sight.

'She was seven! I didn't want to ruin her life, and figured it wouldn't do any good. Then her father sent her away. I think he knew what had happened, that he sensed it. He saw through the lies and couldn't bear to be close to her any longer,' Óskar said, and fell silent. 'I just think that Ásta wasn't a good person,' he said finally.

Ari Thór could hear the notes of 'Silent Night' flowing out of the church, a signal that the service would soon be over.

'Come on,' he told Reynir. 'We need to go.'

He cast a glance at Óskar, standing on the church steps.

He and Reynir made their way towards the patrol car, and the sweet music from the church became fainter with each step.

## XIV

Reynir spent most of the journey in silence. It was only as they were approaching Blönduós that he finally spoke.

'You don't believe all that stuff I said earlier, surely.' His voice was frosty.

'What do you mean?'

'I was terrified of that wretched man. I had to say something to calm him down and I still don't understand why you didn't step in, not that I can be bothered to lodge a complaint about you. You appreciate that I won't say a word until my lawyer arrives from Reykjavík.'

This was the side of Reynir that Ari Thór was already familiar with. He had given way under pressure and was now trying to patch up the cracks; dismiss it all as lies and wriggle out of the situation.

Ari Thór could imagine him overplaying his hand in the same way when Ásta had cornered him in the lighthouse. He'd been like an animal in a cage, putting himself in the role of the victim, and losing control of his temper…

Maybe he would get away with some of this; in fact Ari Thór knew that his confession outside the church was not strong enough evidence. It was as well as that Elín Sara would be able to testify to the abuse. That would be enough to demonstrate just what kind of a man he was.

Ari Thór's thoughts then turned to Óskar. What would become of the old man now? He would hardly be able to stay in the house, and it was unlikely that he had any funds of his own. He would probably have to move away from Kálfshamarsvík, the place he was so fond of, and spend what was left of his days somewhere else. Did he have any other family? If not, he had nowhere else to turn, and would be left all alone. It was a cruel fate.

Ari Thór was pleased, though, that Arnór would presumably be released soon, and would be able to spend Christmas, or what was left of it, with his wife. Ari Thór found it difficult to understand the relationship between those two, but was not inclined to pass judgement on the personal lives of others. He had enough on his plate with his own.

$$\oplus$$

The formalities were over; Reynir was on his way to custody in Akureyri and Tómas had been given the news. Ari Thór was sure he heard Tómas practically choking on his Christmas ale.

'I'm coming up north right away,' were the last words he said, and this time Ari Thór offered no protest.

He hurried back to the hospital. Kristín was awake, but their baby boy was asleep.

'Where on earth have you been?' she whispered, smiling at him.

He paused before replying, peering at the sleeping child.

'Don't worry,' she said quietly. 'He's fast asleep.'

'It's been quite a day. I arrested Reynir Ákason.'

'Really? He killed the woman, Ásta?' she asked in astonishment.

'Yes, and the other one as well, last night. He confessed to both murders. And that's not all. He seems to have more on his conscience … child abuse, including Tinna, Ásta's sister…'

He regretted saying the words the moment he had uttered them. He wasn't ready to answer questions about what had befallen the little girl, not right away. How could he explain to Kristín, the mother of an innocent child only a few hours old and sleeping so peacefully, that a little girl of only seven had come to the conclusion that the right thing to do was to push her own sister off the edge of a sheer cliff? How could he explain that she might have done this to protect her friend, the abuser, because he had promised to take her sailing? All because she was a girl who loved the sea…

'Ari Thór, tell me something—' Kristín began.

He interrupted before she could ask her question. 'Later, sweetheart. I'll tell you about it later.'

'What? Yes, of course, later. But there's something else I was going to ask you.'

'OK?'

'Can you tell me about your father?'

The question caught Ari Thór by surprise. 'What do you want to know?'

'What happened to him…'

Ari Thór hesitated. 'One day, I'll tell you the story. But not now.'

Nevertheless, his mind went back to fifteen years before, to the summer of 1997, when his father and namesake, Ari Thór Arason senior, had disappeared without a trace.

And then, six years ago, in the summer of 2006, Ari Thór had received the ominous letter in the mail: a formal claim document, relating to a £7,000 credit-card invoice from the United Kingdom, made out to an 'Ari Thór Arason'. Ari Thór's first reaction was that he must have been the victim of identity theft, but then he had noticed that the letter contained some personal information about the card holder, including a date of birth: 15 January 1960. It was the date of birth of Ari Thór's missing father. Could it be that his father was still alive? The first thing Ari Thór had done was book a flight to London to try to track down his father …

But as he had said to Kristín, that story would have to wait. Now it was time to focus on the future.

# AUTHOR'S NOTE AND ACKNOWLEDGEMENTS

This story is entirely fictional. The characters and the events portrayed here have no basis in reality.

However, Kálfshamarsvík bay and Kálfshamarsnes point are real places and I have tried to describe the area around them as accurately as possible, although it is difficult to capture the beauty of this area in words alone. The house on the point at Kálfshamarsnes comes from the author's imagination, as does the story itself, and does not refer to any house that may have stood in that place.

The book uses the site of the village that was once at Kálfshamarsvík as its setting, and that village was very real. The information that the characters in the book provide about its history is meant to be accurate. The settlement there was abandoned around 1940; below I have listed the main sources of information about the area. Any departures from fact are the author's responsibility.

The earthquake mentioned in the book was also real. It took place in 1963 and was felt in that area, as well as in Siglufjördur, for example.

It should also be mentioned that the account of alleged malevolent ghostly activities by one of the characters in the book is based on media reports of events at the farm at Saurar in 1964. This farm is a short distance north of Kálfshamarsvík.

The lighthouse described in the book is actually located at Kálfshamarsvík. It was designed by Axel Sveinsson and came into use in 1942. I want to extend warm thanks to Gudmundur Bernódusson at the Icelandic Road and Coastal Administration for granting me access to the lighthouse, in order for me to be able to describe it as accurately as possible.

Police officer Eiríkur Rafn Rafnsson and prosecutor Hulda María Stefánsdóttir are also owed thanks for their help – for proofreading the text and for the wealth of information they provided on the way the police services do their work.

In the third chapter of the book's second part there are two passages, supposedly from a diary written by Kristín's great-grandfather. In fact, these passages are borrowed from a diary kept by my own great-grandfather, Jónas Guðmundsson. In every other respect his diary has no connection with the imaginary one written by Kristín's great-grandfather, as this character and his life are the work of the author's imagination.

As always there are many people to thank for their contribution and help. First, I would like to mention my parents, Jónas Ragnarsson and Katrín Guðjónsdóttir, and my brother, Tómas Jónasson (to whom this book is dedicated), for their constant support and encouragement.

Thanks are also due to my publisher, Karen Sullivan, at Orenda Books, and my translator, Quentin Bates. I would furthermore like to thank my agents, Monica Gram at Copenhagen Literary Agency and David Headley at DHH Literary Agency, as well as my Icelandic publisher, Pétur Már Ólafsson, and my Icelandic editor, Bjarni Þorsteinsson.

Last but not least, my warmest thanks go to my wife María, and my daughters, Kira and Natalía.

Ragnar Jónasson

*Sources of information about the settlement and the lighthouse:*

Bjarni Th Guðmundsson: *Byggð á Kálfshamarsnesi og næsta nágrenni* ('Settlement at Kálfshamarsvík and District'), Húnavaka, 1982.

Guðmundur Bernódusson, Guðmundur L. Hafsteinsson and Kristján Sveinsson: *Vitar á Íslandi* ('Lighthouses in Iceland'), 2002.

Kristján Sigurjónsson: *Frá lífinu í Kálfshamarsvík* ('About life at Kálfshamarsvík'), Húnvetningur 2000–2001.

Kristján Sveinsson: Information displayed on signs at Kálfshamarsvík.

Sigurjón Björnsson: *Skaginn og Skagaheiði*, 2005.

'Ragnar Jónasson writes with a chilling,
poetic beauty ... a must-read'
**PETER JAMES**

RAGNAR
JÓNASSON

SNOW
BLIND

'Seductive ... Ragnar does claustrophobia beautifully'
**ANN CLEEVES**

# RAGNAR JÓNASSON

# NIGHT BLIND

'A classic crime story seen through a uniquely Icelandic
lens ... first rate and highly recommended'
LEE CHILD

RAGNAR
JÓNASSON

# BLACK
# OUT

'Jónasson's books have breathed new life into Nordic noir'
**JAKE KERRIDGE, *SUNDAY EXPRESS***

# RAGNAR
# JÓNASSON

# RUPTURE